Welcome to the

Neighborhood

LISA ROE

sourcebooks
casablanca

Copyright © 2022 by Lisa Roe
Cover and internal design © 2022 by Sourcebooks
Cover design by Olga Grlic

Published by Sourcebooks Casablanca, an imprint of Sourcebooks
P.O. Box 4410, Naperville, Illinois 60567-4410
(630) 961-3900
sourcebooks.com

Library of Congress Cataloging-in-Publication Data is on file with the publisher.

Printed and bound in Canada.
MBP 10 9 8 7 6 5 4 3 2 1

For David, Jackson, and Jordan
And for my mother, Patricia Kaplan

Chapter 1

THERE IS A CHICKEN ON MY KITCHEN COUNTER. BUT IT'S NOT sitting in a roasting pan with a sprig of rosemary and a squeeze of lemon. It is a live, fat chicken scraping its thorny feet across the granite, pecking at the black specks in the tan stone.

"Harri, what the hell!" I yell to my daughter standing just feet from said chicken, her arms out to her sides as if she is protecting the bird from falling off or flying away. "It's going to get *E. coli* all over the place."

Harri wrangles the chicken and tucks it under her arm like she's been living on a farm for all of her eleven years and not, until today, in a fourth-floor walk-up in Woodside, Queens.

"Relax, Mom. I'm showing Mrs. Clucklesworth around her new house. You want her to feel welcome, don't you?"

"Jeff built you a lovely coop. That's *its* new house. Rule #1 of *our* new house is: Livestock stays outside. And besides, chickens don't like kitchens. Too close to the oven for their liking. Don't make Jeff regret inviting us to live here."

Harri pushes her glasses further up her nose with her free hand as Mrs. Clucklesworth pecks at an unraveling braid.

"Mom, he wouldn't... You're married now!"

I look at my hand. The new silver band tries to class up the territory my paint-stained fingernails are dragging down.

I nod, clinking my wedding ring to the matching one on Harri's left hand. "I guess he's stuck with us. Now, get that—"

"Mrs. Clucklesworth!"

"Get that Mrs. Clucklesworth out of here."

Harri slides back the big glass door leading into the yard and skips past an enormous swing set toward the chicken coop.

I open the box on the counter—the one containing the sum total of my kitchen items. Inside are a perfectly seasoned wok, a set of flea-market-find Flintstones jelly-jar glasses, and the mug with the photo of a baby Harri from before the glasses and the dreaded braces but with the same sweet, rounded cheeks I still love to cup in my hands.

The rest of it, the place settings and utensils for two, a few scratched pots and pans, and a stack of ratty dish towels, went to Goodwill. In fact, many of our earthly belongings stayed back, thanks to a deal I made with the landlord, whose next tenant agreed to buy them all for next to nothing— exactly what they were worth.

None of my possessions, collected over years of scraping by, could compare with the stage that has already been set in this house. I could hardly drag in my chenille couch with the worn patches at the arms to compete with the eight-person sectional manspreading in front of the fireplace.

I open each cabinet looking for room to tuck my things. It's like shopping at Williams-Sonoma—thick, cream-colored dishes, service for twelve; chunky glasses of every size; copper-bottomed pots nestled within each other by size like Russian dolls.

As with every other room in this house, every stick of furniture, every scrap of fabric, this kitchen oozes her. His former wife.

The woman I'm replacing.

———

On our third date, Jeff brought me out to his house on Elderberry Lane.

"Come on, Ginny. I'll give you a tour of the estate," he'd joked as we drove from my favorite Thai place in Long Island City over the RFK Bridge and up the FDR.

Jeff's neighborhood was a straight shot west, over the George Washington Bridge and past sprawling New Jersey malls. But when we pulled up to a home that looked like an only slightly pared-down version of Tara, I realized it was no joke.

"Holy shit," I said as we walked through one decorator's showcase room into the next. "My entire apartment could fit in here. Times ten."

In the short time we'd been dating, Jeff Corrigan hadn't struck me as the kind of guy who would live in a place like this. He was handsome in the way nerdy little boys grow up to be handsome. Sweet and down-to-earth, in need of a haircut, the cuffs of his jeans frayed. Not someone who cared about material crap.

But maybe I had gotten him all wrong.

As the tour continued, a familiar leaden feeling sat just under my breast-bone, the one I felt when I realized, once again, this wasn't going to work out.

Dating sucked as a single mom. I spent most of my free evenings with Harri as my plus-one. Online dating was out due to my fear of bringing some creep who misrepresented himself into my house, and my friends had long since run out of fix-up suggestions. I had finally met a guy the old-fashioned way—at my place of business, a field in upstate New York filled with pop-up tents and gourmet food trucks. And things were going so well; I thought Jeff and I were hitting it off. We both loved the Yankees and hated that we loved the Jets. We'd both read the Lord of the Rings trilogy in high school, but Jeff had gotten through the appendices and could recite Aragorn's lineage by heart. We agreed that *Homeland* had jumped the shark after season five. And, we agreed to disagree about who was the better *Great British Baking Show* judge. I was Team Prue. So, based on all that (and the quality of the kissing), I'd stupidly gotten my hopes up about this guy. But this town, this street, this McMansion, was the other shoe dropping.

Or so I thought.

"It's a lot, isn't it?" Jeff said, picking up a bronze statuette of an elephant and turning it over in his hand, studying it as if he'd never seen it before. "I didn't exactly have much say in it all."

He looked around the room and smiled wistfully when his eyes landed on the sectional in front of a pool-table-sized television.

"Except for the couch. I lobbied hard for that one. The rest is all Stacey."

I already knew about Stacey.

On our first date, we played the midlife dating game called "getting the ex's stories out of the way." I told him about Colin, who had resented that unplanned fatherhood had cramped his music career, and how, after a torturous year and a half of trying to "deal," he had chosen his band and the road over his daughter.

Stacey had gone on a girls' vacation to South Beach and returned with a butterscotch tan, a butterfly tattoo on her ankle, and a private equities manager from Malibu.

She left for California a few weeks later.

Jeff set down the elephant and scanned the room. "She became a champagne girl stuck with a craft beer guy. You know how that usually works out."

"I'm a bit of a craft beer girl myself," I said, relieved I hadn't misjudged Jeff after all. "I love Flower Power IPA, although Fiddlehead is my hands-down favorite."

"Shelbourne, Vermont!" He laughed. "I've been there, the Fiddlehead Brewing Company. I used to bring home a few growlers every time I dropped Brendan at UVM. I was heartbroken when he graduated and I had to give it up."

I nodded my chin toward his ex-wife's belongings. "Can I ask you a question? Why is it all still here? If it was her stuff. Not that it's a big deal, I mean."

I was secretly worried that it was homage to an ex-wife he might still be pining for.

Jeff looked around and sighed. "To be honest, it just wasn't a priority at the time. And now I barely notice any of it. It's like a reminder note you stick on the fridge and stare at so many times you stop seeing it."

He turned his back on the bronze elephant.

"Hey, I have a four-pack of Heady Topper in the fridge. Have you ever had that?"

"Who hasn't?"

We abandoned the tour, drank the beers on his back deck, and listened to frogs singing in a nearby pond until Jeff put down his can, took my hand, and said, "There's one more room in the house I forgot to show you."

Then he took me upstairs to the bedroom Stacey had so stupidly vacated.

I take down one of the cups hanging from hooks under the cabinet and replace it with my Harri mug. It stands out in this kitchen, with its French white cupboards, deep farm sink, and ceramic flooring that looks miraculously like wide-planked wood.

I can't help but feel like that mug right now.

Jeff comes in, wrestling the box awkwardly packed with my paints and coffee cans of brushes and collections of palettes.

"This is the last one, Gin," he says.

"Can you put it in the hallway? I've already leaned all my canvases against the wall for now. I guess we have to decide where this will all go."

I have my eye on a spot in the family room just under the Palladian window facing the backyard. The light streaming in is extraordinary. I could throw a tarp on the floor and set up my easel just to the right of the fireplace.

"You know what?" Jeff says with a smile on his face. "I have an idea where we can store all this."

Store? My heart sinks. This has to be a misunderstanding. Jeff knows my art isn't some hobby that I can shove into a closet until I have a little free time. My business of painting pet portraits might be fledgling, but it's growing. For the first time in forty-two years, I get that saying: *Do what you love and you won't work a day in your life.* My things can't be *stored.*

Before I can stammer, "But, but, but…" Jeff hoists the box high on his chest and walks out the back door. I follow him as if he's the Pied Piper.

He crosses the deck and heads to a detached garage. Its shingles are embroidered with moss and a basketball hoop with a torn net sits at a cock-eyed angle, seemingly abandoned since the days when Jeff's son was still living at home.

"The garage is a holdover from before we moved in. Before the previous owners gutted the original house," Jeff says over his shoulder. He puts my box down in front of a side door, reaches into his pocket, and pulls out a key. "Stacey hated that she had to go outside to get into her car. She wanted to tear it down and build something attached. Now I'm glad we never got around to it."

So that's it. I'll be setting up shop out here. My art supplies—greasy oils, toxic-smelling turpentine, jars and cans filled with cloudy paint-tinged water—have no place in a house like this. The decor might be all his ex's, but that doesn't mean Jeff's going to let me fuck it all up with my mess.

We step into a space filled with bicycles and rakes and terra-cotta pots and stacked plastic totes labeled "Christmas," "Halloween," and "Easter" all coated with dusty cobwebs. It smells like potting soil and motor oil. I hear Harri outside laughing. I try not to worry about what the coming winter weather is going to do to the consistency of my paint. A cold garage. Not exactly what I had in mind.

This is what you wanted, I remind myself. *It's a small sacrifice, considering what you are gaining.*

───────

When Harri agreed to the marriage proposal I'd accepted the night before, there was no question we'd move out of the apartment in Queens. I couldn't pack my bags fast enough. But when Jeff asked me to consider moving into his house, I was surprised. I'd assumed he wanted a fresh start, just like I did. Then I found out why he wanted to stay.

"There's almost no equity," he'd said, his head low, his face reddening. "And with the balloon payment and then the second mortgage to renovate the kitchen…"

"You are speaking a foreign language." I laughed, not understanding the seriousness of his admission.

"It means I can't sell the house without losing everything. I'm so sorry, Ginny. This is a shitty thing to pull on you. But, hey," he said, brightening a little, "the school system is top-notch and the street is filled with kids. And you know, *New Jersey Magazine* named us one of 'America's Top 25 Towns to Raise a Family.' Can't beat that, right? Harri would blossom here, Gin. And I'll make it up to you. Both of you. As soon as I can."

It didn't take me a minute to make up my mind. We were sitting on his barge of a couch and I scooted over so my thigh pressed against his.

"I'd live anywhere with you. Here, Queens, Timbuktu. As long as we're together, the three of us."

He leaned back to look at me and raised his eyebrows. "Have I told you how amazing you are?"

"Maybe. But you can say it again if you want."

"It'll be great. I promise you. And you can redecorate—change it all. Only maybe let's hold off until we see what my bonus looks like this spring."

"Jeff, I don't care about any of that, really. Besides, look at it from my point of view. I don't think you realize what a gift you are giving *us*. A beautiful house on a street where Harri can play outside and instantly make friends and go to a great school? I could sell a million dog paintings and never be able to give that all to her. I hadn't thought about it before, but this is the perfect solution."

"So, you don't care about—"

"I love you. I don't care about any of this stuff," I said, sweeping my arms around the room like Vanna White. "Oh, except that elephant statue. That's gotta go."

———

Against the wall of the garage is a set of stairs. Jeff and my box take them two at a time.

"This used to be what they called a granny flat," he's saying. "Or maybe it's a nanny flat. I can't remember. We used it for storage all these years."

I continue to follow him, each step feeling more leaden as I climb, optimism leaching out of me. At the top of the stairs, I am expecting boxes and trunks, old suitcases, and years of dust.

But the room is empty. The floor is new. The walls freshly painted a soft tan. Sunlight pours into the room, throwing long windowpane shadows onto the floor.

"What is this?"

Jeff puts the box on the floor and shoves his hands in his jean pockets. A lock of hair falls over one eye, making him seem young despite his ten years on me.

"It's your studio," he says. "What do you think? I got rid of all the junk, laid down a new floor, threw on a coat of paint. I went with beige. I thought it was the most neutral, but I can repaint it if you want something else. Maybe something brighter? Is brighter more inspiring?"

I circle the space. Jeff watches me, smiling in a charming, hesitant way, as if he is not sure I approve. I am stunned.

"No one has ever—"

"I am going to build you shelves. But I didn't know where you wanted them."

"It's amazing," I say, running my hand across a freshly painted white windowsill.

"Well, if you're going to be the region's premier pet portrait painter, you've got to have the right work space."

Painting dogs and cats in a style I call "folk art inspirational"—think slightly stylized pets with flower wreaths on their heads or angel wings or quirky bow ties— was never going to pay the rent. But now, with this amazing man and this incredible space, who knows.

"I have no words."

"Just say that when Harri goes to school in a few weeks, you'll spend all your time up here."

"Well, I know we talked about this," I say, "but I'll have to get a job at some point."

I was happy to hand in my notice at my day job. Commuting to Astoria from New Jersey was a nonstarter. And JMR Properties could easily find another disenchanted bookkeeper.

"Of course, if that's what you want. But I still think you should take your time, Gin. Get acclimated. Help Harri settle in. Like I've said before, no rush."

I take in this little room above the garage. My mind leaps and dances toward the projects that have until now lived in notebooks, and on scrap paper and the backs of envelopes.

"I honestly don't know—"

"It's nothing really. If I had to bribe Harri to move out to boring old Jersey with a chicken, I figured I had to up my game a little with you. I want you to think it was worth it."

I weave my arms through his and wrap them around him. He smells like coffee and laundry detergent. I reach up on my toes and give him a long kiss.

"Neither one of us needed any bribing. We would have moved here if we had to sleep in our car to do it. But thank you. I love you. This is amazing. I can't even imagine what it's going to be like, spending my days in this beautiful room. Wait, did I tell you I love you?"

When I first started painting, I had to wait until after work, sometimes until after I got Harri off to bed, before I could set up my canvas. I'd sit at the kitchen table with a terrible overhead light and a cheap set of watercolors. At first, I did it to prove to myself there was something left of me, that my whole existence wasn't just raising my daughter on my own and keeping our heads above water.

God, I was terrible at it.

Still, I loved moving the brush across the paper, blending the colors, creating the world as I wanted to see it.

I turn away from Jeff and lean against his sturdy frame. I can see Harri out the window, playing with Mrs. Clucklesworth. She is following the bird as it pecks for insects in the perfectly manicured lawn.

"Ginny, I just want you to be happy here."

I spin around and reach up on my toes until my lips are touching Jeff's ear.

"Oh, I don't think you have to worry about that," I say slowly.

"Hello-o!"

The voice and the perfume race up the stairs before their owner.

"Jeffrey? Are you up here? It's Margot."

Jeff and I step away from each other. The moment that could have been is gone.

"Up here, Margot."

"It's Margot Moss-Marks," he whispers to me. "My ex used to say she ran the street. Queen-bee type. Are you ready for this?"

"Of course," I say, pulling out my messy ponytail and running a hand through my hair.

Before I moved in, Jeff tried to apologize about the women who lived on Elderberry Lane.

"They were Stacey's friends," he had said and raised one eyebrow as if I should know what that meant.

"Don't worry about me." I laughed. "I get along with everybody! And besides, we're all mothers. It's like men and sports. We start talking kids, and we automatically have everything in common. We'll all be fast friends."

But now one of my new fast friends is coming up the stairs and I'm losing a bit of my it-takes-a-village confidence. What if it's not like sports at all? I wish I had a chance to change out of my sweatpants or grab a breath mint or, at the very least, slip a rose quartz confidence crystal in my pocket.

"What on earth are you doing up here?" asks the top of a blond head just before it clears the stairs and is level with the studio floor. "Oh, what is all this?"

When she appears in full, wearing a perfect ponytail and yoga gear that shows off every tanned and tight muscle of her body, I have to bite my cheek to prevent my jaw from dropping. I don't think I've ever been this close to someone so perfect. No stray hair, or uneven skin tone, or any of the little bumps and tiny bulges that populate the bodies of us mere mortals. No, Margot Moss-Marks is a finely curated exhibit.

Behind her is her carbon copy. A tall, lanky teenager, still soft in all the places Margot is hard, wearing shorts so tiny they might be confused for underpants, a crop top exposing a bulging outie, and a bored-already expression.

Margot is holding a small shopping bag exploding with gold tissue paper. Her beautifully made-up eyes scan the empty room and stop on me. She gives me a quick vertical glance, head to toe, before landing back on my face.

"Margot, this is Ginny."

"Don't be silly," Margot says. "We know who this is. It's so lovely to finally meet you. We've all been eagerly anticipating your arrival! We're a girl short on this street, you know."

She looks over at Jeff and winks as if he is responsible for upsetting the gender balance in the neighborhood. Jeff's lips tighten, but he doesn't offer evidence to the contrary.

"Jeff has talked about you nonstop. I feel like I know everything I need to know about you!"

She leans in and gives me a stiff hug. The gift bag in her hand hits me in the back. There is something heavy and solid in there. Finally, she pulls away and hands me the bag.

"This is for you. Just a little moving-in gift."

I take the bag, and I look at the girl standing behind Margot's shoulder.

"Thank you, guys. This is so thoughtful. I'm Ginny, by the way," I say to the teenager who has not been introduced.

Before she can respond, Margot steps forward.

"And *this* is my daughter, Madison," she says as if she's introducing the guest of honor.

"Well, it's very nice to meet you, Madison. I'm going to be in the market for a babysitter soon. How convenient for me that you live right across the street."

Madison's kohl-lined eyes widen and her raspberry-glossed mouth forms a perfect O. Margot lets out a lilting laugh.

"Babysitting? Madison is only eleven!"

I cock my head like a dog who doesn't understand.

"I know, I know," says Margot. "It's the height. She gets it from her father. It's an issue, really, for her acting career. This gargantuan height might be fine for modeling and even manageable for film—you know, bring out a box for the male lead—like they used to do with Tom Cruise. But you can't get away with that on the stage. And Madison is Broadway bound, you see. In fact she's just back from theater camp in the Berkshires, aren't you, darling?"

Madison shrugs and makes no apology for her career-limiting stature.

Margot moves on. "Open your gift!" she sings.

I open the bag and pull out a heavy white candle in a thick glass.

"It's Diptyque," she says. "My absolute favorite. Bulgarian Rose and Black Current. I have this one in my downstairs powder room. But, of course, it's lovely in a dressing room."

I recognize the label of a candle so expensive that it was awarded its own window display at the posh apothecary I occasionally walked past on Madison Avenue. I smell the fruity wax and place it on the windowsill.

"You won't want to leave it out here in the garage," she says.

"I won't," I answer.

"Where will you put it? Not your kitchen. Somewhere where it can be the dominant fragrance."

"Um, my bathroom, I guess?" I am confused by the interrogation over the candle that is now allegedly mine to do with what I please.

"Yes. Good. Fine."

I steal a glance at Jeff who lifts a brow in an I-warned-you kind of way.

"It's lovely, Margot. Thank you."

Margot flaps her wrist, dismissing me.

"It's nothing. Oh dear, we have so much to catch you up on. You missed your chance for class mom, but I'm sure we could get you on the list for party donations, and field trip chaperone, and PTA meeting hostess. After morning drop-off, we do a group walk, unless we have tennis—you play, don't you? Oh, and you're here just in time for the fall fundraiser, and you need to know where we shop, and…"

She reaches up with her perfectly manicured hand and pulls gently at a strand of my hair. "Of course, you'll be wanting a new hairdresser. You don't want your husband seeing those grays."

She laughs and looks over at Jeff in a conspiratorial way. "Am I right?" she asks him. Jeff, to his credit, remains mute on the subject. I'm a second away from telling her I'm all set in the hair-dressing department, thank you very much, that a trim every six months and henna rinse from a woman in Williamsburg, who also creates the most amazing henna tattoos, does the trick, when I hear Harri at the bottom of the stairs.

"Mom!" she shouts.

"And now that Ginny is here, I hope we'll be seeing more of you, Jeff," Margot says, undeterred by the calls of a child. "I think you've been avoiding us."

Jeff looks like he's been caught. "No, not at all, Margot."

"Mom!" Harri's voice echoes up the stairwell.

"Which leads me to my very reason for being here. I'm throwing a little dinner party. To introduce you to everyone. Very casual, of course. This Saturday night."

"Mom!"

"Don't bring anything," Margot commands.

"Mom, guess what?" Finally, Harri gets to the top step. She has the chicken in her arms. Mrs. Clucklesworth's head is making staccato back-and-forth movements, her little eyes wide. I am not versed in chicken body language. But I'll tell you this. It doesn't look happy.

Harri takes in her new audience and stops at Madison. She has the same look on her face I saw last summer when her favorite Nickelodeon star walked past our booth at the Brooklyn Crafts Fair.

"I like your lipstick," she says breathlessly.

Madison flips her hair over one shoulder, but doesn't say anything. Harri looks at me for help but I can only send her a telepathic *don't-ask-me* message. I've already gotten this girl very wrong. A second later my daughter is back on Planet Harri.

"Mom, I taught Mrs. Clucklesworth a trick! Look!"

She takes a step forward, eager to show off her prized bird, but before any performance can proceed, she trips on an untied shoelace. Her knees thunk when they hit the floor. Her arms splay out in front of her, and she drops the chicken. It flaps and cackles as tiny feathers dance with the dust motes in front of the sunny window.

In unison, Jeff, Margot, Madison, and I duck and cross our forearms in front of our faces. Mrs. Clucklesworth, mistaking Margot for an escape hatch, flies up at her and collides with her raised arms before bouncing off and landing on the floor. The chicken skitters and squawks across the room, more tiny feathers scattering in its wake. Harri runs after her, her sneakers squeaking on the new wood. She tries to corral the animal who is done being manhandled for the day.

I see the three long scratches on Margot's arm before she does. Tiny droplets of blood begin to ooze from the wounds. Madison, both hands over her mouth, steps away from her mother as if she now has chicken cooties. Margot examines her arm as I hold my breath. Her face flashes anger but she instantly regains control. She starts to speak but I jump in first.

"I'm sorry. I'm so, so sorry!" is all I can say.

Welcome to the neighborhood, is all I can think.

Chapter 2

YESTERDAY WAS NOT THE ILLUSTRIOUS START I HAD HOPED FOR, what with the chicken attack and all. But Margot left without taking her candle back, so I'm thinking I still have a few more strikes before I'm out. And today is a new day. Today this house and I are getting to know each other. Starting with this kitchen. I want to be so familiar with it that if someone asks me where the melon baller is I can say, "Right of the dishwasher, third drawer down."

After taking time off to move us in, Jeff has gone to work and left me here alone. I relish the chance for the copper farm sink and I to become good friends.

"If that shelf of celebrity cookbooks over there is any indication," I whisper to the Viking stove top, "things are going to be a little different around here. More mac and cheese and scrambled eggs than you're probably used to."

I run my hand along the long countertop.

A trio of thin bottles sits in front of a window. Sealed with wax and string and artfully stuffed with olives and garlic cloves and tiny peppers, they are clearly meant for decoration and not consumption. The sunlight streaming through the jars of oily artwork casts a golden light onto the granite.

Next to them, a tall wooden pepper grinder and a copper saltcellar with a tiny spoon stand at the ready. In the corner, tucked under glass-fronted cabinets is a statue of a pig dressed as a butcher—complete with an apron, a bow tie, and a mallet.

"Oh, that's just not right," I say to the pig. "No self-respecting swine would take a job as a butcher."

I grab the statue, open the cabinet hiding the trash can, and dump the offensive thing in. This is my kitchen now. No cannibalistic butcher pigs on my counters. I cross my arms in satisfaction. Then I open the trash and fish it out. There are coffee grinds on its snout, but it is otherwise intact. I wipe it clean and put it back on the counter. But I turn it to face the wall.

Satisfied with my morning rounds, I pour myself a mug of coffee and look out the open kitchen window. A bumblebee throws itself against the screen. A bird makes the sound of a baby goat somewhere in the trees lining the lawn. Maybe next I'll survey *my* new backyard. I want to hang a wind chime made from bike gears that I picked up at a craft fair in Princeton despite having no backyard in Queens.

And then I see it.

A large, raggedy dog with a coat like a fake fur stole is lying on the deck. I can see his labored breathing, his chest rising and falling as if he ran a mile to end up in my backyard. Is he lost? I don't see a collar.

And then from somewhere around the side of the house, a motor turns over and the hot tub on the deck bubbles to life.

A man wearing a bathrobe and black rubber sandals walks past the kitchen window. My hand flies to my throat as I slink back against the refrigerator, wishing I had my cell phone and praying the sliding glass doors are locked.

The lost dog doesn't even lift his head as the man slides out of his sandals and drops his bathrobe on the deck. He dips a toe into the hot tub, then slides into the water, but not before I see he is buck naked.

"Mom, I just saw that man's penis!"

Oh, shit. Harri is standing in the kitchen doorway, eleven looking like six in her favorite Harry Potter pajamas that haven't fit her in years, hugging her tatter-eared Peter Rabbit, her hair still in yesterday's braids—sort of.

"Harri, come here!"

I wave her over to my hiding spot between the refrigerator and the dishwasher.

"Wait, grab my cell phone first."

Harri hustles over and I tuck her under my armpit like a protective mother swan, but with none of the grace.

"Who is that man?" my daughter asks, craning her neck toward the window.

"I have no idea. But I'm going to find out."

I call Jeff. It goes to voicemail. Jeff works in an open-floor office space, no walls, not even cubicles, just desks pushed up against each other. Better for productivity, he says, shitty for privacy. Of course he isn't going to answer his phone. I'm going to have to deal with this myself.

"Honey, I want you to go back to your room. Just for a little while."

"Nope."

"What?"

"I want to see what's going to happen."

"Nothing's going to happen."

"Then I don't have to go to my room."

Now she's eleven going on twenty-one. The pendulum swinging makes me dizzy. But I have only myself to blame.

"Fine. But stay in the kitchen. I'm serious."

I give her a look intended to prove I mean it, slip my cell phone in my back pocket in case events escalate quickly, and slide the back door open. The naked guy has his eyes closed, face to the sun, so I'm guessing he hasn't heard me walk outside over the noise of the motor and bubbles.

"Excuse me."

Nothing. My heart is racing. I ball up my fists.

"*Excuse me!*"

Naked Guy opens his eyes, shields them from the sun with his hand, and squints in my direction. He doesn't have the startled expression of a trespasser caught in the act.

In fact, he's going nowhere.

He lowers his hand, spreads his arms along the rim of the hot tub and smiles. Friendly as can be. He's an older man, with a full head of shaggy gray hair. Looks like he's gone a week or two without a shave. As he smiles up at me, deep lines, like quotation marks, punctuate light-blue eyes. He doesn't look like a serial killer, quite the opposite really. But you never know.

The dog rises slowly, arthritically, and ambles toward me, a feather duster of a tail wagging slowly. He rams his muzzle in my crotch and slobbers on my jeans. The theme of personal parts—the naked guy's, mine—reddens my face.

"Penny, leave it."

So, Penny is a girl. Weirdly, that makes me feel slightly less violated.

Penny looks over her shoulder at him and returns to her spot on my deck.

"Can I, um, help you?" I ask.

"I'm Wayne." He smiles, as if it's an answer. "Sorry about Penny. She has issues with boundaries."

Penny has issues with boundaries?

"I live next door. You must be Ginny. I thought you were moving in next week."

"Um, no. We're here now. Me and my *daughter*."

I lean into the word *daughter* to emphasize his nakedness.

"Good to meet you, Ginny. Don't mind me," he says. "Just taking my morning soak."

I flap my mouth, but nothing comes out. When Jeff recited the selling points of Elderberry Lane—fresh air, room to run—he failed to mention the nude guy from next door. That was information I could have used from the get-go.

I'm trying to figure out how to tell a perfect stranger that a pair of bathing trunks are in order when Harri pushes past me and rushes up to the dog.

"Aw, he's so cute!" she gurgles. "Can I pet him?"

In a panic, I stare into the bubbling water at Wayne's lap. Fortunately, I see nothing but a distorted outline of his legs.

"That's Penny," he says. "She's friendly. She loves kids."

Penny licks Harri's face. My daughter giggles and wipes her cheek with the back of her hand.

"Harri, go back inside."

"She won't bite," Wayne says.

"I'm not worried about her getting bitten," I say through clenched teeth.

I pick up Wayne's bathrobe and he glances at it, then at my daughter.

"Oh, sorry," he says, blushing so deeply he looks like a lobster boiling in a pot. "I'm not used to anyone being around. Hey, do me a favor, hon?" he says to Harri. "Take Penny inside and give her a biscuit. They're on the shelf in the pantry."

"Okay," she says, slapping her knee at the dog. "Come on, girl."

After Harri slides the glass door behind her, Wayne gestures to his robe. "Do you mind?"

I hand it over and quickly turn my back. Nobody needs to see that twice. I'm done here. This guy can find his way home. I go into the house. But Wayne follows me, making wet footprints on the tile floor.

Harri is on one knee, asking the dog for a paw.

"So how are you settling in?"

My uninvited guest pours himself coffee and then tops off my mug. "Milk?"

Without waiting for an answer, he opens the refrigerator and pours us both some.

"Help yourself," I mutter.

"Huh?"

"I said, it's very different than what I'm used to. We don't have naked guys in our backyards. They're usually wandering the street, waiting for a free ride to the psych ward at Bellevue Hospital."

He laughs. "Sorry about that. Jeff lets me use the tub—for my sciatica. And he leaves the back door open for me, in case I need anything, you know, bathroom or what not. It's a long walk back to my house."

I look out the window past the scant hedges separating our properties. *His house is right there. I could throw this box of dog biscuits and hit it.*

"Mom, can I take Penny to the coop and introduce her to Mrs. Clucklesworth?"

Harri is sitting on the floor with Penny, her arm draped around the dog's shoulder as if they've been BFFs forever. She always did have an easier time making friends outside her species.

"I don't know, Har—"

"It's fine," says Wayne. "She's a friendly old gal. Maybe just keep the pen closed. She is a retriever after all. That's a bird dog, you know."

Harri skips outside. Penny follows at her heels.

"A chicken in a fancy suburban neighborhood," he says. "Nothing personal—it's just a little, what do you call it, incongruent? BMW in the driveway and a chicken coop in the backyard. I guess it's all the rage now. Investment bankers considering themselves gentlemen farmers."

"We don't have a BMW. And the chicken is a pet. Aren't you a little cynical for someone who lives in this neighborhood as well?"

Wayne blows on his coffee, tastes it, looks at like it's insulted him, and then puts the mug in my microwave. We stand in silence as the machine whirs. When it's done, Wayne removes it gingerly. *That one's too cold, this one's too hot. Will Goldilocks be going upstairs to test the beds next?*

"We've been here thirty years," he says after a careful sip. "It was a different place when we were raising our kids. All ranch houses like mine. Lots more trees. But the street's turned over. A couple of times. Every house has been torn down and one of these behemoths has taken its place. Except for mine. I'm the last holdout. And I'm pretty sure the neighbors are looking at their wristwatches, waiting for me to find an old age home. Or worse."

Wayne opens the cabinet to the left of the sink and takes out a package of Oreos. He helps himself to two and offers the open bag to me. *Maybe I should ask him where the melon baller is.*

"Not Jeff. He's one of the good ones."

I watch him dunk an Oreo into his coffee.

"I can't believe anyone around here wants you out of your house."

He might be a noodge, but he doesn't deserve eviction.

He clears his throat. From the look on his face, I don't think it's the cookie gone down the wrong way.

"Have you met the crew?"

"Not really. I met Margot the other day, briefly," I say. "She seemed very, um, friendly. She's having a dinner party, tomorrow night, in fact, to introduce me around. Will you be there?"

Wayne smiles into his coffee cup. "I'll dust off my tux."

"Is that sarcasm, Wayne?" I tease.

Wayne shrugs boyishly and pops another Oreo into his mouth.

"You know," I say. "You remind me of my best friend, Zaria. She's a character too. Not a naked-in-a-hot-tub character, mind you. You two would hit it off. Or kill each other."

"I'd like to meet this Zaria. I'll tell you what, invite her to this dinner party of Margot's and I'll be there."

"Ha, fat chance. Zaria wouldn't be caught dead in the burbs."

"Well, I like her even more now."

I reach for a cookie while my first neighborhood friend—jury is still out on Margot—sips his coffee. *This is going to be okay,* I think. Then we hear Penny barking and Harri shrieking. Through the window we see the big dog lunging at the chicken coop as Mrs. Clucklesworth flaps her wings frantically and throws herself at the far end of the pen.

"That's my cue to go. Enjoy your day, Ginny," Wayne says. "Same time tomorrow?"

He steps back onto the deck and whistles for his dog who gives up on the chicken and comes ambling toward him.

"Same time tomorrow, Wayne." I smile. "And hey, don't forget your bathing suit."

Chapter 3

ELDERBERRY LANE IS A FLAT CUL-DE-SAC IN AN OTHERWISE HILLY neighborhood. Wayne told me it used to be a horse farm and then in the seventies, a street of pretty, brick ranch-style homes like his.

Now his house is like a tugboat in a harbor of luxury liners.

Over the last fifteen years or so, every one of his former neighbors left. In their place young power couples from nearby Manhattan, having outgrown their Upper West Side brownstones or towering Battery Park condos, moved in and tore down the original homes in favor of monstrous boxes adorned with Juliet balconies or Grecian columns or multiple dormers. Or in Margot Moss-Marks's case, all of the above.

We are standing in front of heavy, wrought-iron-embellished double front doors listening to the doorbell play the opening notes of Beethoven's Fifth. I am holding a paper plate of box-made brownies covered in foil.

"Do I look alright?" I ask, not for the first time this evening.

I was standing in the walk-in closet Stacey had evacuated. My limited wardrobe took up a quarter of the space available for someone more interested in fashion. A shoe rack running from floor to ceiling surveyed my few pairs of sneakers, boots, and Birkenstocks and thought, *That's all you got?*

Margot said casual, but since I was the guest of honor I was leaning toward the nicer end of my wardrobe—my favorite long skirt, patches of vibrant, repurposed textiles made by an artist I met at the Rhinebeck Crafts Festival two summers ago and bartered for by agreeing to paint her one-eyed Siamese. It was a Joseph's Technicolor Dream Coat of a skirt, and every hand-stitched square of it made me happy.

I slipped into the skirt and a lavender T-shirt and stepped out of my cavernous closet into Jeff's equally immense one. He had one leg in a crisp pair of chinos.

"How do I look?" I asked.

"You look beautiful," he says, letting his pants fall to the floor.

"Oh, no!" I laughed. "We're expected at Margot's in half an hour."

"So, it's come to this? The honeymoon's over already?"

"Very funny. Be serious." I tugged at the small carnelian stone around my neck, great for creating harmony between the mind and creative inspiration. I wished it were a harlequin quartz or maybe amazonite. I could use more help in the bravery department.

Now at the Moss-Markses' front door, Jeff wraps his arms around me, puts his lips to my ear, and says it again. "You look great. I'm going to have to fight off all the guys. And some of the women."

I smile and push him away playfully, then quickly pull him closer. As we continue to wait, Jeff rocks back on his heels and looks up at the house. "Jeez, I guess it has been a while since I've been to one of these."

I stick my elbow lightly in his ribs. "So, Margot was right. You have been avoiding them."

"Nah," he says. "Okay, maybe. This was always more Stacey's thing."

"Oh, do you want to leave? We don't have to—"

"No, no. Really, it's fine. I'm not the first person these guys call to be their fourth for eighteen holes on a Sunday. Mostly, because I'm in IT, they think I'm their own personal Genius Bar. But when it's one of these couples' things, I'm fine with it. You laugh at some jokes, make a little small talk. You can't believe some of the wild shit I hear. These Master of the Universe types have got insane stories. My strategy is—just *play along*."

"Now you're making me nervous."

"You? I thought you had this. Didn't you say all moms have everything in common? Don't you all wear the same decoder ring or something?"

"Something like that. But still. It's a lot of people at once. And I'm already off to a bad start with Margot. You know, with the chicken attack and all?"

Jeff laughs and pushes the doorbell again. "It was hardly an attack. She got a little scratch. She's not going to hold it against you. It was an accident. No harm, no fowl."

"Very funny." I lean against him again. "I just want this to work out. I want to get along with these people. I want them to think you have stellar taste in second wives."

"No contest there." He gives me a sly smile and a kiss that almost makes me drop the brownies. I catch my breath, smooth out the nonexistent wrinkles on my T-shirt, and get back to business.

"I just want things to be easy for Harri. She's starting a whole new life."

A life I had to convince her would be amazing.

"Why can't we just stay here?" she had asked, meaning our one bedroom in a fourth-floor walk-up with greasy hallways that smelled constantly of soup and garbage, especially when the trash chute that led to the dumpster in the basement opened with a creak and closed with a bang.

"There isn't enough room for the three of us here," I said. "Besides, you'd finally have your own room. Wouldn't you like that?"

For the first half of my daughter's life, we shared a bed. When her long legs and sharp toenails became too much, I created a cozy corner for her—a twin mattress on the floor, an enchanted forest painted on the walls and ceiling, and a bookcase filled with all her prized possessions as a divider between us. A beaded curtain substituted for a real door making privacy simply an illusion.

"I like things just as they are," she had said, lifting her chin.

She was just too young to understand how much I'd already failed her.

Margot's door finally swings open, breaking my thoughts of Harri. A woman in black pants, a white shirt, and a tight bun lets us in.

"Hi, I'm Ginny," I say, holding out my hand.

Instead of shaking it, she takes the brownies and walks away. I look at Jeff for a translation.

"That's the server, hon," he says.

I blush deeply. Sweet, sweet Jeff comes to my rescue.

"Don't mind her, Margot brings her in for all her 'get-togethers.'"

"I thought this was a casual event."

Jeff lets out a little snort. "For Margot, nothing is casual."

As soon as we step onto the white marble floors of a large foyer, I get it. The walls are papered with silver leaf, the circular staircase curls like a comma, and a four-foot-tall vase stands guard at the bottom step. A crystal chandelier the size of a Volkswagen Beetle hangs from a double-story ceiling.

Margot steps out of a small group gathered in a room separated from the foyer by a heavily molded arch.

"You made it," she sings as if we've crossed an ocean and not just the street.

She is wearing a tight-fitting hot-pink sheath dress and holding a cocktail high in an outstretched arm. I can see the long scratches made by the chicken. I look away. She leans in to Jeff and gives him a kiss without touching his cheek.

"Handsome as ever, Mr. Corrigan," she says, laughing. "And look at you!"

She gives me the once-over, reading me with eyes like a supermarket scanner, resting them a beat too long on my beloved Frye boots with their slightly (and permanently) scuffed toes.

"Aren't you adorable," she says.

Jeff puts his arm around my shoulder. He's taking it as a compliment.

"Let's get you a drink and then I'll introduce you around. Daniel is making the most wonderful dragon-fruit martinis tonight."

She turns and walks back through the arches. We follow her into a room with an enormous and elaborate built-in bar and three tall café tables. A couple is sitting at one of the tables. The woman is blond, like Margot, and wearing a similar dress in a lighter pink. Jeff slaps the man on the back, but we don't stop.

I'd assumed Margot's husband was the Daniel who was making the fabulous drinks, but when we press ourselves to the mahogany bar, I see Daniel is a hipster with a man bun, tattooed forearms, and the same black pants and white shirt as the woman who answered the door. So, there are *staff* at this casual get-together. I think about my brownies on the paper plate and hope they're lost before Margot sees them.

Pink dragon-fruit martinis in hand, we obediently toddle after her as she takes us across the foyer. Margot's mules click on the marble floor. My boots feel hot and clunky. We walk through another ornately molded arch into a living room where two women are deep in conversation with a handsome young man in a crisp short-sleeved shirt.

Each of them has one hand pressed against their breastbone and one on their hip. As we approach, they stop midsentence and look over at us. The women's faces are perfect palettes, colors arranged just so, finely blended as if by an artist's hand.

And they've clearly gotten Margot's memo. Dress must be short and tight and in summer fruit colors— tangerine, watermelon, peach—taut arms and tanned knees bared. The guy has a few-days-of-growth beard that is meant to convey a laissez-faire attitude, but is clearly impeccably manscaped.

I don't realize I've leaned in to Jeff, holding onto him as if he were a life raft, until a woman who could be Margot's clone, take away the height and add an obvious nose job, laughs and says, "Jeez, get a room, you two!"

Jeff and I step away from each other like two teenagers caught in the back of a car, and the heat in my face burns as the others chuckle lightly at the jokester.

"Jeff," Margot says resting a hand on my husband's shoulder. "Rand is on the patio with the men."

I flinch for the man standing right in front of Margot who is not on the patio, but his face doesn't change at the exclusion.

"I think they're at the cigars already," she continues. "Why don't you find them?"

I know Jeff hates cigars. And I hate to lose my security blanket.

"Sure, Margot," he says and then turns to me, smiles and mouths, *Play along*. If he can do it, I can do it. This is going to be fine. Just fine. I take a big sip of my martini, tilt my head, and smile.

"Friends, we have a new addition to our little group. Let me make the introductions."

She taps her hand on each person's arm as if she was tagging them for duck, duck, goose.

"Noah, Amber, Colette."

So, Amber is the one with the great sense of humor.

"Noah is married to Brian and has two boys, Jack, six, Liam, four. Amber, two girls, Jacqueline, eleven, Kendal, eight. Colette, married to Glen, has the twins, RJ and Samson. They're eight, no nine. Jacqueline and my Madison are best friends. They've been in the same class since kindergarten, no wait, preschool. Wow, where did the time go? Noah runs membership for the Newcomers Club… Oh, you will definitely join that. Amber is cochair, with me, of this year's fifth-grade fashion show, and Colette runs the Soccer Parents Association. Is yours sporty? Mine isn't. I'm a full-time drama mama. But if yours is, you'll want Colette on your side. You know what they say about those sports parents. Present company excluded, Colette, of course."

The group chortles, yes, chortles at Margot's joke, and the pecking order becomes clear. The names—and bios—whiz past me. I hear the word *eleven*, Harri's age, and cling to that one piece of information.

"So, everyone, this is Jeff's new wife, Stacey. She's an artist, how lucky for us. I've already got a project in mind for her for the fashion show…"

Noah, Amber, and Colette aren't listening to Margot's plans for me. They are all staring at me, mouths agape, watching me turn the color of my martini.

"What are the chances of that?" asks Noah.

"Freaky," says Colette.

"You have the same name as Jeff's ex-wife!" bleats Amber.

"I... No..."

"That's convenient for him, if you know what I mean," Noah says, adding a stage wink.

"Actually, my name is Ginny. Ginny Miller. I didn't take Jeff's... Well, it doesn't matter," I stammer to cover up what must be Margot's embarrassment.

"Ginny? You just said her name is Stacey," Amber says to Margot.

"No, I didn't," insists Margot. "Don't be silly."

No one argues over the faux pas, least of all me. I let my face cool down. It's okay, I think, honest mistake. After all, Stacey lived on this street. Stacey showed up at these dinner parties with Jeff. Stacey was her friend.

"Where do you all live?" I ask. Deflect and distract.

"Noah and Brian are at the end of the cul-de-sac," Margot answers for them. "Amber is next to me. And Colette is two down from you, on the other side of that hideous ranch house."

I scan the room. No Wayne anywhere.

"I have a soft spot for Wayne," Jeff had said after I told him about our unique meet-up and wondered if he'd be at Margot's. "But now that you've met him, you can see why he isn't at the top of her guest list."

"I thought he seemed sweet and kind of lonely," I had said. "Of course, that was after I got past the little show he put on for Harri and me."

"That's Wayne for you. He's always been a little out there, worse since his wife died last year. Cancer. And I don't think he has a lot of family nearby. I like to keep an eye on him."

I make another check on the list of reasons why I was right to marry this man.

"Ugh, when is that old geezer going to move?" demands Amber. "Isn't there a nursing home with his name on it somewhere?"

"I don't think he's that old," I say. "And he's kind of charm—"

"It's bringing down the property values," Margot snaps.

"And he wanders around his yard in a bathrobe," spits Colette. "With that filthy dog."

I'm losing my audience, running the risk of being thrown out of the group before I've even been invited in. If these women don't like me, they could turn their backs on Harri. And they have daughters her age.

"I've seen him naked," I announce and immediately regret it.

"What?"

Four sets of eyes widen.

"No!"

"When?"

"Where?"

Collette leans in, clasping my wrist.

"He could be a child molester. We should call the police. Ginny, you should do it. You were a witness."

What just happened? This was not what I wanted... It was just a stupid, stupid attempt at a little gossip.

"Oh, I don't mean naked, naked."

I force a laugh. Look at me; I'm such a card. Chins lift. Eyes narrow. My new friends wait for an explanation.

"I mean, he had a bathing suit on! Of course, he did. He was helping himself to our hot tub. Scared the bejesus out of me. But ugh—no one needs to see that, am I right?"

Margot is clearly disappointed.

"Stacey, you're such a prude," she says.

I deserved that.

A deep voice behind my back saves me from any further destruction of a poor man's reputation.

"Margot! When are we eating?"

Margot's spine straightens and for a flash she seems not in complete control of the room and everyone in it.

"Rand," she says, recovering quickly. "Come meet our new neighbor."

I smell cigars and cologne before he steps into view. He is, as Margot had accused him of being, tall. He is also broad-shouldered with a JFK hairstyle and deep dimples.

"This is my husband, Rand," Margot says, laying a palm on his chest.

Rand smiles at me as if he is amused by this introduction. I stick my hand out.

"I'm Ginny Miller," I say before Margot can call me otherwise.

He takes my hand between both of his and holds it gently.

"Hello, Ginny Miller," he purrs.

His wife glances at him but I don't see any reaction on her face. If my husband cooed at another woman like this, my brows would be knit like a Shetland sweater. Maybe it's Botox. The woman who took my brownies comes up to Margot and whispers something to her.

"Dinner is served," she announces.

"Ginny Miller, you are going to sit next to me," Rand says into the back of my neck, making me shiver.

He slides his arm across my back and turns me toward the dining room. His reach is so long that his fingers graze the side of my breast.

Chapter 4

THE DEADLINE FOR MY LATEST COMMISSION IS LOOMING. THE owner of a rheumy-eyed shih tzu emailed me the photo weeks ago, but with the move, it got buried in my in-box. I printed it this morning, and it is now taped to my paint-splattered easel.

Harri is sitting in the overstuffed armchair we brought from the apartment. The one Jeff and I had carried up the steps of the studio with an effort that mimicked a comedy routine. I knew I was moving into a fully furnished house, but the chair is our reading nest. Harri and I would sit in it together when we could both fit, and later when we couldn't, Harri claimed it as her own. I couldn't leave it behind.

Now she is sideways in said chair, her legs hanging over a threadbare arm, reading a book about raising backyard chickens. Mrs. Clucklesworth hasn't laid an egg yet, and Harri is concerned.

"Give her a chance to get settled," I had suggested, knowing nothing about chickens but well aware of my own feelings about moving to a new place.

As Harri continues to search for answers, I lean a canvas on the ledge of the easel and look through the cardboard box for my palette. I really should organize everything before I start a new project, but I am just itching to paint. I need it to quiet my mind.

The faces and voices and events of last night at Margot's flip through my head: the women scrubbed free of imperfection right down to their pedicures; the chatter of silverware and voices, talking over me, around me; the familiarity of people who have known each other for years and aren't sure there is room for one more.

And, of course, that touch.

It was unintentional, a miscalculation of male arm length to female torso ratio, I told myself. These awkward things happen. To do anything about it, to have jerked my body away or reprimanded the owner of the hand or told my husband or his wife would have created a scene over something that was clearly nothing. It would have done little to set me off on the right foot with my new neighbors. Best to let it go.

I pry open the battered tin box holding my paint and take out the colors I will use to lay down a background on the canvas before I block in the shih tzu's outline. The dog is black and white, so I choose cadmium red and cobalt blue to make purple, and black and white to gray it down and mute it. It's been so long since I opened the bent and twisted tubes that I need needle-nose pliers to get the caps off.

Harri looks up at me, her nose scrunched. "Do you know a chicken can lay only one egg a day?"

"Well, it's your chicken so it will be your egg," I say as I squeeze the paint into the depressions of the palette. It's an art in itself, estimating just how much to use when my supplies budget is never far from my thoughts.

"Mom, I think we need more chickens. One for each of us. It's only fair."

I make a harrumphing sound and leave it at that. We fall into a comfortable silence. We've been here a million times. We've had years of this, sharing the same air, breathing in sync, like an old married couple. We've spent more time together than most mothers and daughters do. Part of it is habit and circumstance. A lot of it is choice. On both our parts.

But soon the kids on the street will be back from their various summer camps. Harri will have lots of new friends better suited to her than her mother.

It isn't that she's never made a friend, but they rarely stuck around long, and Harri didn't have the social skills to figure out how to keep them. She'd just shrug her shoulders when each little girl eventually went off with someone else and she'd open her book, or we'd go for ice cream, or play dress up with all of our thrift store finds, or stay up late watching movies.

I know it will be different here for Harri. People are different in the suburbs, friendlier, more down-to-earth. Kids lack the street smarts that make city children grow up too fast and harden their edges. At least that's how I remember it from my own childhood and the years of seeing it confirmed in sitcoms and movies.

This is what Harri needs—a place to cradle her soft-boiled shell, like an Easter egg in pink plastic grass.

I use a wide, flat brush to mix primary colors into a hue that until now only lived in my imagination. I pull the color in long strokes across the canvas, building the background of my painting. The almost mechanical act allows my mind to jump ahead to shapes and shadows. When I have paint halfway down the canvas, my cell phone rings. The voice on the other end speaks quickly and hangs up before I get more than a few words in.

"Amber is stopping by," I say to Harri.

I'm torn. I was just getting into a groove. Still, I want to get to know my new neighbors. I rest the paintbrush in the coffee can filled with turpentine.

"Who's Amber?"

Before I can answer, I hear her coming up the steps.

"Hallo!" She must have been halfway down my driveway when she called.

Amber appears before us, one hand on her hip, the other on her heart, as if the climb up the fifteen stairs to my studio led to Everest.

"Well, what's all this?" she asks, not actually out of breath. "I had no idea this was up here."

"My studio. Jeff renovated this old storage space before we moved in. He surprised me."

"Well, isn't that just like Jeff," says Amber. "He's a gem, a real gem."

She scans the room. It's still mostly empty, just the easel and the chair and my supplies propped up on cardboard boxes until Jeff the Gem can build shelves.

"Margot said you were an artist, but I just assumed that meant you were crafty. You didn't say anything last night about being the real deal."

Last night the conversations revolved around Wayne's eyesore of a house, a lunch at Neiman Marcus that Amber hadn't been invited to but wouldn't have gone to anyway, a woman named Babette's vaginal rejuvenation, and most importantly, Margot's daughter, Madison, landing the lead role of Mabel in *Pirates of Penzance* at the same theater camp John Mellencamp's granddaughter attends.

"Mom's a great artist," says Harri, defending my honor. "She can paint any animal perfectly. You just have to give her a picture."

"Amber, this is my daughter, Harri."

"Hi, Amber."

I feel the bloom of pride as my daughter gets up from the reading chair to shake the woman's hand. A lot of kids her age would have just waved or shrugged and turned away from an adult interaction. Amber looks at Harri's hand as if she might have just picked her nose with it and gingerly shakes it.

"Well, hello there, Harri. I'm *Mrs. Franco*. I have a daughter about your age—Jacqueline."

She pronounces the name like Jacques Cousteau and with a bit of a faux French accent.

"I'm eleven."

"So is Jacqueline! How perfect is that? Everyone loves Jacqueline. You'll stick with her when school starts, and you'll fall right in with the popular crowd."

Harri looks at me through smudged glasses, her mouth half-open. For the first time in her life, my daughter doesn't have a quick response.

"That sounds wonderful," I chirp. "We'll have to introduce them as soon as possible. Maybe Jacqueline would like to come over for a play date?"

"My girls are spending August in the Hamptons with their father."

She spits out the words quickly as if they are leaving a bad taste in her mouth. That answers the question of why Amber was alone at Margot's last night in a room full of couples. I want to tell her I get it, I really do. But I barely know this woman; it seems a little early to share war stories.

Harri goes back to her chair and her book. Amber, over whatever emotions her ex-husband in the Hamptons has brought up, surveys my coffee can of brushes, picks one out, and starts bending the bristles back and forth in her hand. I want to take the brush back before she destroys it, but I don't.

"So how about all that Stacey shit from Margot last night?"

She glances over at Harri, who is suddenly much less interested in animal husbandry.

"Pardon my French," she says.

"Hun, why don't you check on Mrs. Clucklesworth? Today might be egg day!"

"Mom, I've heard curse words before. You use them all the time."

"Just go outside, love. Get some fresh air."

Harri makes a show of leaving. Slumping her shoulders, groaning, and dragging her feet down the stairs. Back in Queens she was never dismissed when the grown-ups were talking. But we're not in Queens anymore, and if Amber is willing to bring up "shit" about Jeff's ex-wife in front of my eleven-year-old, who knows what's next.

"I'm sure it was an honest mistake," I say after I hear the door slam downstairs. "The Stacey thing."

Margot had done it a couple of times during the dinner. Each time sent a rush of heat to my cheeks. But she was the hostess. I wasn't going to embarrass her by continually correcting her in public. Amber puts the paintbrush back in the can, walks over to a stack of canvases leaning against the wall, and shuffles through them.

"Margot Moss-Marks doesn't make mistakes. She was pissing on you. Marking her turf."

"I'm not here to claim anyone's turf."

Amber picks up a small painting of a sunflower in a mason jar. She holds it at arm's length and tilts her head.

"Of course, you're not," she says, looking at the painting. "This would look great in my laundry room. Anyway, it's just how things are around here. Margot's a bitch. But she gets a hell of a lot done. She's the CEO of the neighborhood. There's no use in fighting it. You'll get used to her."

It's hard to reconcile the woman who stood behind Margot's shoulder last night, laughing and nodding at everything she said, including allegedly calling me by my husband's ex-wife's name to prove some point, with this person who is standing here warning me about her so-called friend. On the other hand, if it is accurate, I appreciate the inside scoop.

"Thanks, Amber. It's hard when you're new, you know, to know who's who."

"I've got your back. So, if you have any questions about where to go or what to do, come to me first, okay?"

"Okay, sure. Thank you."

"Promise? You'll need an ally on this street. You'll see."

"Yes, of course," I say. "It will be great to have someone who knows the ropes to turn to."

"Yup. That's me. And in return, you can help me. That's why I came over here. I want to recruit you to the fifth-grade fashion show committee. It's a huge yearly event run by the upperclassmen moms. Dinner and a tricky tray and an MC. Some of the best stores in town lend out their clothes and we go all out. The girls get the royal treatment—hair, makeup. They are absolutely gorgeous. And the boys who escort them, they wear real tuxes. They look"—she kisses her fingertips—"*oh-là-là*! The money goes toward a huge graduation party. Can you believe we have kids old enough to graduate? Please don't remind me that I'll have a middle schooler next year. Anyway, we need all the help we can get. And now I find out you have a fifth grader *and* are talented as hell. I mean, look at this sunflower. We need this kind of creativity. We can't do this without it. You'll be saving the whole event. So, tell me you'll do it, tell me you'll be my new best friend and work with me on the fashion show."

I suppress my nagging inner critic asking, *Why would someone like Amber be so hell-bent on being friends with someone like me?* Maybe I'm not the only one who needs a new friend right now. And besides, it's exciting to be courted. I feel like I just got invited to sit at the popular table. I have an overwhelming desire to change into something nicer than my painting overalls.

"Of course, I'll help you!" I say to my new best friend.

"Yay," sings Amber, clapping her hands and smiling so widely she reveals pink gums all the way back to her molars. You'd think she'd won a trip to the moon.

"And you know what?" I add. "I want you to have the painting."

I pick it up and dust it off with my sleeve. It's the last canvas in a series of failed attempts to paint glass. I had finally gotten the reflection of the sun off the jar right.

"Really? Well, let me pay you for it."

"No, no. It's a gift. I want you to have it."

"Ginny, aren't you the sweetest?"

"What are friends for?" I ask.

Chapter 5

THE DOORBELL RINGS AND AMBER AND JACQUELINE ARE AT MY front door. Amber stands behind her daughter, her hands perched on the girl's narrow shoulders as if she is preventing her from making a run for it. Jacqueline's thick, dark hair is pulled tightly off her month-in-the-Hamptons tan face with a pink, sparkly headband.

Her eyebrows are thick and perfectly shaped, but the skin around and between them is red and angry. I can see Amber in her, before salon appointments and surgeon's knife. I wonder if the mother ever fears that standing side by side with her daughter will give away her original self.

"Hallo!" Amber sings, pushing her daughter over the threshold. "We're just back from our waxing, and we thought we'd stop by. Hope we're not disturbing. Jacqueline has only just gotten home from her summer vacay this weekend but she is dying to meet her new neighbor."

Jacqueline looks like she is indeed dying, but from boredom and annoyance and irritation. Harri, who has heard them come in, has a different take on it. She skips into the foyer and stops just short of knocking Jacqueline over. Her arms are wrapped around a stack of fresh library books. Next to the chicken, the library with the beanbag-filled reading nook has helped to seal the move for my daughter.

"Hey, Amber," she says to *Mrs. Franco*. "Hi, Jacqueline, I'm Harri!"

Jacqueline leans back, reclaiming some personal space.

"Do you want to see what books I got today? Do you like Beverly Cleary?"

Jacqueline shrugs her shoulders.

"How about Lois Lowry?"

Another shrug.

"John Green?"

Another.

Harri takes a different tack.

"Do you want to meet Mrs. Clucklesworth? She's my chicken."

Jacqueline wrinkles her nose. Harri looks at me for help communicating with this person who clearly doesn't speak her language. I'm not sure how to help. Harri's floundering feels like my defeat; the weight of it presses against my chest. Fortunately, Amber is there to get us all out of our own way.

"Jacqueline, why don't you go upstairs and see Harri's room?"

Harri brightens at the idea.

"Wanna?"

"Sure," answers Jacqueline, her first word.

Harri turns and thunders up the stairs. Jacqueline follows, taking demure steps. I know my daughter is excited to show off her first actual bedroom.

Instead of the corner of a room, separated from her mother by a few feet and a bookcase, she has four walls and a door and a maple tree outside a window that looks out onto the street.

She has her own bunk bed with a ladder and a desk with a swivel chair on wheels and a lamp shaped like a baseball bat. In fact, everything in the room screams, "a boy used to live here." The walls are papered with a red and blue plaid. A decorative border alternates basketballs, baseballs, and footballs. Nothing has changed since Jeff's son, Brendan, moved out five years ago. Jeff had offered to rip down the wallpaper and put up anything Harri wanted—unicorns or fairies or "Whatever girls are into these days." But she just shook her head, twirled with her arms outstretched, and gave me a Christmas morning smile.

"It's perfect just as it is. Thank you. Thank you." Then she turned to me, holding out a crooked pinkie finger and said, "Best mom ever."

I answered the same way I had a thousand times before. I hooked my pinkie into hers. "Best kid ever," I said.

I hear a thud overheard that means Harri has climbed the ladder and jumped off the top bunk. She says she does it because she can. I can't argue with that. Amber flinches at the sound and looks up the stairs.

"Coffee?" I ask.

Amber follows me into the kitchen, and I pull out the French press I recently found in the back of a tall cabinet. There are a number of coffee makers in this kitchen: a big shiny machine with a stainless steel carafe and enough knobs and buttons to launch a rocket ship, a giant percolator in the pantry that could serve twenty, and an impressive chrome espresso maker squatting on the counter next to the farm sink. But I love the simplicity of the French press—ground beans and boiling water. I fill the kettle, set it to boil, scoop out the grounds, and dump them in the glass carafe. The smell makes me desperate for a caffeine fix.

"Oh, the Miele!" says Amber, standing with her hand to her heart in front of the shiny behemoth on the counter. "I remember when Stacey got this! She was obsessed with espresso and lattes—for about five minutes." She laughs. "I'm all about Starbucks. 'Stacey, let someone else do the work,' I told her."

I feel the zing hearing Stacey's name gives me. It seems like no one around here can stop bringing her up. I guess I am lucky that I'm only just hearing about Stacey and not coming up against her in real life. There have been no family gatherings where we'd stand on opposite sides of a room, trying to one-up each other over who was less bothered by the other's presence. No graduations, no weddings, no third person in our marriage to upset the balance. When Stacey left, she was long gone. And as Jeff tells me, after the papers were signed and the lawyers were paid, that was that.

"Still," Amber continues, "that Miele is a piece of art. Totally worth having if for no other reason than it's a statement piece. I'd hang on to it when you rip out the kitchen."

"What? Rip out the kitchen? Are you kidding?"

"Of course not. You're going to want to put your stamp on the house. As great an eye as Stacey had, you don't want to live with *her* things, do you? You should tell Jeff you need to start from scratch, really. He can't expect you to—"

"Oh, I'd never ask Jeff to change this kitchen. Can you imagine how much it would cost? I don't care about that kind of stuff; it's just not important to me. Besides, you should have seen what we had before all this. My coffee maker in Queens was an old Mr. Coffee I picked up at a garage sale— for five bucks."

I see the grimace starting in Amber's cheek, an otherwise imperceptible spasm, when I mention my secondhand coffee maker. I was proud of that find. Scrubbed out and run through with white vinegar, it made excellent coffee. I decide not to tell her about my toaster oven. Instead, I pour the now-boiled water into the carafe and press down the plunger.

"Suit yourself," she says. "Live with the ghosts."

There wouldn't be a ghost if you guys didn't keep bringing her up, I think.

Moments later there is a thundering down the stairs. Amber flinches again. The girls come tumbling into the kitchen, not so much like a pack of puppies but a herd of baby rhinos. Jacqueline is holding her cell phone toward her mom.

"Madison wants me to come over! Can I go?"

"Sure, why not," Amber says and my heart breaks for my daughter, ever a bridesmaid.

"Can I come?" asks Harri.

"Of course you can go," Amber answers for Jacqueline and me.

The two girls pogo as if they were just called out of the audience of *The Price Is Right* and run out the front door. I feel a sense of relief. That was easier than I thought it would be. Harri will be fine here. I pour the coffee into Stacey's thick ceramic mugs.

"What do you take in yours?" I ask.

"I can't stay. I left Kendal home alone watching *Pretty Little Liars*. And the bad mother of the year award goes to… Don't tell anyone, will you? Especially Margot, with her 'limited screen time.'" Amber performs an exaggerated eye roll. "We can't all be enriching our kids' lives twenty-four seven. Am I right?"

———

Harri isn't home by the time Jeff gets back from work.

"She's been gone a long time," I tell him.

"That's great," he says, pulling me toward him.

I don't relax into his hug and he feels it. "This is exactly what you wanted. She's making friends. It will be great for her to walk into school next week knowing a few kids."

He's right, of course. Still, she's been gone for hours. I decide to text her, just to check in, mind you, but I'm Cool Mom about it, just want to see if she's having fun. She doesn't answer. Fifteen minutes later I try again. Nothing. Ten minutes later. Five minutes later.

"What could have happened to her?" I ask Jeff.

"I'm sure she's just having a great time and not looking at her phone."

"But that's why she has a phone, to look at it when I'm trying to reach her!"

"Gin, relax. She's just at Margot's. What could happen?"

"What if they've gotten into the liquor cabinet? Or wandered into the woods? Oh my God, guns! Damn it, I didn't ask if they have unlocked-up guns. How well do you know Margot? Do you think they have guns in the house?"

"Wow, okay, relax. First of all, I doubt the Moss-Markses have unsecured firearms. But if you are this worked up, why don't you just call Harri and tell her to come home?"

"Yes, that's what I'm going to do."

Screw Cool Mom.

"Okay, but honestly—"

"Shush, it's ringing."

I hear the phone ringing in my ear.

And upstairs.

Harri has left her phone in her room. It is our biggest rule, the one I drill into her over and over again—always have your cell phone with you.

"I need to know where you are," I'd say to her when the cell phone got left on her bed, the kitchen table, the pocket of the jacket she wore yesterday.

"And keep it charged," I'd yell into an empty void.

I go upstairs to Harri's room. Her phone is on the floor next to her new library books, one of which is upside down and open, its spine straining.

"I guess I forgot my phone again," says my daughter from behind me. I swing around, ready for round one thousand on this subject, but when I see her, things change quickly.

"What happened to you?"

My daughter's face and arms are bright orange. There are dark stains on the collar and right sleeve of her T-shirt.

"Jesus, Harri, what the hell did you get into?"

I grab her arm and wipe it with my thumb. Harri looks crestfallen.

"You don't like it? It's self-tanner. Madison and Jacqueline helped me. They said I was too pale and I needed a tan before school started. That way I'd look like I did something cool this summer."

"Oh, Lord," is all I can say.

I lick my thumb and try to wipe at the color again. It's going nowhere. Harri pushes away from me.

"Stop. That's gross!"

"Okay," I laugh, pulling her into a hug and resting my chin on top of her head. It smells like it's time for a shampooing. I take my phone out of my back pocket.

"Let's see if I can find a way to get you cleaned up."

"But then I won't look like I've been anywhere."

"Honey, you've been on the greatest adventure of all this summer. You moved to a new state—all the way to the wilds of New Jersey. Into a new house. You got your own chicken! Your own bunk bed! The top bunk alone is the perfect 'what I did with my summer vacation' story."

I find a site that says a heaping dose of baby oil in a hot bath will help remove some of the color. I run the giant jet tub in the master bathroom and pour in half a bottle. While we wait for it to fill, I wrap her hair in a towel and wipe her face with as much oil as it will take without it running into her eyes and mouth.

"It's like we're having a spa day," I say.

When she climbs into the tub, I sit on the toilet with my feet up on the tiled ledge of the bath. She sinks down low, drenching the towel on her head. I see her knees are dirty and her shins are covered with bruises. I smile at my little country girl.

"Was it fun, at least, meeting Madison and Jacqueline?"

Harri shrugs. "They were fine."

She sinks deeper into the water. The towel unwinds and drops to the bottom of the tub, leaving her hair floating around her head like Medusa's snakes. I'm never going to get this oil out.

"Madison kept asking me what Broadway shows I've seen. She said if I lived in New York I should have at least seen *Hamilton*."

I snort at the absurdity of that statement.

"Clearly Madison doesn't know that almost nobody who lives in New York actually gets to see *Hamilton*."

"She's seen it twice. Her parents took her for her birthday. And then they went back again because she loved it so much."

"No kidding," I say. "Imagine that."

I rub her arm with a washcloth. The pumpkin color starts to fade to cantaloupe. On the surface of the bathwater, the baby oil pools into large circles that bounce off each other as Harri shifts positions.

"I don't know if I like it here," Harri says to the oil circles.

My heart drowns in the cooling tub.

"No? Why not?"

Harri shrugs.

"Just give it some time," I plead, trying to sound like I'm not.

She shrugs again.

"And I know those girls made you look like an Oompa Loompa—"

"Mom!"

"I'm just kidding. But I'm serious about this. They thought they were helping you. Which is sweet if you think about it. That means they want to be your friends."

"I guess," says Harri.

Chapter 6

"You okay with beer? I can make you a G and T. We've got limes. We have limes, don't we, Ginny?"

Before I can answer, Jeff opens the refrigerator and leans in to find the fruit himself.

"No, Dad. I'm good. I've gotta drive back tonight."

Jeff looks crestfallen but catches himself. It's not every day his son comes to dinner. In fact, it's the first time we've seen him since the wedding.

"You can stay over! Harri's got your old room now, but you can crash in the guest room. It's all made up," Jeff says, and the hope in his voice breaks me a little.

"You can sleep on my top bunk," Harri chimes in from her spot at the kitchen table where she has been watching Brendan like a hawk. Her cheeks are flushed, and her eyes are open a little too wide. I think my daughter has a crush on her new stepbrother.

"Thanks, Harri. That's sounds awesome. Definitely next time," says Brendan. "But I'm going out after this."

"On a work night?" Jeff blurts out to the grown man holding a beer in his hand and leaning casually against the kitchen counter.

"Ginny, help me out here," Brendan says with a sly smile.

Jeff holds up his hands. "Okay, I get it," he says, laughing. "I wasn't always this old."

I see a different Jeff when he's with his son. As cool and steady as Jeff is around Harri, he always seems like he's trying too hard with Brendan. Just a year out of college, Jeff's only child works in Manhattan, long entry-level hours, and lives in Weehawken with a tight-knit group of school friends. Life is frenetic and fun and full for him. And coming home, however much he loves his dad, can't be high on this twenty-two-year-old's to-do list. Still, I know Jeff misses him terribly, and the rare sightings make him desperate for more.

"Can someone toss this salad?" I ask, pushing the large wooden bowl toward Jeff and changing the subject. "Dinner will be ready soon. Harri, set the table for me, hon?"

"I'll help you," says Brendan. Harri's eyes light up as he opens the glass-fronted cabinets, takes down four plates, and hands them to her.

"Thank you," she says as if she'd been handed the key to *The Secret Garden*.

Brendan reaches up and grabs water glasses from our spectacular collection.

"Wow," he says. "Nothing has changed. Everything is exactly where it's always been."

I can't tell if he is comforted by this or confronting us about it. Jeff knits his brow as if this is the first time it's occurred to him that we've been playing in someone else's dollhouse.

"No, it's not," he says.

Brendan scans the room and walks up to the counter where Butcher Pig stands facing the wall. "Well, true. This is different. The pig's in a time-out. What'd he do?"

"Mom thinks he's dumb," Harri says as she circles the table, putting a fork at each place. She goes back to the drawer and takes out four knives. Her system lacks efficiency.

"Well, she's right," says Brendan. "No self-respecting pig would take a job as a butcher."

"That's exactly what I said!" I laugh.

"Down with cannibalistic pigs!" declares my stepson.

"Right! Precisely! Okay, who's ready to eat?" I ask. "I made pork chops!"

"You didn't!" Brendan laughs. "That's hysterical."

"No I didn't. I made lasagna. But I should have."

Brendan tips his beer bottle toward me. "Touché."

Harri rolls her eyes. Jeff looks confused. Relief floods over me. Not because I made a dumb joke and it landed. But because I may have jumped a hurdle with this young man. This person who looks so familiar—so like his father, I'll bet their baby photos are interchangeable—that I feel like I should know him deeply. But I don't. Not in the way I hope to someday. And, although Jeff assured me he spoke to and got the blessing of his son before he proposed, I occasionally catch Brendan looking at me as if he doesn't know what I'm doing here. Maybe Butcher Pig has redeemed himself.

Jeff sits Brendan at the head of the kitchen table and peppers him with questions about his job, his apartment, his friends, his neighborhood, his car. Harri eats with her chin in her palm, elbow on the table, absorbing Brendan's answers as if he were telling her about his life at Hogwarts.

It's taken a few days, but the self-tanner has faded, save for a few rough patches on Harri's elbows and knees. She hasn't said anything about wanting to see the girls who got her into that mess in the first place. And neither of them has been looking for her. I've called over to Amber, inviting Jacqueline for another playdate, but I couldn't get on the eleven-year-old's calendar.

"So much to do before school starts," Amber had said. "We are way behind on the shopping. She's got a whole new wardrobe to pick out, you know."

I don't think Harri cares. She seems happy to hang out with her chicken and explore her new house. She's discovered the screeching pull-down ladder stairs that lead up to the attic and has found a treasure trove of old boxes and stored items to keep her busy for hours. I've tried to quiet my anxiety about wanting her to have made some connections before school starts. Very soon she will see Madison and Jacqueline every day. There is more than enough time to click with all her new friends.

After question number eighty-seven from his dad, Brendan turns to me. "So, Ginny, how are you liking it here?"

I don't think this young man wants the true answer—that it's too soon to tell, that I love my new husband and all the promise of this new life, the grin on Harri's face when she climbs on his old swing set or finds a fresh egg or discovers a new reading nook in some new corner of this big house, but that I also don't have my footing, I don't know who's who and what's what and how intimidating and exhausting figuring it all out will be.

"It's great," I say, smiling at Jeff.

"She's met all the neighbors," he says. "And they've already recruited her for one of their committees."

"Yikes," says Brendan. "Good luck with that."

"What do you know that I don't know?" I laugh.

Brendan shrugs. "I don't know, maybe they've all chilled since I lived here."

"Brendan, don't freak Ginny out. Besides, they're lucky to have her." Jeff is smiling but I hear a tinge of defensiveness in his voice.

"It's okay. I'm not freaked out."

Brendan's tone changes. He throws his napkin on the table. "Well, don't let them do to you what they did to my mom."

"What are you talking about?" snaps Jeff.

Brendan sucks in air between his teeth before he says, "Well, she wasn't always like she...like she turned out. It was after she started hanging out with those ladies—"

Things take a quick turn. Now it's Jeff's turn to throw down his napkin. He adds in a push back from the table for good measure.

"Ha," he laughs bitterly. "That's what you call revisionist history. I remember it a little differently."

Jeff and his son stare at each other in stony silence. They both have the same two lines etched between their eyebrows, one shorter than the other like a lopsided eleven. Harri looks to me for guidance and I lower my eyes to my lap, willing her not to share any of her candor on the subject.

"Whatever, it doesn't matter anyway," Brendan finally says. "She's paying for it now."

"Bren," Jeff says, stepping on his son's last word. "The stuff you asked me to pack up for you? To take back to your apartment? It's all boxed up in the garage. Why don't you go make sure I got everything?" His voice is urgent as if the garage were ablaze and all his son's belongings will be lost if he doesn't rush out there.

"Yeah, sure," says Brendan, pushing away from the table.

"I'll come with you," offers Harri. "I can show you Mom's amazing art studio."

After they close the sliding glass door behind them, I turn to my husband. "Are you okay?"

"Yeah. I just can't believe he's still defending her."

I tread lightly. "I'm sure it's not easy for him, Jeff. As an only child, I'd bet in some way he feels caught in the middle. Even still."

I feel a small, selfish sense of relief that Harri was too young to understand what was happening when her father left, too young to feel the pressure to pick a side.

"There shouldn't be a middle. It was pretty clear cut who the shitty parent was. To up and leave your kid, for Chrissake. She missed so many important days in his life: prom, high school graduation, moving him into his dorm. Yeah, she showed up for his college graduation, but you'd hardly know she was there."

Jeff and I quietly clear the dishes from the table. "You know, she's still his mother. Even a damaged mother holds a place in a kid's heart."

My husband shrugs as he scrapes scraps from plates into the garbage.

"By the way, what did he mean by 'She's paying for it now'?"

"Nothing. Just that now she's married to a jerk."

Jeff goes outside to help Brendan load the boxes into his car. Through the open kitchen window I hear the basketball bouncing in the driveway and the thwack of it hitting the old hoop over the garage. I smile to myself. All is forgiven. Jeff and his son are strong and always will be. They share a hard history that belongs only to them. They were the two who were left behind. I get it. I know how they feel.

After Brendan leaves, Jeff and Harri come back inside a little sweaty and a little out of breath. "That was fun," Harri says. "Can you and me play basketball again someday?"

"Sure. Anytime you want, Har."

My daughter runs up to her room with a huge smile on her face. I start stacking the dishes into the dishwasher and wipe down the counters.

"The pig is pretty dumb," says Jeff, walking over and picking it up.

"It is a poor choice of occupations for a swine."

"I'm sorry, Gin."

"About what?"

"About all this crap lying around. All Stacey's crap. Why didn't you say anything to me about it? Just because I'm blind to things like this doesn't mean you should have to look at it day after day. You must think I'm so insensitive."

"Jeff, no! Not at all. I don't care about any of this," I say, pointing toward the family room where, frankly, a lot of *this* is lining the shelves. "Harri and I are so very happy here. Some bric-a-brac someone else picked out isn't going to change that."

"Nope, that's it," he declares and goes to the bottom of the stairs. "Harri, can you come down here?" He walks back into the kitchen and right out the sliding door he just came in through.

Harri thunders down the stairs and looks at me standing at the sink with my mouth open. "What's happening?"

"I have no idea."

A minute later Jeff is back with an empty Rubbermaid box labeled "Easter" and a glint in his eye.

"What's going on?" I ask. "Where are the Easter decorations?"

"On the garage floor."

He walks over to Butcher Pig and puts it in the box. "Harri, I need your help. I'll hold this box and we're going to go around and you're going to help me decide what to pack away. It's going to be like a reverse scavenger hunt."

Harri's eyebrows raise over her glasses. "Okay!" She giggles.

"Jeff, what are you doing?"

"What I should have done before you two got here. I'm getting rid of this ancient history and making room."

"For what?"

"For whatever you want. Your work, all the great stuff we've collected at craft fairs, some of Harri's sand art."

Harri claps her hands and skips into the family room to get to work. "Don't forget the bronze elephant," Jeff shouts to her.

I watch the two of them fill the Easter storage box and go back to the garage to get the Halloween container. It is one of the most romantic things anyone has ever done for me.

Chapter 7

THE WHITE MERCEDES BEHIND ME LEANS ON ITS HORN. THROUGH my rearview mirror I see the driver, a woman with a severe ponytail and ginormous glasses, raise both palms in a what-the-hell-are-you-doing gesture.

I can't hear her, but I can imagine she's calling me some not-so-nice names. This is what I get for not committing to memory Acorn Avenue Elementary School's drop-off flyer that arrived with a thick packet of papers including not only a complex system of traffic patterns and loading and unloading procedures, but also a mission statement, student code of conduct, fundraising calendars, meeting schedules, health forms, and an order sheet for the school T-shirt, sweatshirt, and matching sweatpants.

I let the car roll forward a few inches and then slam on the brake as indecision about whether I turn right here or at the next entrance overwhelms me. In Queens we walked to school. There was none of this.

White Mercedes barks out two angry blasts.

"Mom! You're giving me whiplash!"

"Give me a break, Harri. I can't remember which way to go."

"But it's my first day. I don't want to be late."

"Okay, relax. You're not going to be late. We're right here. I just have to figure out—"

Honk!

Damn it, White Mercedes, where's the fire?

I make an executive decision and take the first turn. I swing into the driveway that curves in front of the school and lurch to a dead stop. I picked the wrong right. And now a white Cadillac Escalade is staring me down.

The driver, a woman with another tight ponytail, another pair of ginormous glasses, and an angry gash for a mouth, leans on her horn and gestures emphatically, pointing in the direction opposite to the one I am heading in. A line of cars forms behind her. I look in my rearview mirror and see a swarm of kids crossing behind my car.

"Mom!" yells Harri, because that is definitely helping.

Adding to my humiliation is a crowd of moms, students, and teachers on the sloping, grassy hill in front of the school with front-row seats to my performance. Trapped and flustered, a cacophony of horns blaring at me, I spot an open space on the narrow lawn separating a real parking lot from the driveway. I spin the wheel, pull up onto the grass, and turn off the car.

"Mom!"

"It's fine. It's only for a minute. Grab your backpack."

Harri groans and tumbles out of the car. I get it. I'm embarrassing my daughter on her first day of school. It won't be the last time. I grab her hand and we quickly cross the driveway as the other parents, the ones who know the routine, roll up to the front steps, pause as their kid jumps out, and wave to them lovingly as they set off on their day.

Everyone seems to know exactly where they are going. This drop-off business is a well-oiled machine. Harri squeezes my hand and my heart catches just a little as I realize the situation I've gotten her in. My daughter, whose only moments of real social confidence seem to occur when she's with generous, nonjudgmental adults, is getting thrown into this mosh pit of a school where she knows no one. Well, save for two little girls who I now see at a distance, holding court with a group of kids who look like they were all created on the same assembly line.

"There's Madison and Jacqueline," says Harri, pulling me toward them. I want to warn my daughter about circles of girls, how you cross into them at your own peril, how stumbling into them uninvited could get you barred for life. But I don't.

Harri lets go of me and dashes toward the group. She leans slightly forward as she runs, pitched against the weight of her backpack, filled with every single one of her shiny new school supplies: good old-fashioned yellow Number 2 pencils, colored markers, a stack of single-subject notebooks with matching folders, erasers, a clear plastic protractor, and a sturdy wooden ruler.

It's one of our favorite days of the year, school supply shopping, the thrill of a fresh new notebook making us both giddy. For me it is rivaled only by a trip to the art store with its rows of brushes and stacks of fresh canvases and the intoxicating smell of oil and charcoal and possibility.

Margot's daughter, Madison, her long, stick-figure arms and legs jutting out of a pink and lime-green shift dress, ignores my daughter. She is telling a story, and no one is going to stop her midscene. She seems very comfortable in the spotlight—maybe Margot is right about her Broadway potential.

Harri stands just outside the circle. Her worn but loved clothes look like an eraser smudge against the landscape of fruity colors her new classmates are wearing, the pinks and greens, the orange shorts, the bright-yellow tops, as if plucked from a J. Crew catalog. This morning Harri picked out her gray sweatpant shorts, a favorite because they don't cut across her belly, and her lucky T-shirt, a vintage Mr. Bubble found at the bottom of a box at a thrift store in Chinatown.

I tried to get her to wear something else for her first day of school, something less, well, less Harri.

"How about this cute striped top?" I asked as I touched the hole near the neck of the paper-thin, secondhand T-shirt she had laid out on the bed. "Madison has one just like it, doesn't she?"

"What? No, Mom. Mr. Bubble brings me good luck. Remember I was wearing it when I won Goldie the Goldfish? Besides, why do you want me to look like Madison? I want be the real me on my first day."

I felt guilty even suggesting it. But just this once I could see the merit of walking in as a piece of their puzzle, something that just snapped into place. There would be time for the real Harri tomorrow, after everyone had been charmed by her specialness. In the end, my daughter would have none of it. It was Mr. Bubble or bust.

Amber walks up to me, arms crossed with the confidence of someone on familiar turf. "Relax, Momma," she says. "She has Mrs. Parson, who's been here since the Stone Age. You've got to love tenure. But she's a sweet, old granny type. That'll be a nice soft launch for her. And besides, Jacqueline's got her back."

Jacqueline is literally standing with her back to Harri, inadvertently (I hope) blocking her from the circle of children. I appreciate my new friend trying to reassure me, but I might save my momma relaxing for later.

"I know," I say anyway. "I'm sure she's fine."

Soon a loud bell rings and children scatter. A young teacher in a pencil skirt and skinny heels that pierce the grass opens her arms wide and shepherds Harri's group toward the front door like a border collie rounding up sheep. I want to give Harri a thumbs-up or a reassuring glance, but she doesn't look back. I watch her back as she disappears into the school, and even though this is exactly the best send-off she could have, I feel like shit.

As the mothers scurry back to their cars, no one lets me back out of my illegal parking space. The crossing guard, in her bright-orange vest, glares at me. I'm sure if she had the authority and a citation pad, she'd write me up.

As I sit there—waiting for those well versed in traffic patterns to file out and thinking about how those girls are going to eat my sweet, sweet daughter alive—I see Amber, Margot, Colette, and Noah on the walkway with their heads together. Amber and Margot, in matching tennis dresses with the same gold and red crest over their left breasts, seem conspiratorially close.

Amber, with one hand on her chest and one on her hip, looks up at Margot who is gesturing empathically with outstretched hands. Noah, with his fingers on his chin, seems to be concurring. Then they all turn and look at me, sitting dumbly in my car, trapped. Amber points at me like I'm an attraction in a zoo and they all nod.

A space opens up in the exit line and I reverse out too quickly, leaving tire tracks in the soft grass. In my rearview mirror I see my new neighbors watching. As I try to remember if I take a left or a right to get home, I take a deep breath and try not to be paranoid. I want to believe they aren't talking about me.

I have definitely made another wrong turn. Is it left at the brick Georgian colonial with the semicircular driveway and the barrel-sized copper pots of flowers trailing down the stagelike front steps or at the Italian villa knockoff with the life-sized stone lions guarding the front door?

I should have just followed Amber. Or Margot. Or Colette. Or Noah. We each drove our own car to school this morning. So much for our carbon footprint.

I see a street called Blackberry Lane, then Mulberry Court, followed by Huckleberry Drive. I must be getting close.

Finally, at a sprawling white farm-style house with a wraparound porch, I find my bearings. Ours is the next street.

I pull onto Elderberry Lane just after the others do. Like a presidential convoy, Margot's Lexus SUV, Amber's BMW SUV, Colette's Porsche SUV, and Noah's Land Rover file down the street and turn into their respective driveways.

Our driveway leads to our detached garage. And while Stacey may have hated it, coveting the three bays all her friends had, I couldn't be more grateful for this little building and the space up the stairs that is all mine.

I'm going to spend the whole day up there. Today is a gift. Harri is tucked into her new school. I will myself to believe she's going to do great, that my decision to bring her here was the right one. And now a delicious day is laying itself at my feet. A day saying, "I'm all yours."

It's the first time I haven't dropped Harri off at school, hopped on the bus, transferred to the Number 7 at Queens Plaza, and hurtled myself to a job where I would worry all day about getting back on time to pick her up at after care, or about the books I couldn't read to her class, or the class trips I couldn't chaperone because I couldn't afford to miss a day of pay.

But now there is no job. And my time is my own. And I'm going to spend it in the beautiful space, the art studio my amazing new husband built for me. I'm going to paint in daylight. I'm going to start something that isn't for someone else (although I still have that shih tzu painting growling at me).

And at three o'clock I'm going to go back to school (entering the driveway in the right direction this time) and be standing there when the doors open and my daughter comes out.

Chapter 8

"WHERE ARE YOU?"

"Hi, Margot."

I can see it is Margot from the caller ID. And I guess Margot can see I can see. Still, a greeting would have been less off-putting and would make me feel less like I've done something wrong.

"The meeting has started."

"The meeting?"

"The meeting of the fifth-grade fashion show committee. Everyone's here. We talked about this. We're all waiting for you."

We hadn't talked about this.

I take the old tomato sauce jar filled with charcoal pencils and place it next to the coffee can of paintbrushes on the new shelf Jeff has just put up. The shelf runs the length of the room, under two windows. I can fill it with the contents of Marty's Art Supply, if I want to.

"I'm sorry, Margot. I don't remember you telling me about a meeting this morning. And I'm kind of tied up right now."

Today is a gift. Today is painting day. I'm going to unpack the supplies still sitting in the cardboard box, open my oils and inhale their earthy smells. I'm going to introduce them into each other—Scarlet meet Cobalt—and watch them evolve into a new, breath-stopping, magical color.

And then, I'm going to take that new color and let it explore a blank canvas. I'm going to let it skip and roll and stretch itself in the sunlight of this beautiful room, listening while it tells me what it wants to be.

"Oh, but Ginny. That just won't do. We absolutely need you."

Calling me by my real name stops me. For once, I don't feel like Margot is staking out her position—her higher position. It disarms me.

But still. Today is a gift.

"It's just I was planning to—"

"I get that there has been a misunderstanding, and I blame Amber for that. Inter-committee communications is her job. But we need our artist! We can't do this without you!"

She is singing all my greatest hits, including but not limited to "Recognition as an Artist," and "You Are Needed," and featuring the world-renowned, platinum-selling "Someone's Counting on You."

"I guess I can come by for a few minutes," I say.

Margot hangs up without so much as a goodbye.

She told me to let myself in, so I bypass the Beethoven's Fifth doorbell orchestra and follow the sound of voices back to a sunroom off the kitchen. Glass walls and ceiling, like in an English manor conservatory, tower two stories over large wicker couches with thick, oversized floral cushions and a glass coffee table laid out with plates of pastries, fresh fruit, and a stainless-steel coffee carafe. Trees in pots the size of oil drums guard the corners of the room, and on every surface is a floral arrangement that matches the fabric.

In the backyard, the late summer flowers continue the color scheme. The pool, with its white paving stones and line of chaise lounges with coral-colored cushions, also cooperates with its decorator's grand plan.

"Here she is," sings Margot.

Amber, Noah, and two women also in tennis whites look up. I recognize one of them as the person I almost collided with at drop-off. She doesn't seem to make the connection, which is fine by me. Margot doesn't bother to introduce us.

"Now, I'm sorry, Stacey, but you're late so you'll have to catch yourself up. We all have to be at the club at ten and there is so much to get through."

Well, that was short-lived. Amber throws a quick eye roll my way but doesn't correct Margot. I sit down and Margot gives me a sideways glance as if she's concerned my painting overalls are going to ruin the chintz. It's true, they are smeared with dried paint—but just on the thighs where I have a tendency to wipe my hands while I'm working, so she's safe.

"Alright then," she says. "Now that we have the date and the venue, it is time to divvy up the responsibilities. Amber, make sure you write this all down. I don't want anything falling through the cracks and someone accusing me of not telling them what I wanted right from the get-go."

No one flinches. No one argues back. No one says, "Margot, you're not the boss of me." Amber opens a notebook and raises her pen. Margot begins to pace and ticks off her list.

"Noah, everything financial of course—ticket sales, vendor payments, final tally. We've got our own accountant; we might as well use him."

"Former accountant," he says, holding up one finger.

"Noah worked for Deloitte before he became a SAHD," Amber tells me. I'm confused. "Sad?"

"S-A-H-D," explains Noah. "Stay-at-home dad."

"Oh." I laugh. "I thought you were *sad*, like depressed. Although, that's not funny. I'm sorry. I don't know why I'm laughing."

"L-O-L," says Noah. "It is actually a little funny. But have no fear, I'm a happy SAHD."

Everyone cracks up except for Margot, who is losing the room.

"Amber," she says after clearing her throat, "you'll be coordinating with the stores, pulling the outfits, creating the catalog. Neiman Marcus is on board this year, thanks to my close personal relationship with them, and every outfit that walks will be linked back to them for sale."

"Wow, Neiman's," says the woman from the drop-off line. "That's a huge get."

"Yes, it is, Evelyn. They will be supplying all the formal wear."

Until now, the woman sitting next to Evelyn, the one whose name

I don't know because Margot couldn't take the time out of her precisely packed schedule to introduce us, had been quietly eyeing the pastry but had neither taken one nor said anything. The mention of Neiman Marcus formal wear brings her into the fold.

"Oh! And how are we going to decide who gets to model that?" she asks. "Everyone's going to want it."

"It will be our children, of course," Margot says. "We are doing all the work, so they should be the stars of the show."

Everyone nods and murmurs in agreement. She turns to me and says, "I'm going to need your daughter's measurements ASAP."

I hadn't really connected the two—me being recruited into this committee and Harri walking the catwalk in formal wear—yet. Maybe she'll enjoy it, like a spectacular game of dress-up. Or maybe she'll want to kill me.

"Moving on. Evelyn, you will coordinate with the PTA and the BOE. I want them informed just enough to keep them out of our hair. And I don't want to hear about any of their tacky ideas. Remember how Adrienne Costello's Uranus cookies almost took down Space Exploration Day last year? Nip it in the bud, Evelyn. Nip it in the bud."

Evelyn's thumbs fly over her phone, presumably typing, *nip in bud*. Margot points to the woman who really wants a pastry, but her cell buzzes and stops her before she can delegate again.

From where I'm sitting, I can see Margot's husband's photo pop up on her caller ID, and I feel the color in my cheeks deepen. I think about Rand steering me to the table as if I were the main course. I feel his fingertips on my breast. If I'd been anywhere else—the subway, a bar—I'd have given him a good hard shove, no questions asked. But this was different. I'm the newcomer. I'm the one, like Harri, trying to cross the threshold of an established social circle. Accusing the husband of their leader, especially without proof it wasn't an innocent, unintended graze, could be putting a big, bloody bullet hole in my own damn foot.

Margot answers the phone with a smile, but her face changes quickly. She presses a finger to her nonphone ear and dips her head. Then she leaves the room.

"I hope everything's okay," I say to the others.

"Oh, please. It's Rand," says Amber with a swat of her hand. "No one gets Margot off her high horse faster than him."

I press my lips together. I'm not shocked Amber would say something like that about Margot. You don't have to be Sigmund Freud to figure out these two have issues. But I am surprised she'd say it in Margot's house, in front of Margot's friends, and so loudly.

After a minute, during which the unnamed woman finally succumbs to a pastry, takes a demur bite, makes an I'm-in-heaven face, and then puts the Danish down, holding up her manicured hands as if to say, *Keep it away from me*, Margot returns to the sunroom with a less-than-sunny look on her face.

"Okay, let's wrap this up," she says. "Amber, where were we?"

Amber dutifully reads from her notes. "All things money to Noah. Fashion liaison, me—"

"Yes, yes, yes," Margot snaps, back to business. "I got it. Okay, so that leaves decorating the venue and publicity. Both of which I've decided to leave in the hands of our newest recruit."

Everyone looks at me, groomed eyebrows raised.

"Normally, I wouldn't assign something so *visible* to an unproven member, but you are a professional artist. We can't let an opportunity like this slip away."

"You're a professional artist?" asks Evelyn.

"Well, um, I do have a small business painting—"

Amber pipes up. "She's amazing. I've got one of her pieces. Sunflowers. They are *so* realistic!"

"I'd love to be artistic," says the woman who's thrown caution to the wind and taken a second forbidden bite of her pastry. "I can't even draw stick figures. Oh, this is *so* exciting. A professional artist. We are *so* lucky to have you!"

Although I am blushing and protesting, I have to admit I'm eating it up. Creating art doesn't always come with many accolades. Sure, if a customer is happy with their pet portrait they might leave me a note on my website or a review on my Etsy page, but making art is more often than not long stretches with no feedback and a lot of second-guessing your own ability—including whether you have any at all.

"So just to be clear," says Margot. "There will be eighteen tables of ten. We'll need centerpieces for each. The rest of the room I'll leave up to you. But the theme, which was voted on at the last committee meeting, so it's nonnegotiable, is Modern Day Cinderella. In addition, we'll want posters for around the school and all the local stores, as well as the school and PTA websites. We're going for one hundred percent fifth-grade-mom attendance—plus guests. Whether they have a child walking or not."

"Oh, Ginny!" says Noah. "This sounds right up your alley. Please say yes. I doubt there is anyone who could do a better job than you."

It does sound like a lot. The most I ever did at Harri's old school was send Rice Krispies Treats for a bake sale and fashion together a turkey costume with thrift store finds for the Thanksgiving parade—neither of which I could attend because I had to work. Still, it sounds like a fun project. If I had to be assigned a job, arts and crafts is the one to get. And the confidence these people have in me is intoxicating.

"Happy to take it on."

"Yay!" chirps Amber. "How lucky are we that Ginny moved onto our street?"

Look at me, saving the day. I'm killing this suburban mom thing. And all for a couple of posters and a few centerpieces? How hard can it be?

Chapter 9

HARRI AND I SIT OPPOSITE EACH OTHER AT A WHITE FORMICA-
topped table sprinkled with pink and turquoise fifties boomerang shapes, a
Nutella cupcake with a peanut butter center in front of her, poppy seed with
pistachio frosting in front of me.

Buttercupcakes, a bakery/café that makes unicorns and rainbows and
fairies look dull in comparison, was one of our discoveries when we moved
here, and after that first visit, we declared it "our place."

I didn't end up spending today painting. By the time Margot dismissed
us—by standing up abruptly and carrying the tray of uneaten pastries into the
kitchen—my mind was swirling with ideas for a Modern Cinderella theme.

I decided a trip to Goodwill (where else would a modern Cinderella
shop?) and the craft store were in order. I was excited and I knew the ham-
ster running on the wheel in my head wouldn't rest until I had figured out
whether my seemingly genius ideas could actually be executed.

Before we left, Margot assigned Pastry Woman, who I then found out
was named Kim, to assist me.

"I'm looking forward to working together," said Kim as we walked to
her car. "But I have to let you know, I'm not creative. I'm not really an *idea*
person. And I suck at art. And crafts."

"That's okay," I said. "I'm actually going to do some shopping now, you
know, to see what's out there. Why don't you come with me and we'll do
some brainstorming?"

"Oh, I'd love to. But I have to be at the club. We've got tennis. But you
let me know what you find."

I realized immediately there would be limits to Kim's assistance. At least I knew I wouldn't be fighting her for creative control of the fifth-grade fashion show. Buzzing with the same excitement I felt when I started a new painting, I headed out. By the time I got home, it was too late to go up to the studio and it was almost time to pick up Harri.

At three on the dot I was outside the school. I had come in the correct entrance and parked the car in a legal spot, feeling a sense of accomplishment and the satisfaction of learning the routine. Tomorrow it will be old hat. A bell rang and the children tumbled out of the building. Harri walked out alone and scanned the parking lot. When she found me, she ran, her head bent forward, a hand on each of strap of her backpack. When she reached me, we hugged and I felt relieved she made it through the day and guilty that I had been so involved in my new project I hadn't been thinking about her every minute she was gone.

Harri held onto our hug too long. Every Harri hug has its own timing— the good-night hug, the thanks-for-the-gift or the help or the pep-talk hug, and the I-missed-you-today hug. There is a rhythm to each. I know their timing like a bird knows to start singing as the sun rises. And this one was too long.

"Tough day at the office?" I asked when she let me go.

"It was okay."

She shrugged out of her backpack and climbed into the car. I drove straight to Buttercupcakes. I didn't need to ask her if she wanted to go.

I stick my finger in the pistachio buttercream and lick it off. Holy cow, a cupcake like this could solve a lot of world problems.

"So, tell me about your day."

Harri breaks her treat in half and puts the bottom on top of the frosting, turning it into a cupcake sandwich. She holds it in both hands, takes a huge bite, and then talks with a mouth full of peanut butter and chocolate crumbs.

"They have a display of dioramas in a glass case in the hallway. One was of the Mesozoic Era. It had actual plastic dinosaurs instead of making them out of clay, like we did that one time."

"Well, it all sounds very professional."

"Yeah, I'm sure whoever's parent made most of it for them. We hate that."

"We do hate that. What else?"

"My teacher is okay. Mrs. Parson. One of her eyes goes the other way." She puts her hand up to her glasses and points her finger off on a diagonal, leaving a smudge of chocolate on her cheek. "You know, like Ethan Claypoole's did before he had that operation."

"You're not planning to suggest to her she have an operation?"

I know my kid.

"I'm thinking about it. It fixed Ethan."

"How about you wait a bit, 'til you get to know Mrs. Parson a little better?"

Harri shrugs. Her cupcake is gone. She is eyeing mine.

"Oh, and get this, right?" she adds. "So, all the English books we're going to read this year are lined up on the ledge of the blackboard. And guess what? I've read all of them!"

"Did you tell your teacher that?"

"Yup, and guess what? She said I can go to the library and pick out all new books. I still have to participate in class discussions on the books she has. But she said I could read new ones and write my papers on those."

"Well, that is very nice of her."

"Yeah, that part is good. I guess."

"But?"

Harri licks a bit of frosting from her upper lip. I slide my half-finished cupcake toward her and she looks down at it but doesn't eat it.

"But, I don't think this is going to work out."

"What do you mean?"

"I don't know," she says, but she does. "The girls, they're okay, I guess. But I don't think they like me."

I feel the crack in my heart, but I press my lips so it does not show on my face.

"Oh, Harri, it's just the very first day. They just need a little time to get to know you. But I guarantee they are going to love you."

I think about that closed circle of girls. Like a jar of vibrant jelly beans, different colors but all the same. "Hey," I say, extending my pinkie across the table. "Best kid ever, right?"

She doesn't take my finger. She doesn't "best mom ever" me back. She leaves me hanging and touches the blue lace agate necklace I lent her this morning to ease her first-day jitters.

"This girl asked me about my crystal," she says. "When I explained, she laughed at me and asked me if I was a hippie. And then the other girls started laughing. Including Jacqueline. What's wrong with being a hippie?"

"Wearing a crystal doesn't make you a hippie," I say. "But even if it did, hippies are cool. Some of my best friends are hippies."

That coaxes a small smile from my daughter. "Like Aunt Zaria?"

Zaria is not Harri's blood aunt, but she is my closest friend. She and I had shared a pop-up tent at crafts fairs across the Northeast—she with her exquisite hand-blown glass and me with my pet portraits, which I don't actually sell, but which have garnered some nice commissions, especially from the second-home set who stroll through the rows of booths in their expensive field clothes, often with the very dogs who *absolutely must* have their portraits painted.

It was Zaria who elbowed me into talking to the cute guy lingering over a painting of a blue pit-bull with a crown of flowers on its head. And it was Zaria who walked away—suddenly realizing she had to talk to a weaver at the other end of the fair—leaving me to have my first real conversation with Jeff. And yes, I guess with her masses of long, thick hair, her beautiful makeup-free, wrinkle-free (even at almost sixty) skin, her warm earth-mother body enveloped, almost always, in rich caftans, if anyone was going to be categorized as a twenty-first-century hippie, it would be Zaria.

"So, speaking of Aunt Z," Harri says, "that brings me to my plan."

I lean in. "You have a plan?"

"Yes. So, what I'm thinking is, maybe it isn't a good idea for me to start a new school."

"It isn't?"

"So what if I stay with Aunt Zaria in the week—you know, live at her studio—and I could go back to my old school, and she could take care of me, just for the weekdays, and then you could come get me on the weekends and I come back and be with you and Jeff."

I take a beat.

"So, you want me to give Aunt Zaria joint custody of you?"

Harri shrugs. "Maybe."

"And who's going to take care of Mrs. Clucklesworth while you're gone?"

Harri lowers her head. She realizes she can't abandon her beloved chicken.

"She's finally started laying eggs. Who's going to eat them if you are away all week? Not me. And not Jeff. He has to watch his cholesterol."

I smile but my daughter doesn't see it. She is watching herself press her thumb into what's left of my cupcake.

"You could homeschool me."

"Harri."

"Mom, *please*. Just listen. If you homeschool me, we can hang out together all day."

I slide the now-demolished cupcake out of her reach and hand her a napkin.

"You know there is nothing I'd rather do than hang out with you," I say, truly, achingly, meaning it. "But there is a list of reasons as long as my arm why homeschooling isn't a good idea. My terrible math skills being one of them. Look, like I said, it's only the first day. It's a lot. New home, new school, new friends. But you have to give it a little more time. What do you say?"

All I get is another shrug. Time for a new tactic.

"Oh, hey, listen to this. This morning I went to a meeting of the parents working on the fifth-grade fashion show. I'm going to be helping with all the artsy stuff. Decorations, posters, that kind of thing. And I'm definitely going to need a brilliant creative mind by my side. You in?"

"I am good at artsy stuff."

"You are amazing at artsy stuff. And get this, right? All the kids of the committee members are automatically in the show. Everyone else has to put their name in a hat. And because of your elite status—like you know some-one on the inside track—you get to wear the formal wear—like ball gowns and what have you—from a really fancy store."

"That sounds terrible."

"What? Really?"

"Why would anyone want to dress up in weird clothes and have every-one stare at them? And what if you trip and fall? Or what if your dress rips and your underwear is showing? Or what if you get nervous and barf all over yourself in front of everyone?"

"Well, that all sounds bad, but I don't think any of it would happen."

"You don't know that."

What I do know is the fashion show as distraction was not the right move. Maybe I played that card a little too early. I have plenty of time to convince her it would be fun and a great way to make new friends.

"I have an idea," I say. "How about we go to the mall. Isn't that what all the suburbanites do for fun? And aren't we card-carrying suburbanites now? You know, I noticed all the girls at school were wearing these white sneakers with black stripes. They must be all the rage. Why don't we go see if we can find you a pair?"

Harri finally smiles.

At the mall, minimal detective work reveals that the sneakers all the girls are wearing are Adidas Superstars. They don't look like anything special to me; in fact they are downright granny-like. But Harri thinks they're cool and that's enough for me.

Of course, Harri being Harri, she insists on the sneaker with the rose-gold stripe and not the black stripe like the girls at school have. I'm not going to argue. After all, I may have the not-so-hidden agenda of finding a way for my daughter to fit in with the pack, but that doesn't mean she has to disappear into it.

Chapter 10

IT'S BEEN RAINING SINCE NOON. IT'S A HOT, SOUPY, LATE SUMMER rain that doesn't clear the humidity, but thickens it; the kind of rain that makes me want to cancel all plans and curl up in our old armchair with Harri, our respective books on our laps.

Instead, I am standing with Jeff in the entrance to the Taj Mahal Grill, the heavy scents of curry and cardamom settling into my damp hair.

"Do you see them?" Jeff asks.

The restaurant is dark, like a speakeasy. Wall sconces cast circles of light onto eggplant-colored walls. Selfish votive candles illuminate only their own tables. I scan the room, trying to block out the opus of chatter as if that will improve my vision.

"Thank you," I say. "I know you'd rather be anywhere else."

"That's not true. I'm happy to do it. If you bond with the Big Cheese, she can make life a lot easier for you."

"Life is going to be hard for me?"

"Of course not. That's not what I mean. Oh, there they are."

We make our way across the restaurant, my dripping raincoat rubbing across the backs of diners at tables that are too close together.

"I'm sorry we're late," I say to the Moss-Markses who are sitting at a square table set with a basket of untouched papadums and two half-empty martini glasses.

Rand stands and claps Jeff's shoulder. "Don't worry about it. We got a head start on you."

As I lean down to her, Margot stretches her long neck toward me and kisses the air near my cheek. She smells like Givenchy and gin.

"Martinis on a school night. Brave of you," Jeff says, laughing.

As if to prove a point, Margot sits up taller and brings her glass to her lips. Her hair, nails, and dress are all the same champagne color. It's a brave move in an Indian restaurant. My outfit is more strategic: jeans and a dark-patterned blouse, both excellent for camouflage *and* washability. After all, I've never met a rogan josh that didn't end up splattering my shirt or landing in my lap.

I pull out the chair closest to Margot—better for girl talk or whatever bonding with the queen bee of the neighborhood looks like—but Rand protests.

"No, no, no. Boy, girl, boy, girl. Ginny, you come sit by me."

I look at Jeff and he smiles in a fine-by-him sort of way. Rand pulls out my chair but a nanosecond before my butt hits the seat, he repositions it just a skosh closer to him.

"You know what? That martini looks good, Margot," says Jeff. "I think I'll have one too. Why not?"

I raise my eyebrows. *Martini on a school night, brave indeed.* Rand finishes off his drink in one gulp, calls over the waiter, and orders four more Bombay Sapphire martinis.

I beg off. "Ah, no thank you. I'll have a Kingfisher. The small bottle, please. Looks like someone is going to have to drive us home."

"Thanks, hon," says Jeff, covering my hand with his. "I had a day today. I could use a drink. Or two."

Jeff hadn't said anything about "having a day" on the ride over. I search his face, but I don't see any concern other than when his drink is going to get here.

After the cocktails and my beer arrive, Rand offers a toast. "To our new neighbors!"

Margot presses her lips together in a begrudging smile as our husbands clink and cheer. I'm not sure why we've been invited to dinner tonight. It's not as if Margot and I have built a budding friendship over the never-ending fashion show meetings she runs as if she were the commandant of elementary school fundraisers.

In fact, I'm starting to think she might want me booted off the team.

After wandering around Goodwill hoping for something "modern day Cinderella" to jump out at me, it finally did. Against the back wall I found rows and rows of old shoes, tons of which were stilettos, and that's when it hit me.

I would buy up all these high heels. Sure, they were pretty beat up, but with a little Lysol, some silver spray paint, and a ton of hot glue, I could fashion them into a tower of Cinderella's lost slippers.

I was so excited with my genius plan that I called Margot as soon as I got home. I had bought four bags of secondhand shoes and dumped them on the never-used dining room table. I cradled my cell phone in my shoulder as I tried to figure out the architecture of the tower.

"They are going to be the most unique centerpieces ever," I said.

"Old shoes?"

"Yes, isn't it awesome? Perfect for our theme! I'll have to scour every secondhand store in the county to collect enough. But how fun will that be? Like a scavenger hunt."

"Old shoes?"

She sounded like I had told her I was collecting roadkill to decorate her event.

"Margot, just wait and see. You'll love it. It's not only right on theme; it's socially conscious, using recycled materials. It's a great message we can send the kids."

"I just don't think dirty shoes on a table where people will be eating…"

"Margot, don't worry about anything. This is going to work out."

"I have very strong reservations."

"It will be fine." I laughed.

"Very. Strong. Reservations," she insisted.

"I'll prove you wrong," I sang. "You'll see."

I hung up before we could go around again. They wanted a professional artist; they got one. Now they had to leave me be to work my magic.

The waiter lumbers to our table under the weight of an enormous tray carrying too much food. He repositions the votive, the salt and pepper, and the empty glasses to make room for steaming dishes: buttery chicken tikka masala, searing lamb vindaloo, colorful biryani rice, wicker baskets of naan, small bowls of chutneys and yogurt. Right behind it all comes another round of drinks, which causes more shuffling of the tabletop. Another beer is placed before me. I haven't gotten halfway through the first one yet.

We dig in, the men heaping food onto their plates and tearing off pieces of the warm flatbread. Watching Margot take small, careful servings, I fall somewhere in between. But unlike my cautious friend, I add the rice and bread. Rand puts a spoonful of vindaloo on my plate.

"You've got to try this," he says. "But be careful, it's a ring stinger."

Jeff almost gags on his martini as he laughs at Rand's warning. I'm well aware of what a "ring stinger" is—our apartment was only a few blocks from Little India in Jackson Heights where you could get a vindaloo that would make you breathe fire—but Rand explains it anyway.

"It burns just as much on the way out as it does on the way in!"

"Rand!"

Margot's tone is scolding, but she is wearing a small half smile. It looks like the second martini is doing the trick, smoothing her around the edges. She spears a piece of chicken tikka with her fork, brings it halfway to her mouth, and then rests it on her plate.

"It was Rand's idea to have this dinner," she says, her words ever so slightly slurred.

She picks up her drink and looks at her husband, and I see a flash of defiance that fades quickly. So, Margot isn't interested in bonding with *me* to make *her* life easier.

"That's right," he says. "I thought we should to get to know Ginny better."

I glance at Margot who is studying her glass.

"And Corrigan," he continues, "we haven't hung out in ages. Not since Stacey—"

He stops himself. "Sorry, Gin."

I hold up my hand, giving him a pass.

"Although I must say, Jeff seriously landed on the right end of that deal."

He winks at me. Margot leans back in her chair. I can almost hear her groan over the din of closely packed diners and "Bridge over Troubled Water" coming out of hidden speakers overhead.

"I couldn't agree more," says my husband, covering my hand with his and beaming. The drink has brightened his cheeks and put a twinkle in his eye. He is just adorable.

Rand starts talking about his golf game, and Jeff nods and smiles and quips back. He's really leaning into his *play along* bit. I'm impressed. I know the only thing Jeff hates more than cigars is golf.

"It always comes down to the nine iron, doesn't it?" Jeff says with a surprising degree of confidence.

Suddenly, I feel something—or someone—under the table, leaning against my right thigh. It's not Jeff, who is on my left. It's Rand. The pressure is warm and steady and unrelenting. Maybe he thinks he's resting his knee against the table leg. I wait for him to shift on his own, but he doesn't. I feel a rush of heat in my face. He doesn't miss a beat, talking about "something-something under par" to a nodding Jeff. I glance at Margot who is looking bored and restless.

Slowly, I move my knee away from his. I feel a cool patch where our bodies are no longer touching. I take a long drink of my beer, gone warm with me trying to pace myself. And then the heat is back, the knee is back, pressing even harder into me.

Rand is nodding at Jeff, pointing his finger at him and agreeing with something that is only funny to the two of them. This time I move my knee away quickly, without concern about being noticed, and Rand flashes a glance at me but then quickly adds a punch line to Jeff's joke.

Earlier this week, I called Amber after I got the unexpected dinner invitation from Margot.

"I don't understand. Why us?" I asked.

"Have fun," she said, her voice brittle.

I'd struck a nerve. That was dumb of me. I could only imagine that when you are single in the suburbs, your dinner invitations are few and far between. It might have been a godsend for Jeff, but I'm sure to Amber it feels like nothing short of total ostracization.

"Just watch out for Rand," she said. "He gets handsy after a few."

"I can handle Rand," I said, thinking of his errant fingers at Margot's party and how I had handled or, more accurately, hadn't handled that.

"Whatever. You've been warned."

Amber's warning now plays in my head. *Handsy, but harmless*, I convince myself, shifting my chair as stealthily as possible toward my husband. I squeeze Jeff's hand and lean in close enough to feel the heat from his body. I'm staking my claim, showing my dinner companion who belongs to whom at this table. Margot gives us the once-over and her eyes land on my hand, and for a moment she looks like she's lost something. I glance over at the chasm between her and Rand, and it makes me push back from Jeff. For some reason the intimacy between us feels like gloating.

Our plates are stained from oily curry sauces, grains of rice speckle the table like pebbles tossed on a path, and the naan basket is empty but for its greasy wax-paper liner. Rand pushes his plate away and holds his empty glass up toward the waiter. I don't think anyone needs another, but that's probably because I'm stone-cold sober.

The drinks arrive. I don't bother to wave mine away this time. I'll just let it sit there. Jeff picks up his martini glass by the stem, and the alcohol splashes over the sides. He transfers the glass into his other hand and licks his wet fingers. Man, is he drunk. I've never seen him like this.

When we were dating, there was always a level of control to our drinking. We were often with Harri. And when we weren't, the nights she would stay with Z or I could find a babysitter that Harri would approve of, Jeff still had to drive back to New Jersey at the end of the evening. Sharing a bedroom with my daughter put the kibosh on sleepovers—unless he wanted to take the couch.

So it was always a few glasses of wine here, a couple of beers there. Except for that weekend in New Paltz at the Mohonk Mountain House. Harri had stayed at Zaria's loft and Jeff and I got a precious overnight alone. But even the two bottles of wine, brought to us by room service and drunk in bed wearing thick, white terry bathrobes, didn't bring out the guy I'm seeing tonight. Maybe it's the gin.

"Wait, wait, wait," says my husband after he's sorted out his sticky fingers. "Another toast!"

I have to laugh at his excitement. "What are we toasting?"

"We are toasting DFP's next chief technology officer for new and emerging business."

"Jeff! No way!" I squeal. I push back my chair and throw my arms around his neck. "Why didn't you tell me?"

"I wanted to make a big deal... I mean, a big reveal."

"Well done, old man," says Rand as he claps.

Even Margot gives a rare wide smile. I'm excited for him. He's talked about the frustrations of being passed over, about feeling stagnant at DFP for as long as I've known him. But I also can't help but feel just a little cheated. I would have liked to share this news with him, just the two of us. Harri would have loved to hear it before the neighbors did. Still, he deserves an audience.

I pick up my beer, the new one that hasn't gone warm, and we all raise our glasses.

"So, 'new and emerging business,'" says Rand. "That's a great get."

"Exactly!" Jeff says, holding up one finger in an I'm-glad-you-asked kind of way. "They are sending me to help launch a new office. Brand-new operation, build it from the ground up, set up a team, the whole shebang."

The cold beer does a dance with my undigested dinner, spinning and dipping it.

"Sending you?"

"So, this part is so cool," he says, squeezing my hand. "You're not going to believe it."

He waits a dramatic beat. Looks around the table at his audience. His inebriation has turned him into a game-show host. When we've all sufficiently held our collective breaths, he makes his announcement.

"I'm going to Dublin!"

"What?"

"We're going to Dublin, Ginny. How amazingly cool is that?"

He leans back in his chair as if he is ready to take questions and receive accolades.

"Dublin? As in Ireland?"

"Yes, Ireland. It's been a huge trend over the last couple of years, maybe more, for American companies to open offices in Ireland. Great cost cutting, tax savings, opens new markets. Oh, you don't want to hear about all that. I've heard Dublin is an amazing city, and the Irish countryside… Think of the painting opportunities!"

"Jeff, I can't just take Harri out of school. I mean, if it's just a week, maybe."

"It's not just a week."

"How long?"

Jeff looks down at his lap. So, this is why he waited until now to tell me. He didn't want an audience; he wanted a buffer.

"A month, six weeks tops."

"Six weeks! Jeff, we just moved in. Harri is just getting settled. Barely. And she can't leave school. What were you thinking?"

Jeff looks heartbroken. The news that moments ago buoyed him now weighs him down, flattening his features, his shoulders, his spine. He suddenly seems exhausted.

"This is what I've been waiting for," he says quietly.

I glance over at the Moss-Markses, who have the good sense to avert their eyes. Margot searches her purse and pulls out a lipstick. Rand flags down the waiter and signals for a check.

There is no question of who between the two of us will drive home. We sit in the car, still parked behind the Taj Mahal Grill. The rain, appropriately, thrashes against the windshield, turning everything outside the glass into the transition before a dream sequence.

"I'm sorry," Jeff says, slumping in the passenger seat. "I handled that all wrong. I wanted to surprise you. I didn't think through the Harri piece. I've been waiting for an opportunity like this for so long, and I guess I got caught up in it. And honestly, it's been forever since I've had to factor a child's schedule into my life. I guess I'm out of practice."

I turn on the car. Immediately the windows begin to fog.

"Of course, my decision is based on all of us. You, me, Harri. It's a family decision."

I feel torn in two. One tattered half belongs to my new husband whose joy is my joy, whose success is my success. The other and larger piece is for my daughter, whose well-being I must protect at any cost. I look out the window and see the blurred figures of our dinner companions running to their car. Rand jumps into the driver's seat, leaving Margot to fumble with her umbrella and wait for him to unlock her side.

"It's huge though, chief technology officer," I say with a small smile meant to meet him partway.

He offers a half laugh. "I was shocked, I'll tell you. I'd given up any hope of moving up at DFP. Stacey hated that I didn't push harder, but she didn't get it. It wasn't as easy as walking in and making demands. Anyway, they were doing this big corporate re-org and my name came up, my year-end evaluation impressed them, and they thought I was the right guy to go do it."

"Took them long enough to figure what the rest of us already know," I say. He deserves this so damn much.

He takes my hand and smiles.

"So, it has to be Dublin?" I ask, knowing the answer.

"It wouldn't even be six weeks, really. That's a worst-case scenario. It's set up the team, get it going, come home."

"You know Harri and I can't go."

"I know."

"You are going to text me every day. And FaceTime with us before Harri goes to bed."

His eyes widen. "Really?"

I take my hand back and twist my wedding band around my finger. I love Jeff, it will only be a month, I can do this for him.

"Harri and I have been on our own for a long time. We know how to do it. And this time we'll be in a beautiful house, with a pet chicken and great neighbors who will watch out for us. Piece of cake."

"Are you sure?"

"Yes, you should go," I say. "You should definitely go."

Chapter 11

PENNY IS LYING AGAINST THE THRESHOLD OF MY SLIDING GLASS door. Her rib cage rises and falls as if an oppressive heat is stealing her breaths, but when I open the door, I feel a cool, early fall breeze. Penny doesn't move; in fact, she doesn't even lift her head, which leaves me to perform clumsy acrobatics as I step over her with a cup of hot coffee in each hand.

"Don't mind me," I say to the old dog.

"Penny, move your lazy butt," barks Wayne from the hot tub. The dog raises one ear and squints at him but promptly closes her eyes and falls back to sleep with a deep sigh.

"Too little, too late," I say as I pass over her, avoiding twisting an ankle.

I hand Wayne his coffee, roll my jeans up to my knees, and sit on the edge of the tub with my feet in the water. I can see my neighbor's bright-yellow bathing suit and skinny legs. I appreciate the effort he's made to cover up.

I let myself get lost in the bubbles. I should be painting. The light will be perfect in my studio right now. I have three commissions waiting. But I feel heavy, wet sand where my heart should be, and my muse does not care to appear under these conditions.

"You alright?" Wayne asks. "Late night? If you don't mind my saying so, you do look a little green around the gills."

Last night Jeff and I drove home in silence even though the news he shared should have left us looking for an all-night liquor store and a bottle of chilled champagne. I want Jeff to be happy. I want Jeff to be successful, whatever his measure of success is. But I also want Jeff here. This wasn't how I expected our new life together to start out.

This morning my husband left early for work, smiling because he couldn't help himself, but staying quiet, and I joined the women on their post-drop-off walk to clear my head, which it most certainly did not.

"Ha, yes, late night," I say, wanting to leave it at that.

Wayne tsk-tsks me, but winks. *I get it, I'm old, not dead,* his look implies. My cell phone rings and Zaria's face pops up on the screen. I escape to the kitchen, away from any further interrogation by the hot-tub police.

"Hey, you."

"Hey, yourself," she says. "How's it going? You the new cast member of *The Real Housewives of New Jersey* yet?"

Boy, do I miss Z.

Out of the window, I see Wayne climb out of the hot tub and wrap himself in his robe. He waves to me, snaps his fingers at Penny, and the two wander back through the hedge to their own yard.

"Ha. I didn't get a callback."

"Just so you know," she says. "I'm not calling for a chitchat."

"Um, okay. So, what's up?"

"I have a bone to pick with you. How come you never said anything about the wedding gift I sent you? I'm not asking for a big formal thank-you. But you could let me know it arrived in one piece."

"What wedding gift? I haven't gotten anything."

"Oh, shit. You're kidding me. I sent it almost two weeks ago. Now I'm going to have to try to track it down."

"I'm sorry, Z. But on the bright side, you got me a wedding gift! Yay! You didn't have to do that."

"I might not have. Not if it's lost. Damn it, it was a one-of-a-kind."

"Oooh, one-of-a-kind? What is it? Tell me. Don't leave me hanging."

"Okay, fine. It's the Hummingbird."

The Hummingbird is my favorite piece in Zaria's collection. It's a tall vase with the wings and vibrant coloring of a hummingbird worked into the glass.

The lip of the vase is drawn out to resemble the bird's long beak. It is light and whimsical and it won her Best in Show at the Peters Valley Craft Fair.

"No way, Z! You could sell it for a fortune. I can't accept it."

"Well, my dear. It's mine to give. Now you'll have a part of me in that new home of yours. If I can track it down, that is."

"You know, Z. I could really use the *actual* you here right now."

She laughs. "You know how I feel about the burbs."

"I know. Like you'll be abducted by body snatchers. But still…"

I fill her in on Jeff's promotion and upcoming posting in Dublin.

"Between you and me, and I'll deny it if you tell him I said this, I really don't want Jeff to go. I told him we'd be fine here on our own. And we will. I can handle myself, you know that. But we *just* got married. Harri and I *just* moved in. This wasn't how I imagined us starting out our new life together. With him thousands of miles away. And to be honest, I think he's going for all the wrong reasons. But I can't tell him that. Not after what I just heard."

Every other morning, when they don't have tennis or Pilates or boot camp class, the women on my street drive straight from drop-off to a park with paved paths that wind around the town's municipal buildings, past softball and soccer fields, and through a thick wooded area where signs of underage drinking are scattered in the tall grass and ferns along the walkway.

This morning when I pulled into the parking lot, I saw I was the last to arrive.

Margot, Amber, and Collette were gathered in a small circle, but when Margot spied me, she started walking. The others quickly tucked in behind her. I guess there were no social pleasantries for latecomers. I scooted to catch up to them and ended up next to Collette, the narrow path allowing for only two abreast.

"Congratulations," she said to me. "Margot told us everything."

I watched Margot and Amber's matching blond ponytails peeking out of their baseball caps swing in unison and wondered how Margot had skewed the news.

Did she tell them about my wholly unsupportive reaction? Did she share the look of disappointment on my husband's face? Or was she just drunk enough to see it as one big celebration like Rand had?

"I mean, good for him," said Amber over her shoulder. "Long awaited, much deserved. But man, I'm not sure I'd let my husband go away for *that* long."

Margot snapped her head in Amber's direction. Her large sunglasses covered her face from cheekbone to cap brim, but her smirking mouth spoke volumes. Amber, the one with no husband at the moment, had no credibility on the what-a-husband-was-allowed-to-do subject. Collette looked at me and rolled her eyes.

"He isn't going to be away *that* long," I said, feeling the need to defend the very thing that was upsetting me. "I'm a big girl."

"And," squeaked Collette, "you've got us. We've got your back if you ever need anything. Right, girls?"

"Right," said Amber.

As we rounded a corner, we passed two young moms with strollers. Amber took the opportunity to hang back a beat so she could switch places with Collette.

"Don't get me wrong," she said as she fell in step with me. "This is awesome for Jeff. I was just being protective of my friend, I guess."

"That's sweet of you," I said, thinking about how lucky I was to have made a friend like Amber. "We'll be fine. I'm not thrilled about him leaving because I'll miss him like crazy. But I've got this. And it's great to know I can count on you guys."

"Ha," laughed Colette over her shoulder. "You'll hardly know he's gone."

Our pace quickened and our elbows pumped as we tried to keep up with Margot's long stride. We came up behind another group of walkers and Margot picked up speed to pass them, startling one woman who hadn't heard us coming.

A trickle of sweat rolled down my temple. I didn't realize we were doing a half marathon. Finally, we circled back around to the parking lot. Margot stopped so abruptly I almost knocked into her. She turned on her heel to face us.

"You know, I'd love to be a fly on the wall when Stacey hears about the new Jeff."

My face was already too red to flush any hotter. Here we go.

"Margot," said Collette in a stage whisper that fooled no one.

"I'm just saying," Margot continued. "It's so ironic. I mean that was it, the very reason she left. You all were there. How many times did she complain to us about how Jeff couldn't provide for her the way *our* husbands did?"

No one answered her rhetorical question. They kept their mouths shut and their eyes on the ground as if they were searching for a lucky penny.

Margot kept going. "She'd say it to anyone who would listen. And even those of us who were sick of hearing it. 'If only Jeff made enough money for this. And if only Jeff made enough money for that.' I don't know how he put up with her. And then she left. She was tired of waiting around for him to step up, as she put it. So, she went out and found someone who could give her what she wanted. A mergers and acquisitions guy from Goldman or Credit Suisse, I think. Terribly emasculating if you ask me. I'm going to assume Jeff was doing the best he could."

———————

"She sounds like a bitch," says Zaria after I finish telling her about my morning.

"She was. I don't know how Jeff stayed married to her for as long as he did."

"I'm not talking about the ex. I'm talking about Margot. That's a story she should have kept to herself, for God's sake. What good can come from sharing that ridiculous gossip with you? What kind of messed-up street did you move onto?"

"It's not like that, really. Most of the women are super nice. It's just Margot. One minute she's welcoming me to the neighborhood with open arms, and the next she's acting like I killed her best friend, Stacey, and took her place."

"That Margot and Stacey sound like a pair. Imagine talking smack about your husband? Especially about Jeff. Jesus. They don't make them any better than Jeff."

"I know," I say wistfully.

"Does Jeff know about this little backstabbing PR campaign his wife was on?" asks Zaria.

"I hope not."

"Are you going to say something? Maybe when he realizes what a psycho gold-digger his ex-wife was, he'll realize he doesn't have to leave and take this crazy job to prove anything to anyone."

"I can't say anything to him. If he doesn't already know, I don't want him to find out from me. It will humiliate him. And it will humiliate him if he already knows and I just drag it back out into the open. No, I've got to just let him go and do this. I'm going to support him in every way I can. I'm going to help him succeed, even if I'm going to miss him like hell."

"I hear you. And look, it's six weeks tops. Isn't that what he said? You and Harri were on your own for a lot longer than six *years*. This will be a walk in the park."

"And you'll come out and visit me often."

"Now, let's not get carried away," she says, laughing.

Chapter 12

"WHY ARE YOU LEEEE-VVVING?"

Harri balls her fists, straightens her arms, and belly flops onto our bed where Jeff has laid out his suitcase. Folded piles of clothes bounce and wobble. A rolled-up belt and a pair of sneakers fall on the floor.

I am standing in the doorway, leaning against the doorjamb. I've already told her where Jeff is going, why he needs to go, and when he'll be back. I'll let him take it from here.

"It's just going to be for a little while, Har."

"Six weeks is not a little while," she groans into the mattress.

"You'll barely know I'm gone. You'll be having so much fun at your new school with all your new friends."

She lifts her head just long enough to shout, "Ha! Good one."

Jeff looks at me for help.

I guess he thought things at school were going better than they are. Over dinner the other night, Harri told us that while she was waiting on the pizza line in the cafeteria, three girls had stopped as they walked past her to say her new sneakers, the Adidas Superstars with the rose gold stripe, were cool.

"See," Jeff said. "You're killing it."

To him, that one point of reference was enough to assume Harri was fully adjusted and thriving. I shook my head and reminded myself that Jeff had only raised a boy.

"Harri, let Jeff pack, hon. His taxi is coming soon."

I didn't offer to drive Jeff to the airport. I had my excuses lined up like dominoes. He's taking the red-eye to Dublin. It will be late by time I'm back from Kennedy Airport. It's a school night. Plus, the company is sending a car, which will save me gas and the sixteen-dollar toll on the GWB.

"It's actually a town car," he says to Harri.

She rolls herself up into a sitting position and crosses her arms over her belly.

"Big deal," she grumbles.

"Hon, give Jeff a big hug and say good night. You will talk to him on the phone tomorrow."

Reluctantly, Harri stands and then hurls herself at Jeff as if she is trying to hurt him. He laughs and picks her up, her bare feet dangling like a rag doll.

"Hey, do me a favor while I'm gone," he says into her hair. "Keep an eye on Mrs. Clucklesworth. And your mom."

She looks over at me. "She doesn't need my help," she grumbles, but she's just being difficult. How many times have Harri and I told each other we had the other one's back? She's had a close watch on me for eleven years. She doesn't need to be asked.

"And think of something you want me to send over from Ireland. Anything you want."

"A souvenir is not going to make me not upset," she says over her shoulder as she leaves our room.

I pick up the belt and sneakers and lay them in his suitcase.

"She's just really going to miss you."

"I doubt that. Sounds like she's got a pack of new friends. She'll be too busy to realize I'm gone."

"I don't think a compliment on her sneakers translates to a pack of new friends. I'm worried. I just want this to be easier for her."

"Give it some time," he says, kissing me on the forehead. "She'll be Miss Popular in no time."

"Do you even know her?" I ask with more aggression than I intended.

I've never shared parenting with anyone. After the first "I didn't sign up for this," I didn't expect much from Colin even when he was still around. And after he left, when I could have used the help, I had nobody. No siblings. No cousins within driving distance. No old college roommate one town over. Colin's family wasn't an option.

My own parents had migrated to Myrtle Beach, an early retirement after the years of running their dry-cleaning business had worn them both down to the bone. Right away it was bridge games and movie nights and events at the community center in their town-house complex. Coming up almost never fit into their plans. "How I'd love to see more of that darling girl," my mother would say when I'd bring Harri to South Carolina for Christmas. "Maybe in the spring, when the weather up north is better." Spring would turn to summer that would turn to fall. So, raising my daughter was all on me. Over time, I felt lucky I didn't have to share her with anyone. Never needed a second opinion.

But things are different now. Jeff and Harri have become great buds. I know he loves her. But I also know I need to take a half step to the side and let them be more than just friends. I need to let Jeff coparent his stepdaughter. Keeping Harri to myself isn't fair to her—or Jeff. Then again, Jeff is on his way to the airport, if we are talking about fair.

We see headlights turn into the driveway. Jeff zips up his suitcase and pats his breast pocket.

"That's it, I think."

"I should have driven you to the airport," I say, regretting the send-off I'm giving him. Either I'm excited for him or I'm not. Pick a lane, lady.

"I'll be back before you know it," he says, hugging me for the last time in a long while.

"Of course you will."

Jeff's cell phone lights up. The driver telling him he's ready when Jeff is.

I step out of my husband's embrace and say, "Don't worry about us. I can handle everything here. You go do your thing. Go kick Dublin's ass."

"Thanks," says my husband. But he is only half listening, his mind now focused on the travels ahead. He carries his bag down the stairs with me trailing behind like a kitten following a ball of yarn. At the door he kisses me quickly and distractedly.

"Hey!" I say.

"Oh, sorry," he says, and he gives me a kiss meant to make up for all of this. Which it doesn't. He wheels his bag out the front door and down the walk to a black town car. The driver gets out, puts Jeff's suitcase in the trunk, and opens the door for him. Jeff gets into the back seat and I wave. But he doesn't look back. He's already gone.

"She was a cranky mess this morning," I say to Jeff when he calls around noon our time to tell me he'd landed. "She came downstairs with one sneaker, then went back to get the other and came back down without it. She spilled milk on her favorite sweatshirt, that tie-dye one she loves so much, and refused to change into a clean one. All I got was a lot of groaning and eye rolling."

"I blame myself," Jeff says but he's laughing.

"I blame you too. But I miss you."

He says something that may or may not be "I miss you too," but his voice is drowned out by the sound of a loudspeaker announcing a flight to Belfast and the incessant beeping of a golf cart passing him by.

"What?" I shout, holding a finger in my open ear as if that is going to block out the noise from Dublin Airport.

"I've got to go. Heading to customs. I'll call you later. Good luck with Harri today!"

When I arrive at Acorn Avenue Elementary School at three, having circled the lot twice only to be relegated to street parking, I am expecting a gelatinous blob in the shape of my daughter to ooze down the school steps. Walking up from parking purgatory, I see Amber, Noah, Collette and Margot standing under a shady maple tree, shouldering out anyone else who might think they deserve this coveted waiting spot.

I pick up speed, zigzagging around little ones who are running toward me as their mothers shout, *Slow down! Wait at the curb! Walk, please!*

By the time I reach the group, Harri is coming out the door. I expect her to be alone. As I said to Jeff last night, even her cool, new rose-gold-striped sneakers haven't garnered her enough social capital to give her a buddy to leave school with. But as she steps out into the sunlight, I can't believe what I'm seeing. Harri is walking side by side with Madison and Jacqueline. And Madison is holding Harri's hand.

"Mom!" shouts my daughter as the girls come down the stairs. "Can I go to Maddie's after I do my homework?"

I look at Margot, who is staring at her daughter as if she doesn't know who *Maddie* is.

"Madison," she says, her hand to her heart. "What on earth are you wearing?"

Everyone looks at the girl's tiny waist, around which is tied a faded tie-dyed sweatshirt. It's the milk-stained sweatshirt Harri was wearing when she left for school today. Madison presses her lips together and lifts her pointed chin but doesn't answer her mother.

"Oh, I'm letting her borrow it," says Harri.

"Well, you can give it back now," says Margot. "It clashes with your outfit."

"It's okay," Harri says quickly. "I can get it later. Come on, Mom, I want to get my homework finished fast." Then she walks away quickly, ending the conversation about givebacks.

"What was that about?" I ask when I catch up to her.

"Mom," she says, resting her hand on my arm and leaning toward me. "Today, at recess, Madison got her *period*. And she didn't know it."

"Oh, yikes," I say. My mind goes back to the ten thousand times that's happened to me and every woman I've ever known.

"Yup. She was climbing on the jungle gym and I saw the blood on her, you know, butt. I didn't want her to be embarrassed so I went over and told her I had a really important secret to tell her, but she had to come down from climbing to hear it."

"That was very considerate of you."

"Yeah, well, at first she made a face at me. I guess she didn't believe me, but I said, 'It's a really good secret,' so she came over. And then when she did, I tied my sweatshirt around her waist and said louder, in case anyone was wondering what I was doing, 'Here's my sweatshirt that I promised you could borrow.' Then I told Mrs. Schubert, the recess aide I didn't feel well and needed to go to the nurse, and asked if Madison could walk me there."

"That was quick thinking."

"At first she didn't want to go with me. She looked mad. But I kind of pulled her arm and said, 'Trust me,' and she did! When we got inside the school, I told her about getting her period and the blood on her pants, and she started crying so I held her hand and brought her to the nurse.

"It was the first time she ever got her period, Mom. She was so upset and said she would probably die of embarrassment and she would never be able to go back to school. I patted her back and told her it happens to everyone, and then the nurse came and got her and Maddie asked if I could wait right there for her and the nurse said I could so I did. And when she came out, she was still sad because the nurse tried to call her mother and she didn't answer the phone so Maddie couldn't go home like she wanted to. So, I told her she could keep my sweatshirt for the rest of the day and she seemed happier and then she asked me if I wanted to come over after school."

I don't always consider myself the world's greatest mother. I've spent the last eleven years worrying that with our financially limited life, I haven't exposed Harri to enough, or I've exposed her to too much by allowing her to spend so much time with adults. I worried about her growing up without a father, and then I worried about marrying again and forcing a stepfather on her. I worried that our insular relationship has ruined her chances for dealing with the outside world and I worry that the outside world, with all its harsh surfaces and sharp corners, will ruin her sweet and trusting soul. But right now, after hearing Harri's story, I know I must have done something right, or just gotten damn lucky with the daughter I got.

"You are a good kid, Harri Miller," I say, giving her a squeeze. "These girls are lucky you moved to town."

Harri smiles. "I was just trying to be nice. I didn't want her to be upset."

As we climb into the car, my phone buzzes. It's a text from Margot.

Sorry M not available for playdate.

Jeez. Harri can't get out of the gate with these people.

Has a mani appt but wants H to join her. Will pick her up @4.

I'm surprised at Harri's reaction. She looks down at her fingers. There are bits of dried blood on both thumbs from the picking and gnawing I have no power to stop.

"Yes!" she sings. "Tell Maddie I say, yes!"

When Margot pulls into our driveway at five to four, Harri skips out the door. I follow her, and when Margot sees me, she lowers her window and hands me Harri's sweatshirt.

"Thank you for this," she says, her face uncharacteristically soft. "I wasn't expecting it. I thought there was more time."

"I know. It's so hard to see them growing up because it means we'll have to let them go. And right now, that seems unbearable."

Margot gives me a strained but thankful smile.

After they leave, I go up to my studio. That shih tzu isn't going to paint itself.

I'd finished the purple background and gotten the dog roughly blocked with a burnt sienna outline. Now, I fill in the body with white mixed with a hair of cobalt and a skosh of raw umber. It looks more like a snowman than a dog, but that's the beauty of painting. Each layer, each brushstroke, brings the form into view, like focusing a camera lens.

I can usually get lost in my work. In the apartment, when I'd have to wait until Harri was asleep to be able to concentrate uninterrupted, I could find myself stepping away from the easel only to realize it was three or four in the morning. Since we've been here, it hasn't been the same. Flashes and images of the day punch holes in my concentration. Being the newcomer tips your center. There are so many new rules and personalities, ropes to learn, tight spaces to fit into. And that's before your husband takes a new job three thousand miles away.

I dunk my wet brush into a coffee can of turpentine and wipe my hands on my jeans. Shih-tzu white streaks appear like claw marks on my thighs. Harri isn't home yet. How long can it take for two girls to get their fingernails painted? I check the time on my phone. I need to chill.

This is exactly what I wanted—Harri to find a friend her own age, someone who likes her for being Harri. Even Madison recognized my daughter's true nature. Other girls might have just pointed and laughed at the fallen princess bee. A true friend, the kind of friend every girl needs, would come to her rescue. This is how Harri is going to find her place here, by just being Harri.

Still, I check my phone a couple more times before I hear Margot's car pull up. I cover my palette with Saran Wrap and meet them in the driveway.

Harri is in the back seat giggling with Madison. Her hands are held in the air as if she is saying, *Don't shoot.* On each fingertip is a bright-pink one-inch dagger. She looks ridiculous. I feel my eyebrows rise before I can neutralize my face.

"Thanks for bringing her, Margot," I say. "I can see she had a great time."

"Madison insisted," she says, glancing over at my own embattled fingernails. "You're welcome to come with us next time."

"Ha, occupational hazard," I say, shoving my fists into my pockets.

Margot twists her mouth disapprovingly. I open the back door for Harri and she slides out of the car, hands still in the air.

"Mom, let's go. I'm starving. I told Mrs. Moss-Marks and Madison about our cupcake place, but they didn't want to go. Can we *please* get me something to eat before I *pass out*?"

Harri side skips up the driveway, her glasses sliding down her nose, and waits at the front door. Apparently, her new nails have rendered her incapable of letting herself in. I wave goodbye to Margot and let Harri into the house. She heads to the kitchen and stands in front of the pantry like a dog waiting for its dinner.

"So, you had fun?"

I pour some cheddar-cheese rice cakes into a small bowl and put them on the counter. I cross my arms, watching her trying to pick one out with her Edward Scissorhands.

"So much fun. Madison is really nice. She likes to talk a lot, mostly about plays she's in, and oh, she modeled for a Children's Place ad, so she's kind of famous, but still, she was super nice to me."

"That's awesome."

She pops a rice cake into her mouth. Orange crumbs fall on her sweatshirt.

"By the way—that's quite a manicure you've got there."

She holds out her hands. "Madison says they're just like Cardi B's."

"Who?"

Harri doesn't answer my question. I wonder if she knows herself.

"Don't you just love it?" she asks, moving on.

"To be honest, no. You look like a dragon lady, not an eleven-year-old."

I specifically remember a time when Harri and I were watching a movie in which a woman with extremely long, manicured nails had to use a pencil to dial a phone. (This was back in the day, when people had actual telephones and pushed buttons instead of tapped screens.) Harri had laughed. "Why would anyone have nails that long if they couldn't *do* anything because of them?"

Harri finally lets her hands rest by her sides. She looks crestfallen. "Mrs. Moss-Marks said these were trial-run manis for the fashion show. All the girls will get 'hair, nails, and makeup.'"

"I thought you didn't want to be in the fashion show."

"Well," she says, brushing away a piece of hair that escaped from a braid and is starting to tangle in her glasses. "I changed my mind."

Chapter 13

THE MUTED BUZZING OF A VIBRATING CELL PHONE ON A BEDSIDE table sounds like a five-alarm fire in the dead of night. It can only mean a few things. None of them good. My first thought is of Harri until I remember she is safe in bed. I sit up quickly and grab the phone, fighting the dizziness and mild nausea that comes with being dragged out of a deep sleep. The screen glows and I see who it is. And what time it is.

"Jeff! What's wrong?"

"Gin! What a crazy first day I had. Wait 'til you hear this!"

The moonlight throws a dull rectangle of light on the rug next to my bed. The rest of the room is cloaked in darkness, like a towel thrown over a birdcage. "That's great, hon. But you know it's three in the morning. You scared the crap out of me."

"What? Oh shit. I'm sorry, Gin. I got it wrong. I thought you were five hours ahead. Ugh, must be the jet lag. Go back to sleep."

"No, no. I'm up now. And I've gotta pee."

I throw off the covers and shuffle into the bathroom, one hand holding the phone to my ear, the other out in front of me, lest I become the thing that goes bump in the night. Without turning on the light, I find the toilet and reach down, a habit born out of getting a cold, wet butt in middle of the night, to make sure the seat isn't up.

"How are you?" Jeff asks. "How's Harri? Was she okay after this morning?"

"I'd say. She saved someone from social purgatory and made a new best friend today."

I tell him the details of Madison's menstruation misfortunes.

"Well, uh, that's…great."

"How about you?" I ask, saving him from having to weigh in. "Tell me everything."

"Okay. I'm about to leave for my first day in the office. Yesterday was insane. When I got to the flat, I unpacked and then passed out. Later, they sent a guy from DFP, Ian, to take me around."

"A flat, huh?"

"You should see this apartment, Gin. You'd love it."

My eyes have adjusted to the dark. The bathroom is a muted black and gray canvas of its daylight self. "They put you up in an apartment for just a month?"

Jeff ignores my question and whatever the meaning behind it is. I'm not even sure myself. I just don't want him to get too comfortable. *And now I feel guilty.*

"The city is gorgeous, Ginny. I mean, I haven't been beyond this neighborhood yet, but you should see it. Rows of beautiful brick homes. Pubs on every corner. According to Ian, my local's called The Bath. Although, apparently the lads from work go to Nancy O'Shea's across from the office for a pint after a long day." His voice speeds up, jet lag be damned.

"The lads, huh?"

"Oh, and we're a stone's throw from Aviva, the rugby stadium. Ian says you can hear the roar of the crowds in the stands on game day from right here in the flat. They're playing France next week. He's got an extra ticket. I'd better bone up on my rugby knowledge. Which is nonexistent at this point."

"Wow," I say, crawling back under the covers. "Sounds amazing. You'll never want to come home."

"No, Ginny. That's not true. I just wish you were here."

The adrenaline rush of being woken up quickly and before I was ready has faded, and a deep exhaustion comes over me. I close my eyes and listen to Jeff tell me about the beef and oyster pie he had for lunch and the claw-foot tub—no shower—in the flat, and that the sink has separate faucets for hot and cold water and how, even though he burned his hands the first time he turned it on, it was just so damn charming.

It might be the hour, or the sound of something scurrying on the roof (or is it in the attic?), but my mind takes the thing he's not saying and runs with it. His bachelor pad is great, the city is magical, his life is his own. He can come and go as he pleases. So much to see, so much to do. No wife and her daughter to hold him down. Maybe this trip is about to fill Jeff with regret. Regretting the loss of his freedom. The regret of having gotten married too quickly.

———————

Jeff and I did everything we could to spend time together in those early weeks and months of dating. Even with two rivers, two jobs (plus one fledgling painting business), and one little girl's schedule doing their best to keep us apart. Our first solution, come to my place of work. Jeff started joining us at craft fairs. He didn't mind getting up at the crack of dawn; he carried our boxes and wrestled with the folding tables and hung my paintings on the wire grid panels that we stored at Zaria's studio and schlepped with us everywhere.

After a few weekends I gave him an out. "I don't want you to feel like you're an indentured servant," I said as he'd carefully unpacked one of Zaria's bubble-wrapped glass pieces and set it, ever so gently, his hands hovering close in case it toppled like a Jenga tower, on the batik cloth she'd laid over the table.

"Are you kidding?" He laughed, admiring his work. "I'm having the time of my life. This is the closest to being an artist I'll ever get."

Then he'd take Harri's hand and they'd wander off, down the rows of pottery and wearable fiber and leather and jewelry, returning with a jar of grainy mustard or a hand-dipped candle or a figure made out of discarded kitchen utensils. And there was always another a gift for my daughter: a wooden puzzle, a stuffed bear made from a repurposed sweater, or a dazzlingly colorful woven scarf.

"You're going to spoil her," I would say every time, but my heart would sing as I watched them smile at each other conspiratorially.

"Good," he'd say.

But after some time, weekends spent in a cow pasture or a snowless ski mountain or a high school parking lot weren't enough. I talked to Zaria, who wanted Jeff in our lives almost as much as I did. With her blessing, I sublet my half of the tent to a potter named Patricia whose free-flowing glazing technique was aesthetically more in line with the cool-jazz fluidity of Zaria's glasswork, and who had a loyal following that actually brought more foot traffic to the booth.

Jeff, being so talented with technology, helped me build a website and linked it to an Etsy page that attracted more eyes to my work than any weekend at a craft fair ever could. When I shared my online success with Zaria, she said, "I'm too old for this shit," and Jeff did the same for her. We promised each other that we'd go back to one or two of our favorite venues, but only when we wanted to get back to our roots, absorb the culture, and see our old friends. Plans are under way for the Berkshire Crafts Fair next summer.

After that we had our weekends to ourselves. We took Harri to the Brooklyn Botanical Garden and the Turtleback Zoo not far from Jeff's house. We'd sneak in a romantic dinner out when we could. But we still only had the weekends. And every outing ended with a drive back over two bridges to our respective homes or, on a very rare occasion, a guest on a couch. And soon that didn't seem tenable either.

"The only sensible thing to do is get married," Jeff said.

"Is that your proposal? Because if it is, I've got some reservations." I laughed.

"No, when I propose for real, you won't see it coming," he said with a sly look and a finger in the air.

And he was right.

He called my parents and, despite never having met them, somehow convinced them to drive up north. I thought the shock of seeing them pull into Jeff's driveway was the end of the surprises, but I was wrong. They tumbled out of their car, arching their backs and stretching their arms while Harri, clearly in the know, ran out to greet them.

Jeff and my dad talked Yankees and shared their identical dream of someday making the trip to Tampa for a spring training game. My mother was overcome by his home and elbowed me in the doorway of every room on the house tour. As soon as my parents had unpacked and come downstairs, Jeff looked at me and tapped his watch.

"Let's go," he commanded as I stared at him open-jawed. "Steve, Marion, thank you for offering to stay here with Harri. We'll be back tomorrow night."

"Wait? What? Where are we—"

Jeff opened the front door waved me outside. "Your chariot awaits," he said with a bow.

We drove to Shelbourne, Vermont, the home of Fiddlehead Brewing Company, the maker of the beer we both said we loved the first night I came to Elderberry Lane. We bought a growler and took it to the pizza place next door. Then we drove to Burlington, where Jeff had booked a lovely bed-and-breakfast, and we walked along the shore of Lake Champlain as the sun set.

"Ginny, I know we've only known each other a short time," he said. "But I've been in love with you since the moment I met you. I wanted to ask you this on our first date. And every day since then. But Ginny Miller, will you and Harri spend the rest of your lives with me?"

The wedding was at a brew pub in Brooklyn with a rooftop bar and twenty IPAs on tap. Jeff had secretly bought three rings from a silversmith he met at the Hudson Valley Arts Festival. We made our vows—Jeff, Harri, and me—with my parents, Zaria, Brendan, and a few friends looking on. We had only known each other five months on the day we were married.

———————

I wake up with my cell pressed between my cheek and the pillow. I lift my head and the phone sticks for a moment before dropping off and sliding under my shoulder. I must have fallen asleep while Jeff was still talking. He had been regaling me with his new life in a shiny new city; with his new "local" and the frenzied sports fans and the thousands of years of history just outside his door. I wonder if it all made him think about how quickly his life had changed. How easily he'd given up his freedom and saddled himself with a new wife and someone else's child, now relegated to staying on a street where he does his best to avoid the neighbors.

I push my pillow up against the headboard and lean against it, my chin to my chest. I can hear Harri's shower running. She's up before me today. Unheard of. I'm just exhausted, I think. Maybe it's just the tectonic plates of my new life shifting under my feet. The change in plans that I wasn't expecting. Jeff never said any of those things. I'm creating my own ill-informed narrative. He's happy. Harri's happy. I'm just being silly for a reason I can't quite put my finger on. I throw back the covers and swing my feet onto the floor. I'm fine. Everything is fine. Still, I think I'll wear my black tourmaline crystal today, perfect for absorbing any negative energy, just in case.

Chapter 14

"I STILL DON'T KNOW WHY YOU DIDN'T ASK MARGOT TO DO THIS with you," I say.

The stack of books Amber asked me to bring her from the disorganized, heavily laden shelf weighs as much as a slab of marble.

I drop them on the table with a thud to avoid pinching my fingers under the pile. I lift the cover of the top one, *Toiles of Provence*. The paper is thick with a slight plastic texture. I turn the first few pages. Pastoral scenes in mauve, pastoral scenes in navy, pastoral scenes in dove gray. It goes on and on like that.

"The only thing I know about wallpaper," I say, "is that if it starts to peel off your bathroom wall and you don't stop yourself from picking at it, you are going to end up with a huge shredded mess."

Amber is swiftly turning pages of fat vertical stripes in jewel-toned colors. She closes the cover and gives the book a dismissive shove across the table. Then she grabs one called *Watercolour Bouquets* and looks up at me.

"The last thing I need is Margot and her *expert* opinion on decorating. I get enough unsolicited advice from her. I can't imagine how unbearable she would be if I actually asked her for help. Besides, you're an artist. This is your department."

"Speaking of my department, I'm feeling really good about the decorations for the fashion show. My shoes towers are coming along. They're tricky; I'm not going to lie. I could use a degree in bridge building to get them to stack up right. But I'm working on it."

Amber continues to turn pages and doesn't look up. "How's Jeff?" she asks instead of discussing my crafting genius.

"Fine, great, splendid," I say too quickly. Every afternoon, now that Jeff has got his time zones right, I get a daily update. "Did you know that you can go on a tour at Guinness and take a class on pulling the perfect pint?"

Talking to Jeff is becoming like scrolling through TripAdvisor.

"I don't know what that means," she says. "But it sounds like he's having fun."

She makes a face I assume is meant to express empathy but comes off as patronizing.

"You just don't want him to have too much fun."

I clasp the black tourmaline hanging on a leather string around my neck and press my lips together. Moving on. "What are we picking out wallpaper for anyway?"

"I'm redoing the bathrooms. All of them. The master needs gutting. I can't even walk in there without thinking of You-know-who; I swear to God I can still smell his piss. But I think I can get away with just a makeover for the other two upstairs." Amber flips pages as she talks, tilting her head at a Monet-inspired paper. "Then there's the powder room off the foyer—it's so country-casual blah—and the back bathroom behind the kitchen—too juvenile. How did I let the kids convince me to go with a barnyard theme? I mean, I know they were the only ones who used it, but still, I shudder. Oh, and the basement—ugh—too man cave, way too man cave!"

In our old apartment, Harri and I pressed our bodies side by side in front of the single often-dripping sink of our only bathroom.

For years, a secondhand wooden stool that I'd painted with moons and stars helped her see herself in the mirror in front of an old, and in places rusty, metal medicine cabinet.

Now we have three bathrooms. "One for each of us!" Harri had said when Jeff gave her the grand tour.

And indeed, Harri does have her own bathroom, complete with her old wooden stool. So much has changed since we arrived at Elderberry Lane, but I'm not ready to let all of our old life go.

"No," Amber says. "I'm going all midcentury this time. It's very in. And gray. Everything is gray. Look in any magazine; that's all they are showing."

I go back to the shelf and find a book called *Gray Gardens*, and Amber squeals in delight.

"See, I told you you'd be good at this."

I am soon lost in *Gray Gardens*—page after page of smoky and icy and steely hues and soothing patterns. I run my hand over the thick pages, feel the textures, the embossed surfaces, the hard sleekness of the metallic papers.

"I'd love to use this in my design somehow," I say. "It would look great with the silver shoes. Maybe I could decoupage some with the paper? I wonder if I they'd sell me a sample book. Maybe they have old ones, or extras?"

Amber sighs and closes her book. "Listen," she says. "About the shoes."

"What about them?"

"This isn't me talking, it's coming from Margot... The shoe thing is a no-go."

"A no-go?"

"Margot just thinks the shoe thing is kind of, you know, tacky. Used shoes? She doesn't want stinky old shoes on the tables."

"They're not stinky old shoes. They will be cleaned and spray-painted. I've talked to her about that."

"I'm sorry. Margot's a bitch. But she's chairwoman of the committee. I know, I know. We're cochairs. But do you really think she'd let me wrestle any power away from her? And besides, she knows you've got another better idea in that creative head of yours."

I feel the twist in my gut and the heat in my face.

"Jesus, Amber. I've already bought almost a hundred shoes!"

"Just return them," she says with a flip of her skinny wrist.

"Return them? Half of them are sprayed already! And I've been to almost every thrift store in the county. And they're thrift stores! You don't return to thrift stores!"

"Okay, okay, don't shoot the messenger."

I fold my arms and sulk. They asked me to handle this. They said, *You're the artist. We're so lucky to have you.*

I take a deep breath. It's just a stupid school fundraiser. "Fine," I say. "But I'm getting reimbursed for those shoes."

"Of course. Just give your receipts to Noah. He'll take care of it."

She seems pleased with herself. I, for my part, am still stewing.

"You've got a million ideas. I know you," she says with a wink.

"Yup, a million," I grumble.

"Oh, look at this," she says, sliding a wallpaper book toward me. "This would be perfect for your kitchen. It would break up all those damn cream cabinets."

I guess that's that. "What's the matter with the cream?"

First the shoes, now my cabinets?

"They're so very twenty-fifteen. Everything's white now."

"I thought everything was gray?"

"It is. And white."

A saleswoman with glasses hanging from a gold chain checks on us. "Did you try Schumacher?" she asks as she drags another two tons of books over to our table and then leaves us to it.

Amber pulls one of the new books closer and rests her elbows on it.

"I know you said you don't want to redecorate, that you don't 'care' about these types of things." She makes finger quotes around the word *care*, her long, pointed nails scratching the air. "But you are making a big mistake. You've got to put your stamp on that house. It's only fair, for God's sake."

I think about Jeff's face the night he told me moving out of the house would ruin him. He felt like he was letting me down, but he couldn't understand how wrong he was.

"Everything is fine the way it is," I say. I don't tell her that Jeff insisted we toss some of Stacey's decor into the attic and put out our craft fair finds. That won't satisfy the woman who is redoing bathrooms because her ex-husband peed in them. "More than fine. I never thought, in my wildest dreams, that Harri and I would end up living in a house like this, in a neighborhood like this. When Colin left, it was all I could do to scrape by, no matter how hard I tried. And then I met Jeff and we ended up here. I consider myself lucky. So really, I don't need to redo anything."

"Even with Stacey's stink all over it?"

"Is that what that is? I thought it was black mold."

Amber laughs. There, I've defused the tension from earlier, giving her permission to go back to her boss and tell her "mission accomplished."

But the mention of Stacey's name has touched a nerve. Ever since I heard the story, the real story of her campaign to squeeze more and more out of Jeff, I've had an ever-growing sense of dissatisfaction about my surroundings. It's not that I want to make a statement, to claim my turf, to prove what is now mine.

It's that I see the trappings (and I now understand just how much they are *trappings*) of wealth and status surrounding me—the granite countertops, the six-burner Viking, the precious and professionally maintained landscaping. All as Stacey chipped away at Jeff, making him feel less and less as she wanted more and more.

And now I am the one who is paying for it. My husband, after years of being led to believe he wasn't enough, feels compelled to prove himself to a woman who is no longer here by leaving the one who is.

"Did you find anything you like?" asks the saleswoman, returning. She eyes the stacks and stacks of sample books scattered across the table like a fallen house of cards. "You can sign out up to five books. If you'd like to take them home and see the papers in the space."

"I'm afraid not," says Amber, pushing her chair away from the table.

She stands, heaves her enormous salmon-colored bag onto her shoulder, and starts to walk out of the store. Since she drove, I have no choice but to follow her. As I do, I throw an apologetic glance at the saleswoman who has already flattened her face in resignation as she stacks the heavy books and starts to lug them back to the shelves. Looks like there are two of us disappointed with this shopping trip today.

Chapter 15

HARRI AND MADISON PLAY ON THE FLOOR OF THE STUDIO WHILE I focus on the shih tzu's face. I bite my bottom lip and hold my breath. It's always the eyes that give me a hard time. A dog can go from "good boy" to Cujo just by leaning too heavily on the brush.

The girls have found the pile of rejected high heels in the corner. According to Amber, there was no appealing to a higher power to save my project. Eventually, I will donate the unpainted ones back to Goodwill, but for now the girls can have at it. Madison is wearing a mismatched pair, sashaying across the wooden floor as if she wears stilettos instead of bedroom slippers. Harri is teetering, arms helicoptering at her sides like a tightrope walker. The long, pink nails are long gone, snapped and chipped and peeled off within days.

"Arch your back!" instructs Madison. "Shift your gravity!" She does a catwalk away from and back to Harri.

Harri shuffles forward, taking small, tentative steps. Madison laughs.

"Harri, you are so weird! Pick up your chin. Don't look at your feet, look where you are going!"

Kids repeat what they hear adults say, I think to myself. It's no surprise to me that this little girl will have heard these same instructions multiple times before.

The shih tzu looks at me disapprovingly. *You got me all wrong*, it seems to say. I'm going to have to let the paint dry and go over it again tomorrow.

"Hey, girls. Are you hungry? I've got some cookies in the kitchen."

Harri kicks off the secondhand shoes. "Let's go. We made slice and bake."

Baking cookies is a Saturday morning ritual we brought with us from Queens. The twelve-minute start-to-finish time that turned a log of raw dough into "homemade" was all a three-year-old Harri could focus on, but even when her attention span grew, we couldn't give up our beloved ritual.

"What's slice and bake?" asks Madison.

Now it's Harri's turn to laugh.

The kitchen island is covered with brainstorming supplies grabbed as I ran through the craft store like I was on some supermarket-shopping game show. I'm not going to let Margot and the committee shoot down another idea. I shove aside felt and pipe cleaners, Popsicle sticks and glitter glue, Styrofoam balls and stems of plastic silver flowers to make room for the girls, who sit on the stools at the counter. I place the plate of cookies in front of them and pour milk into two Flintstones jelly-jar glasses. I put Pebbles, Harri's favorite, in front of Harri.

"Madison can have Pebbles," she offers, sliding the glass toward her new friend. Madison shrugs. The Flintstones mean nothing to her.

Harri quickly devours a chocolate chip cookie and grabs another. Madison's sits on the paper plate I placed in front of her, untouched.

"You sure eat a lot of carbs," she says to my daughter.

I'm washing my hands in the sink, my back to them, but I quickly turn off the water. I need to hear what comes next.

"What are carbs?" Harri asks.

"Carbs stands for carbo-hydrates," Madison says with authority. "They're in white foods."

She ticks off a list with her long, thin, still manicured fingers. "White flour, white rice, white sugar, or food that has white things in it, like *cookies*."

Harri looks at her chocolate chip slice-and-bake as if carbohydrates are slithering through it like insects.

Madison's eyes widen with the secret to life she is about to share. "Basically, they stick to your body and make you *fat*."

It gives me an unsettled jolt. I'd heard similar declarations all my life from my own mother as she precisely measured out her half cup of cottage cheese and sprinkled it with Sweet'N Low and raised an eyebrow at my second helping of chocolate pudding. I pivot from the sink on one heel, my hands still wet, and grab a cookie from the plate on the island top. I take a ferocious, oversized bite.

"But carbohydrates are delicious," I say, spitting crumbs.

Madison laughs at my clownish display. I think I've successfully put the kibosh on the fat talk. They are eleven, for God's sake. Demonizing a cookie is the last thing they need.

"Let's go see Mrs. Clucklesworth," says Harri. She slides off her stool. Madison shrugs and follows.

As they head out the door, I hear Harri say, "Hey, most eggs are white. Are eggs carbohydrates? But my chicken's eggs are brown. So, are they okay to eat?"

Jesus Christ.

I wolf down what's left of my cookie (hey, carbs *are* delicious) and clean up the mess I made by spitting out the crumbs. When the doorbell rings, I throw the damp dish towel over my shoulder and head to the door. Through the frosted-glass panels, I see the top of a tall head, clearly a man. My heart skips a beat. Years of living in the city have trained me not to open the door unless I'm expecting someone. I'm not expecting anyone. But, as I remind myself, this is Elderberry Lane, not Queens Boulevard. I'm pretty sure I can take my chances here.

I open the door and there is Rand. He's standing with one straightened arm leaning seductively against the doorjamb like a model on the cover of a romance novel. I definitely am not expecting him. You don't see many men on the street during the day around here—except for Noah, of course. But even Noah doesn't randomly knock on doors. He'll do the normal human thing and text me from three houses away.

"Ginny," Rand says, stepping over the threshold.

"Hi, Rand." It dawns on me why he's here. "Madison is out back."

His face twists as if he doesn't recognize that name.

"Who?"

"Madison. She's in the backyard with Harri. Do you want me to call her?"

Rand catches up. "Oh yeah, right, Maddie."

"Hang on, I'll go get her."

"No, wait," he says. He grabs my arm and lets his hand slip down until he's grasping my fingertips. I pull back and shove my hands in my back pockets. We stare at each other in silence for a beat.

"I'm not here to pick up Maddie."

"You're not?"

He gives a half-snort laugh. "I didn't even know she was here."

Of course, you didn't, I think. I put my hands on my hips, an alpha move that belies how I'm feeling inside. This guy makes me uncomfortable, to say the least. He takes up far too much air in my foyer, as if this space belongs to him.

"What's up?" I ask.

"I'm here to see you."

Anxiety buzzes between my shoulder blades. "Oh?"

"Well, Jeff's gone and…"

The buzzing travels up to my head as if my ears are filled with wasps. I take a step back.

"And I promised I'd keep an eye on you. So here I am."

I can't believe Jeff asked this guy to look in on me.

He was probably trying to appease his guilt for leaving us, like piling bags of rock salt in the garage in case it snowed in October or printing out the recycling schedule from the town website and taping it up next to the back door.

Now Rand looks around my empty house. He glances toward the dark living room that we almost never use. He scans the staircase leading up to the bedrooms. He peeks over my shoulder into the kitchen where the cookies still sit out on the counter. I hear the girls laughing outside, but the chicken coop is out of my line of sight. Rand takes a step forward to fill in the space I had just tried to create.

"So, how are you?" he asks.

If we were on the F train, I would strongly consider kneeing this guy in the groin. But we're on Elderberry Lane. And this is Margot's husband, Harri's new best friend's dad, and I have to give him the benefit of the doubt. Some people are just so oblivious they don't realize they're crossing a line—a close talker, a space invader, a boundary buster. Yes, that's the explanation I'm sticking with.

"We're great." I laugh. "I spoke to Jeff yesterday. He's just been on a tour of Trinity College and seen the Book of Kells."

The mention of my husband's name does not make Rand back off. He leans in. I can smell his cologne and morning coffee. I feel my heartbeat in the hollow of my throat. Maybe the kneeing thing will actually be required.

"Well," he purrs, "if you need anything..."

"Daddy!"

Rand's head jerks back as if I had slapped him. Madison is standing in the threshold between the kitchen and the foyer, her hands balled up and dug into nonexistent hips. Harri is behind her holding a dull-brown egg.

"No, Daddy, it is not time to go home!"

Rand flinches and then recovers.

"Maddie! Mom sent me to get you. Let's pack it up, chickadee."

"No. I'm allowed to stay until my voice lesson at four o'clock. Mom said."

She pulls the latest iPhone out of her back pocket and holds it up to her father.

"It's two forty-seven."

Rand smiles at me. *Kids*, his eyes say.

"Sorry, angel, I guess Mom changed her mind."

Madison stomps a foot and crosses her arms. "Not fair."

Rand clamps a hand on his daughter's shoulder and moves toward the door.

"Mom's mean!" Madison growls.

"I don't know what to tell you," he says, letting Margot take the fall. "Let's move it."

"Madison, don't forget your egg," says Harri. "Bye, Madison, bye. See you tomorrow, okay?"

"Nice talking to you, Ginny," Rand says after he's moved the stomping and whining Madison out the door. "Remember, whatever you need."

Chapter 16

PIZZA THURSDAY IS A HARD GIG TO GET AT ACORN AVENUE Elementary School. Every parent wants the opportunity to see their child in action in the most important room in the school—the cafeteria. That's where you can take their temperature in real time: are they anxious, are they energized, do they have someone to eat with? Not to mention, who doesn't want to be the person handing out hot slices of pizza? You get cool mom status just by standing next to the stacks of greasy white boxes. So when the random generator gave me a slot this early in the year, I was thrilled. I knew I wouldn't get another chance until the spring.

I was told I'd be serving with Noah today, and I'm looking forward to it. I get the sense the women on the street have cast him as the GBF—gay best friend—in their reality TV show lives, and I have this need to let him know I don't buy into that. Plus, I can ask him how to get reimbursed for the shoes.

But when I walk into the cavernous room that smells like prepubescent sweat and disinfectant, with *Lunchroom Rules* and *Be A Buddy, Not A Bully* posters on the walls and long, folding tables with connected seats, I find Margot Moss-Marks running her finger down the list of pizza recipients.

"I thought I was working with Noah," I blurt out in lieu of a hello. It has only been a few days since Rand stopped by to "check on me." His "handsy but harmless" routine has left me feeling awkward around his wife, as if I've done something wrong, which I certainly have not.

"I needed him to switch with me. I have a tennis club board meeting next Thursday." Her face shows neither embarrassment nor accusation. So, she has no idea about her husband's visit.

I step behind the table used to serve the pizza. Thanks to the specific directions in the email I received from Christy Neustadler, the head of the pizza lunch committee, I feel prepared for the job. When the bell rings, the fourth and fifth graders will file in. The brown baggers will find their seats and the pizza kids will line up. I am to ask their name, find it on the list, put the number of slices indicated on a paper plate, add a napkin, and check the name off the list. *No deviations*, wrote Christy. A few of the boys, particularly the bigger and bolder ones, will try to get back in line for seconds. *Don't fall for it*, I was warned.

Margot takes a pair of latex gloves and hands me the box. She is wearing tight jeans, high boots and a deep-raspberry-colored sweater, having traded in her summer sorbets for more seasonal jewel tones. A large, round diamond solitaire sits on her breastbone. She places an invisible escaped hair behind her ear. Her half of the pizza boxes are stacked neatly at her end of the table. The paper plates are lined up. The pile of napkins is squared off. She is ready. My area is much less organized. I might have to borrow a pen from one of the lunchroom aides to check the names off my list. And my outfit was chosen for the ease with which I can wash out pizza grease.

The bell is going to ring any minute now and the stampede will start. I look over at Margot, who has summoned a lunch aide. She is pointing to the clock on the wall and to her watch. The aide looks intimidated by the Great Margot Moss-Marks. *Get in line*, I want to tell her. I watch my neighbor, her spine rod straight with self-assurance. I'm going to let the Rand thing go. What exactly am I going to accuse Rand of? Assholeishness? I think about the social currency of our little cul-de-sac, about Harri's new friendship with Madison, and how I am finally seeing real, authentic smiles coming from my daughter.

I decided the same was true about saying anything to my husband about Rand. During our last call, placed after Jeff had been "down to the pub" in Temple Bar, a neighborhood of narrow streets and plentiful bars, I listened as he extoled the virtues of a pint of Guinness. "Supposedly," he told me, "Peter O'Toole once said, 'my favorite food from my homeland is Guinness. My second choice is Guinness. My third choice—would have to be Guinness.'"

As Jeff chuckled at his joke, I tried to work out exactly what I'd say to him about our neighbor. And why. I had been adamant about being able to take care of myself. Telling him would only worry him, and possibly for no reason. And what was I expecting Jeff to do about it from three thousand miles away? So, in the end I let it go. I listened to his slightly slurred recounting of his day. The system wasn't getting set up as quickly as he'd hoped. Staffing was tough. It was hard to find great candidates with everyone going to Microsoft. The chip shop across the street from St. Ann's Church has the best fish he's had so far.

At three minutes past the official lunchtime the fourth and fifth graders pile into the cafeteria, surrounding our table like piranhas.

It's not as easy as it looks, this pizza dispensing. Hungry children are demanding and sometimes picky. "No, not *that* slice, *that* one." Finally, the moment I've been waiting for, the reason I'm here feeding other people's children, arrives. I see Harri. She comes up to the pizza table, arms linked with Madison and Jacqueline. Something seems different about her since I last laid eyes on her.

"Hey, Har," I say, trying not to upset the assembly line I've created. Pizza, plate, napkin. Check off name. Pizza, plate, napkin. Check. A girl in an oversized sweatshirt that is sliding off her shoulder doesn't want the slice with the bubble on it.

Now I see it. Before school I had put Harri's hair in her signature braids. It's been our morning routine since Zaria came into our lives. To entertain the little girl who had to wait patiently at craft fairs on long, warm days, Z often braided Harri's hair, once giving her a headful of long plaits woven with ribbon. After that Harri begged me to re-create the full look. "Like how Aunt Zaria does it!"

"Start with two and work your way up," she told Harri, seeing the look on my face. Two was about the most I could handle, and even those were never good enough to last a whole day.

But now Harri's hair is brushed back off her face into the same tight ponytail her new friends are sporting. She is running her hands down the length of it, as if she's pulling taffy. There is something about the severity of it, the way it pulls slightly at her eyes and cheeks, that makes her look older. I don't like it. I don't like it one bit.

"Wow, your hair looks pretty, Har."

"Madison did it."

Madison seems uninterested in her beautician skills. "One slice of gluten-free."

The line is growing. I've gotten my glimpse of Harri in action, and now I need to get back to my job. I scroll down my paperwork. There is a short list of children who need the gluten-free pizza. Madison's name is not on it.

"Sorry, honey. You get a regular slice."

Madison wrinkles her nose at me, but before she can chastise me, her mother does.

"Just give it to her," Margot says while turning around to the pizza box placed behind us so not even an airborne speck of gluten can land on it. She takes a slice and hands it to her daughter. Then she looks at me.

"What? It's less carbs."

"Can I have a gluten-free pizza, Mom?" asks Harri.

"No sweetie, you can't. That's for someone else. Here, I'm giving you the biggest slice. There are advantages to knowing people in high places."

Harri's face falls. *Over pizza?* Her ponytail must be too tight.

The girls go to their table and the line slows to a dribble. I peel off my latex gloves and keep an eye out for the one child who isn't getting their special dietary needs met today. I'm sort of hoping they show up and make a scene. I'd like to show my daughter you can't get away with this kind of stuff.

Margot and I clean up our stations. We stack the extra pizzas. At the end of the lunch period, if no stragglers show up to claim them, the leftover slices will be sent to the teachers' lounge. I'm sure on their salary even cold pizza once a week is a godsend.

Now seems like a good time to broach the subject of my new centerpiece idea with our chairwoman. After that last debacle, all the wasted time and work, I don't want to get ahead of myself.

"So, what do you think of this," I ask Margot. "Mini pumpkins with fairy godmother wands stuck in them?"

Margot wipes pizza crust crumbs off the table, catches them in her still gloved hand, and looks at me. "What for?"

"For the new centerpiece idea. I'm thinking hundreds of pumpkins, different sizes for visual balance—spray-painted silver and another color, maybe pink. I can buy glittery wands at the dollar store—so super cost-effective—and drill holes in the pum—"

"What on earth are you talking about?"

"The new centerpiece idea. For the fashion show. You know, Amber said you hated, I mean, you had an issue with the shoes, so I've been racking my brain to come up with something new."

Margot pulls off her gloves with a sharp snap and tosses them into an overflowing garbage pail. "Jesus, classic Amber getting it wrong again."

"Excuse me?"

"I didn't *hate* the shoe idea. I had concerns. I asked Amber, as cochair on the committee—although I use the prefix 'co' loosely—to address them with you."

I feel the seething rise. I don't know who I'm mad at. But the list is short. It consists of one willowy blond and her willowy blond mini-me.

"But Amber said it was dead. And there was no convincing you otherwise."

"Why would I kill an idea I'd already approved? I simply told her to make sure the shoes were hygienic. That woman. Honestly, no wonder her life is such a mess. She can't follow through on the simplest of tasks. I'm sure she must have adult ADHD. Someone needs to medicate her."

These two need to get their shit together.

"It's my fault really," she says. "I keep trying to have faith in her because I feel sorry for her, but she keeps disappointing me. After what she's been through, I thought it was the least I could do to keep her involved in the group. Some people wouldn't, you know."

Margot steps so close I can see a fallen eyelash on her cheek.

"You know her backstory, don't you?"

I shake my head, no.

"Her husband, Mitch, left her for a *man*."

"Oh, that sucks," I say. It's not as shocking as Margot's wide-eyed per-formance would imply. I've heard stories like this before, but it still sucks.

"She turned him gay," she says with a nod.

"That's not a thing."

Margot ignores my correction.

"It's why she is constantly flirting with our husbands. I've seen it. It used to drive Stacey mad. And she needs a leash around my husband. She's trying to prove she isn't responsible for, you know, the gay thing."

"Again, that's not a—"

"Well, in any event. She's given you the wrong information. Continue on as you were. We have a deadline looming."

"That's going to be a problem. I don't have enough shoes anymore. Amber said, well, I mean, I re-donated most of them. It's going to be cheaper and easier to just go with my new idea at this point."

"Just get them back. I've already given the Board of Ed liaison a com-plete proposal. Including the decorations you presented to us. I'm not going to go back with something different now."

The bell rings and we pause for the thunderous sound of children gathering their belongings and lining up. I watch Harri grab her backpack and throw out her half-eaten slice. *That's a first,* I think. Harri's never met a pizza she didn't like. Even the crusts don't go to waste.

I stop myself from going over and giving her a big hug and a kiss on top of her tight ponytail and throw her a small wave instead. She smiles at me but is quickly distracted by something Madison is whispering in her ear. I feel a tinge of loss as my daughter walks away from me. I take a breath and turn back to Margot. I've still got a case to make.

"I can't just ask for them back," I say. "That's not how it works. I'm going to have to buy the shoes all over again. If they are even still there. I'm going to have to run all over the place, again."

"Well, you are going to have to figure it out yourself. The budget is approved. Noah doesn't have room in it to cover mistakes like this."

"But I didn't—"

"I'd suggest you discuss it with your dear friend Amber."

Chapter 17

AMBER IS LYING ON A PINK PADDED TABLE. A WOMAN IN A surgical mask leans over her from behind her head, gluing eyelashes, one by one, to her lids. The Lash Stop, a narrow white room with midcentury-modern lighting and a row of pink padded tables, is tucked into a strip mall that also houses a nail salon, a waxing place, a blowout bar, a Pilates studio, and a juice bar. One-stop shopping for the suburban beau monde. I'm only here, watching sharp tweezers come dangerously close to Amber's eyes, because she promised she'd go Goodwill hunting with me. I have to try to buy back as many shoes as I can. And she owes me one.

I was seething when I left the cafeteria. If Margot's story checked out, Amber had some things to answer for. And her excuse better not be she turned her husband gay. I sat in my car outside the school, smelling like pizza and watching the afternoon kindergarteners get dropped off, and called my so-called "dear friend" Amber.

"Oh my God. She's such a bitch," she growled after I repeated what Margot said. "Either she's lying or she's a shitty communicator," she continued. "Both of which we know are true."

"Whichever it is, I don't appreciate being the ping-pong ball between you two," I said. "Next time can you guys figure it out before weeks of work go down the drain?"

Now Amber lifts her head from the pink pillow, causing the lash artist—according to her monogrammed black smock, Tiffany, Lash Artist—to glue a false eyelash to her forehead.

"You're on my side about this, right?" Amber asks, not for the first time.

She's been complaining about Margot since we arrived at The Lash Stop. I don't even care anymore who said what. I just want to buy the damn shoes and get this project over with. I twist the white howlite ring on my finger, hoping to absorb some of its calming properties.

"Yes," I sigh.

When I think about it, Amber doesn't have a reason to lie to me. She's been a good friend since we arrived on Elderberry Lane—wacky, brusque, and often annoying—but a good friend. Margot's motives, on the other hand, are cloudy and questionable.

Amber seems satisfied that she is cleared of any wrongdoing and finally stops talking and moving and giving the woman with the tweezers a hard time. When it's all done, she sits up and admires herself in a hand mirror. "Are you sure you don't want to get a set? Even partials will make you look a lot younger." She holds a hand up to her cheek and bats her new lashes at me.

"I'm good," I say.

Amber puts two fingers on my chin and lifts it. "You can get away with it for now—with that skin and those cheekbones. But if you want to keep your husband happy, don't wait until it's too late."

So much about that statement is messed up that I can't even go there with her. "Maybe in my next life," I say.

"That will definitely be too late." She laughs as she jumps off the table and hands a gold credit card to a young woman behind a Lucite desk. "Okay, let's go thrifting! I want to see how the other half lives."

I cringe and twist my ring again as I follow her into the parking lot to her white Mercedes and head to the part of town none of my new friends will ever have frequented.

———

For an artist, thrift shops, secondhand stores, and even dollar stores are an exciting adventure—like walking into the cavernous prop and costume warehouses on a movie lot. Treasures are everywhere. You just have to know how to find them amid the chaos.

"Oh, P U!" Amber pinches her nose as the door of the shop closes behind us with the jingle of the bells hanging over it. "It's like we just walked into my aunt Carmen's basement."

"*That* is the smell of possibility!" I say, gazing in awe like a child who just entered Mr. Magorium's Magic Emporium.

If I remember this store correctly—I've been to so many—the women's shoes are in the back corner. We walk past the glass cases holding the valuables—watches that may or may not work, jewelry that may or may not be worth anything, a series of pocketknives that may or may not be sharp enough to do some serious damage. We pass rack upon rack of clothes, organized by gender and age group. A young mother with a toddler crying at her feet sifts through children's winter coats. Two college-aged girls pull jean jackets from their hangers and model them for each other. More than any other part of the store, this section, where clothes have been collected from attics and garages and the backs of closets, gives off a strong odor of mothballs and mildew. I know for a fact it takes at least three washings to get rid of the smell. Amber stops in front of a selection of cocktail dresses.

"Michael Kors, good Lord," she says.

"A lot of wealthy people clean out their closets," I say. "If you shop near a rich town, you can do very well in a Goodwill. And it's a responsible way to repurpose clothes. Believe me."

Amber touches the sleeve of the black lace dress but pulls her hand back as if it's been burned.

"No, thank you. Nordstrom Rack, okay. Even TJ Maxx in a pinch. But, *used* clothes? No."

"Suit yourself. Besides, we're not here to shop for you. The shoes are against that wall behind the kitchenware and bric-a-brac."

"Bric-a-brac? I love bric-a-brac! I'm going to look."

"Okay, fine. I'll go see what shoes are left. Fingers crossed they haven't sold many."

I leave Amber in front of a forehead-high shelf piled with china, teapots, mix-and-match glasses and salt and pepper shakers, and head to the shoe racks. There are seven pairs of high heels and one lone stiletto. It's about a quarter of what I dropped off. Damn it. I scoop up as many as I can fit in my arms and look down the aisle for Amber. She'll have to carry the rest. She is mid-aisle holding a floral teapot in one hand and its lid in the other. Before I can call her name, she slips the lid into her pocketbook.

"Amber!" I bark and she startles. I march over to her, taking short staccato steps so as not to lose all the shoes balanced in my arms. "What did you just put in your bag?"

She is still holding the topless teapot in her hand.

"Nothing," she says with all the innocence of a child who hasn't taken a cookie before dinner.

"I just saw what you did. Amber, put it back."

"Relax, Ginny." She laughs. "It's just a piece of junk."

I suddenly feel protective of that piece of junk and all the pieces of junk in this store. These things might be old or used or cracked but a two-dollar teapot might be just the thing that someone who can't afford a bright and shiny new one has been looking for. But if it doesn't have a top, because some wealthy lady slumming it at the Goodwill thinks it's okay to just pocket, it truly is worthless.

"Put it back, Amber. Please."

The mother with the toddler is now at the front of the store at the checkout counter. The college girls are gone. An old and bent woman one aisle over is engrossed in a toaster. She has turned it upside down and is shaking it. No one has seen Amber's pilferage.

"It was just a little game," she says. "To see if you'd notice. And look at you... Top score for being observant."

"That's a weird game."

"Whatever," she says, laughing.

I take my armload of shoes to the register. A moment later Amber is by my side with the rest of them. A girl in a Black Sabbath T-shirt and tattoos snaking up her neck rings us up.

"I can't believe Margot's making us pay for this," I grumble. "We've got to be able to appeal this. Maybe go to the Board of Ed and ask for an extension of the budget? How suicidal do you think it would be to go over Margot's head?"

"Wait, hold on," says Amber, placing a hand to her chest. "What do you mean making *us* pay? How did I get dragged into this?"

"Are you kidding? You're the one who told me the project was dead."

"Because that's what Margot told me. I was just the messenger."

"So you've said."

"Because it's true. I can't help it if Margot's playing some kind of f-ing power-struggle mind game with you. But I'm not paying for it."

"That'll be thirty-seven fifty," says the cashier.

Amber makes no move to take out her wallet. We square off, just for a second, until I remove two twenties from mine and hand them over. But Amber is not ready to let it go.

"I'm a single mom with two kids. You, on the other hand, are the classic Cinderella story. From rags to riches, aren't you?"

"Excuse me?"

"It's obvious to everyone," she says, her eyes dancing. "You always talk about how you were a poor, starving artist. 'Barely making ends meet,' I think you said. And suddenly, one day you meet your prince. A rich guy from the right kind of town and it's love at first sight. How *lucky* for you."

She leans into the word *lucky*. The cashier hands me two dollars and fifty cents but she's looking, eyes wide and mouth ajar, at my friend. I want to fling the change at Amber.

"Are you suggesting I married Jeff for his money?" What the hell? Is this payback for stopping her little klepto game?

"I'm just saying, no one ever heard of you and then there you were. I guess it was a 'whirlwind' romance." She raises her fingers in quotation marks for emphasis.

It's a slap in the face. No, it's a roundhouse punch I didn't see coming. I want to tell her how fucking dead wrong she is. I want to tell her the only reason I'm on this street, palling around with women like her, leaving real, genuine people like Z behind, is because my knight in shining armor has no money—thanks to his ex. But I won't say it. I won't be goaded into betraying Jeff. No matter what Amber thinks she is accusing me of.

"You've got it all wrong, Amber." That's all I'm giving her. I grab the two plastic bags filled with secondhand shoes and fling open the door with so much force, the bells above it clamor and toll. Behind me I hear laughing.

"OMG, Ginny! I was *kidding*! I was just pulling your leg. Wow, I thought you had a sense of humor. My goodness, girl, you've got to lighten up!"

Chapter 18

WAYNE PLACES A BOX ON MY COUNTER.

"Special delivery. This was leaning against the garage door."

"That's weird," I say. "They usually drop the packages at the front." My mind flashes to Zaria's missing wedding gift. "Although, maybe it's safer back there."

"It's for Harri," Wayne says as he inspects the postmark. "From Ireland."

"Another gift from Jeff. They've been showing up every few days. First it was a claddagh ring, then a Seamus the Sheep stuffed toy. Oh, and the Guinness socks with the toucan on them. What's that about? Tropical bird? Ireland? Whatever."

"I'll bet she's happy about that."

"Well, let's just say she's forgiven him for going away." I laugh as I hand him his morning coffee.

Wayne and I have fallen into a comfortable morning routine in the few weeks that Jeff has been gone. Even with the weather turning colder, he starts most of his mornings in the hot tub while Penny, who doesn't seem a fan of the falling temperature, lies under my kitchen table and waits for Harri to drop some of her breakfast—something she conveniently started doing as soon as Penny showed up.

But this morning Harri is taking her sweet time coming downstairs and the dog is looking indignantly at me as if I should sit in as the relief food-dropper. I break off a piece of the banana I just peeled and offer it to Penny. She sniffs it and turns her head.

"I beg your pardon, Your Majesty," I say.

"I think she's waiting for her Cinnamon Toast Crunch," Wayne says, laughing. "Normally, I wouldn't let her have it. Mary was pretty strict with giving her 'people food.' But she's gotten so picky over the last few months, I'm just happy to see her eat."

I kneel down and scratch the top of the dog's head. I can see the crescent moons of cataracts in her eyes. "At her age she's entitled not to have to watch her figure."

"Ha, right," he says. "Still, I'm a little worried. I took her to the vet last week. They did some blood work. Haven't heard anything back yet."

I give the dog a tickle on her shaggy side. I can feel her ribs. "Well, you'll let me know what they say."

Wayne looks down at his dog. "Thanks, Ginny. Jeff's a lucky guy. And an idiot for going away. Although, his loss is my gain. It's nice to have someone to talk to in the mornings."

"You are welcome anytime. Even when Jeff gets back—which is soon by the way, yay!" I top up his coffee. "Besides, it's nice to have someone *normal* to talk to around here," I add.

"Ha, you moved to the wrong neighborhood for that."

"Honestly, it's like being in high school all over again. The popular girls just have bigger boobs and Botox." I tell him the on-again, off-again shoe story ending with, "Maybe this is why Stacey really left. Margot and Amber Bickerson drove her off."

"Doubtful. Stacey was the matriarch of the Bickerson family."

"Funny. Man, I thought this was going to be easier."

"Moving here or working on the fashion show?"

"Both."

"Why are you doing it—the fashion show? Why don't you just quit and let them tear themselves to pieces without you?"

"I tried," I say. "I thought about it and realized this whole thing was becoming less and less fun and more like a chore. I figured they didn't really need me anymore. My quote-unquote assistant Kim could assemble the centerpieces and hang the twinkle lights as well as I could—if I left her instructions. All I needed was Harri's blessing. Now that she's excited about being in the show, I didn't want her to be disappointed. But she's a reasonable kid, or so I thought."

That was before I'd talked to my daughter about it at bedtime last night.

"What? No, Mom! You can't quit. I want to be in the show."

"I'm not saying you can't do it. You are still in it."

"But all my friends' moms are running it."

"If all your friends' moms were jumping off a bridge…"

"Mom! Stop!"

"Okay, I'm sorry. I don't think it's such a big deal."

"*Please*, Mom. Don't quit it."

I pour coffee into my Harri mug and say, "So, I'm in for the long haul."

"Well, hang in there. I'm sure the worst is over. And look, your kid wants to spend time with you. Not every mom can say that."

"Speaking of kids and time, where the heck is Harri? She is going to be late for school. And Penny needs her breakfast," I say with a wink.

I go to the bottom of the staircase and yell up. "Har, let's get a move on!"

I expect to see her appear at the top of the stairs, full of classic excuses about how she had to finish a chapter of the last John Green book or she was watching a spider spin a web outside her window and lost track of time. But instead I hear a thud like she's fallen out of bed, and then she roars, "I'M NOT GOING TO SCHOOL!"

I'm stunned. I've heard Harri complain about going to school before, but it's always been in small catlike whines or exhausted fever-laced pleading—never in an angry, explosive shout. I jog up the stairs and stop in the threshold of her room. She is standing in T-shirt and underpants, her hands balled up and pressed to her thighs, in the middle of what looks like a tornado aftermath. Almost every piece of clothing she owns is on the floor. Her desk chair is covered with more clothes and has toppled over.

"What on earth is going on in here?" I ask, righting the chair.

Harri folds her arms across her belly and stomps her foot. "I'm not going to school and you can't make me."

"Excuse me? What happened?"

"Nothing," she says.

I look around the room. It's as if she has emptied every drawer and dumped its contents on the floor. "This doesn't look like nothing. Harri, what's going on? This isn't like you."

"Forget it. You don't get it."

"Ah, the old 'Mom doesn't get it' routine," I say, trying to steer this stampeding herd into a different direction. "Here's what I do get. I get that you are going to put some pants on and get ready for school. And I get that when you come home later, you're going to clean this all up."

"Mom!" Harri twists her body like an Olympic diver and falls onto her bed. "You. Don't. Understand. I can't go to school today!"

"Are you sick? Do you have a fever? Here, let me feel your head."

"No, Mom. Get off. I just can't go because…because…because I'm too FAT!"

She throws herself into her pillow and tucks her long legs up to her chest.

"Wait, what?" I ask, so confused. "You're fat? You? Since when?"

"I'm not going to fit into my formal wear."

"Your formal wear? What formal wear?" I feel like I've walked into the middle of a conversation in someone else's life.

"For the fashion show!"

"Oh Christ, Harri. Okay, you're being silly. You are not fat. You've never been fat. You are a completely normal-sized eleven-year-old. Where did you even get this idea?"

"I can see it," she says, pointing to her stomach.

I think back to Madison putting the fear of God into Harri about carbohydrates and white food. Oh no, this is getting shut down right now.

"Well then, I think you need new glasses."

"Mom!"

"The very last thing you need to think about at your age is your weight. And don't listen to anyone who would suggest otherwise. Now please, the show's over. Get your perfectly normal-sized eleven-year-old butt dressed and come downstairs."

When I get back to the kitchen, Wayne and Penny are gone, scared off by Miss Hyde, no doubt. It takes Harri another ten minutes to appear, wearing the same T-shirt she had on earlier, the same jeans she wore two days ago, and a ponytail that is already escaping its confines. She looks just as she did yesterday. And the day before. Fat, my ass.

She refuses breakfast, and I let it go. We are so late already. Now Harri will need a note to bring to the front office explaining why she couldn't get to homeroom on time. I consider writing, *Dear Mrs. Langston, Please excuse Harri for being chubby*, but I don't. The old Harri, the one who wasn't having more and more of these wacky mood swings—although this morning's outburst took the cake—would have thought that was hysterical. I decide to save the joke until *that* Harri gets back. Instead, I grab the notepad I use for making shopping lists and take the blame. *Dear Mrs. Langston, Please excuse Harri for being late. My alarm didn't go off and I overslept.*

"Do you want me to fix your hair real quick?" I ask as I hand over her backpack.

She whips her head away from me. More hair falls free.

"No."

"Okay, suit yourself."

We take the five-minute ride to Acorn Avenue Elementary in chilly silence. I drop Harri at the front steps of the school and watch her trudge up them and disappear into the building. Then I lean on the gas to get to this morning's after-drop-off walk. Today we are having a fashion-show committee meeting while we walk. Margot needs to be efficient with her time this morning—she has a Juvéderm appointment at ten. Of course, that's not what she told us. But Amber sent me a text message that read: Margot = the spa-lady emoji + hypodermic-needle emoji, and I figured it out.

I see the group, clustered like a skittish herd of sheep, across the soccer field and moving fast. I have to wait for them to come back around; I'll never catch up to them. I stretch my quads for no other reason than it's a thing to do and get ready to jump into the group. As they round the corner, I see it's the full committee. Even Evelyn and my "assistant" Kim, who often miss meetings, are there.

I step in next to Amber. I have forgiven her for her terrible sense of humor at Goodwill the other day. I've had a joke or two fall flat from time to time. Maybe if we become closer, someday I'll give her my famous comedy tip borrowed from Rowan Atkinson. "What's the secret of comedy?" I'd ask my sidekick Harri, and before I could say the word *comedy*, she'd step on my line and yell, "Timing!" Yes, maybe I'll tell Amber that calling me a gold digger while I'm still getting my footing on this street isn't the best timing.

"Where've you been?" Amber asks. Sweat is beading on her upper lip and threatening to run into her cherry-red lipstick. "We've already discussed fittings and rehearsal schedule. Speaking of which, you never gave me Harri's measurements. I can't pull her gown without sizes."

"Today is not the day to take a tape measure to my daughter's waist," I tell her. "Let's just say it was a tough morning."

"Welcome to my world," she says. "I can't get my girls out of bed without threatening their lives anymore."

"It wasn't that. She didn't want to go to school because she thinks she's *fat*. I mean, what the hell? She's just a kid."

Margot, who is, of course, leading the pack, turns her head back toward me without breaking stride. "Actually, she's not a child. She's a preteen now."

"Preteens, don't get me started," says Kim from behind me.

"Preteen *girls*, you mean," adds Noah. "Boys are actually easier at this age if you ask me."

"Yes," laughs Evelyn. "Caleb is a piece of cake. All he needs is food and sports. Feed him, tire him out, and I'm good to go."

"Laugh all you want," says Amber. "As soon as my sister's son hit puberty, he locked himself in the bathroom twenty-four seven, if you know what I mean."

"That's vile," says Margot.

"What's vile about it?" Noah says, laughing. "At least I'll know where they are."

"That's not funny," says Evelyn, suddenly sounding less confident in the ease of raising a boy.

Amber lays a hand on my forearm. At the pace we're traveling, it almost trips me. "Listen, now is the time girls get a little crazy. They start noticing boys and start caring about what they look like. Just wait, it gets worse."

"None of that describes Harri," I say. A month ago she was building a fort out of couch cushions and blankets for her stuffed animals.

"There's no fighting it. And there's no point worrying about it," says Amber. "It's all perfectly *normal*. This is what you want, a normal kid—no offense, Noah."

"None taken, bitch," He laughs as he throws an imaginary scarf over his shoulder. "I was about as abnormal as they come."

We all laugh. I'm relieved Noah is gracious enough to *just go with it* after Amber's homophobic comment.

Maybe that's what I should do, *just go with it*. As much as I'd like to, I can't keep Harri from growing up, but I can also try to let it go, move along, nothing to see here.

Chapter 19

WHEN I WALK BACK INTO THE KITCHEN, IT'S JUST AS I LEFT IT. Uneaten and soggy Cinnamon Toast Crunch floats in now tan milk. The cereal box has fallen over and spilled out onto the table. The coffee maker is still on. What's left in the carafe smells burned. Remnants from lunch making—an open jar of mayo, the box of sandwich bags, a dirty knife—lay on the counter. Only Wayne's coffee mug is washed and tipped into the dish drainer, as it is every morning, bless his heart.

I feel better after the walk. Listening to everyone share their lumps and bumps of child-rearing makes me feel less alone and less like I don't have a clue. Being part of a group shows me none of us do, really. We're all just winging it. And being able to bitch and moan and laugh about it will hopefully make the next crazy outburst or sullen mood easier to deal with.

I dump out the dregs of the ruined coffee and put up a new pot. There is a lot to do today. After Noah told a story about finding seven smelly socks (where was the eighth?) stuffed between the couch cushions, Margot took back control of her meeting. She berated Amber for not having all the children's sizes ready to give to the stores (which in turn gave Amber the perfect opportunity to give me an I-told-you-so look.) Then Margot spent an entire lap of the field talking about the menu before she turned on—I mean, to—me.

"Where are we with publicity? We need Facebook, Twitter, and Insta. I want to see the graphic before you send anything out. We're behind on this."

So instead of collecting a few ruby and golden leaves from my backyard, the colors of which I'm using for a portrait of a smiling pit bull named Violet, I'll be on my computer, cursing at a graphics program I can't figure out without Harri's help.

I am about ready to throw my laptop against the wall when my cell phone rings.

"Thank God you're coming home soon," I say to my husband before hello. "Don't ever leave me alone with a computer again."

"Is everything alright?"

"No." I laugh. "I'm technologically challenged. How did I get assigned this job? I can't get the type thing to line up with the art thing. I need Harri to help me but she's hardly around. She spends all her time at Madison's. And when she finally comes home, she's got her nose in her phone. She won't even look up when I talk to her."

So much for my newfound rolling with the punches over Harri's preteen antics.

"Sounds like she's having fun with her new friends."

"I'm concerned about what kind of influence they are having on her. Do you know that her library books are overdue? When have you known Harri to be late returning a book? I'm worried."

"I don't think that's a reason to call out the cavalry."

"And, she wants an Instagram account."

"Is that good or bad?"

"Jeff, she's eleven."

"Okay, so bad."

"Forget it. I don't know why I'm so upset. I guess things are changing too fast for me. I'm not ready for it. Seriously, I'm fine. How are you? Wait, it's four o'clock there? You never call me when you're at work. What's wrong?"

"Nothing," he says. His voice reverberates like he's in a stairwell. "Nothing terrible."

Nothing terrible never means anything good. "What's going on?" I ask as flatly as possible.

"Well, um, so…"

I wait. I can hear my heart beating in my ears as I mentally catalog the million ways to die in Dublin.

"Scheduling stuff. You know, screwing with our timelines."

Wait? That's it? The pounding in my head subsides. "I'm sorry, hon."

"Yeah, I think I've mentioned the hiring issues we're having here. We're struggling to find the programmers we need. And with Brexit, now the people we thought we could recruit from Belfast have to get visas and that's gumming things up, putting us behind on setting up the system. Which means we're not hitting our target dates."

"That sucks."

"It does suck," he says. "It also means I need to stay a little longer."

And the thumping is back.

"How much longer?"

"I'm really sorry, Gin, I know I said—"

"How much longer?"

"Another few weeks. Four at the most."

"Four *more* weeks? Jeff, you promised. You said four to six, and you were done!"

"I know, I'm really sorry, Gin. I am. But there were circumstances out of my control. You have to understand."

"I do? I *have* to?"

"You know what I mean. It's my job."

"Why can't someone else do it? Get one of your guys. Or do it remotely. Come home and work on the computer. Everyone does that these days."

"It's not that simple. Look, I've got to see this through. I don't have a choice."

His voice is no longer echoing through a stairwell. He must have taken this conversation outside.

"You made the choice to leave," I say. "You made the choice to change everything for us when no one wanted it except you."

"Wait, I don't get it. You were supportive of this before I left."

"Of course I was. I am supportive of it, of you, Jeff. I want you to be happy. I want you to feel successful and fulfilled and not have to live under some false narrative Stacey created for you."

I had been pacing the kitchen floor, circling the granite-topped island, my strides getting stronger and longer as the conversation escalated. But now I freeze in my tracks.

"What is that supposed to mean? Do you think I took this job to prove something to my ex-wife? That's insane."

Shit, why did I say that?

I take a deep breath. I'm not going to say more about Stacey. I'm not going to talk about the gossip I've heard. The stories that have been told behind his back. This is not a rabbit hole I want to go down with Jeff. Not right now. Not with thousands of miles between us. I decide to switch ammunition. I throw my daughter at him.

"You said four to six weeks. What am I supposed to tell Harri? She's expecting you to come home in ten days. Now, you're going to miss her fashion show."

"You told me husbands didn't go to that."

"Well, you won't get to see her in her outfit before she goes."

"I'll talk to her. And you can send me pictures. *She'll* understand I have to work."

I don't respond. We've talked in a circle. He has got to work. I heard him the first time. The silence between us burns. The only sound I hear coming through the phone is a siren. Someone in Dublin needs saving.

Jeff finally breaks the standoff. "Look Ginny, I have to go. We have a meeting with the COO in five minutes, and we're going to get our asses handed to us. I'll call you later night. Or tomorrow. Probably tomorrow. Please don't be upset, it's all going to be okay," he says.

"Fine," I say.

But it's not fine. It's not fine at all.

"I hope you are calling me to tell me the package finally turned up," says Z.

"The package?"

"The wedding gift. The Hummingbird?"

After the phone call I just had, the word *wedding* makes me burst out into tears.

"I'm sorry," I blubber. "I completely forgot about it. I'm a terrible friend."

"Okay, okay, breathe," Zaria says. "It's not the end of times. These things happen."

"It's not that."

She waits as I wipe my tears on the back of my hands and then onto my thighs.

"It's stupid, I'm sorry," I sniff.

"Is Harri alright?"

"Yes, of course. Just growing up too fast."

"Uh-huh, they do that," says the woman who raised three amazing sons, now grown men.

I tell her about my phone call with Jeff.

"Four more weeks? I'm sorry, baby, that's disappointing."

"'Disappointing.' Yes, that's a more diplomatic way of putting it."

"As opposed to? Do you think Jeff wants to be away from you all this time? Try not to forget who that man is. The guy who got up at the crack of dawn and followed you all over upstate just to spend the day with you? He loves you."

"Well, he's not doing that anymore."

"Now don't be persnickety. Neither are you."

I wipe the remaining tears on my sleeve. "I guess. I just can't help but feel like this has been one big 'bait and switch.' This isn't what I signed up for."

"Women's husbands, hell, husbands' wives have been leaving to worse places for a lot longer."

Damn her pragmatism. I feel deflated.

"He didn't have to go," I offer up as one last offensive.

"That's a different story."

"And this, this being here is more challenging than I thought it would be. The women, they're… I don't know. I'm out of my comfort zone here, to put it mildly."

"Now, that sounds like the headline."

"Everyone is just so different than me. So different. The things they think are a big deal. The clothes, the hair, the nails—and the razor-sharp teeth. No one is safe. I'm not sure I'll ever fit in. I'm not even sure I want to."

"Uh-huh."

I tuck the cell phone between my ear and shoulder and start to clean up the mess left behind in the chaos of this morning. I wipe the spilled cereal into my palm and toss it into the sink.

"And oh God, Z, I said the worst thing to Jeff about his ex-wife. What's the matter with me?"

"Ginny, you're human. We all do it. We say hateful things to the ones we love. Sometimes we mean them, sometimes we don't."

"I think I meant it," I whisper.

"Marriages are the hardest relationships," she says. "Harder than parenting, which believe me, we think can be the death of us. But marriages have escape routes, which means you have to work harder not to use them."

"I'd like an escape route from Stacey. She's everywhere."

"Exes are part of the marriage. Even if you both swear they won't be, they are."

I walk over to the sliding doors and press my forehead against the cool glass. Wayne has covered the hot tub to prevent the turning leaves from clogging up the works. Already, those that have fallen are bouncing on the canvas, like children on a trampoline.

"Can you just come live with us, Z? I need a daily dose of you."

"Not on your life, darling. You think *you* don't fit in."

As she chuckles, I scan the backyard of this home. The grass is still green even as the trees turn orange and gold. The swing set, larger than those in many playgrounds in our old neighborhood, stands lonely, all but ignored by the little girl who now has big-girl things to do. The chicken coop, built by Jeff to entice Harri into loving it here, sits in the weakening autumn sun with its door wide open. Wait, what? The coop door is swung wide open. A panic rises in me as I scan the lawn. And then I see, a few yards from the cage, a rust-colored mound, like a deflated basketball or an overturned terra-cotta pot.

"Z," I say. "I have to call you back."

Chapter 20

MRS. CLUCKLESWORTH'S NECK IS TURNED LIKE THE U-BEND under a sink. There is no blood or obvious wound, just small rust-colored feathers surrounding her like rose petals on a bed. She could be asleep, if chickens slept on their sides, their heads twisted behind them, out in the open grass with no protection from predators. But she's not asleep. She's dead. *Shit.* I tap her gently with my toe.

"Get up," I plead.

I look at the coop. The door to the enclosure is open and banging gently against the fencing with a breeze that kicks leaves and feathers across the yard. Last night I came out here to shovel the manure, lay down fresh bedding, and pick up the lone brown egg. It's Harri's job, really, but after asking her twenty times I couldn't wait for her anymore. The smell of chicken poop was wafting up toward the house. So that means I'm the one who left the door open.

It's my fault the chicken is dead. *Shit.*

Harri is going to kill me. And I don't need another reason to be on my daughter's bad side. This morning it was making her go to school when she was having a fashion crisis. The day before it was for the egregious offense of not agreeing to contact lenses. And the day before that it was for taking her phone away when I caught her texting with Madison after midnight.

When we bought Mrs. Clucklesworth we were warned of the constant danger of suburban predators. The list included coyotes, raccoons, hawks, and of course the proverbial fox. "Make sure the gate is properly latched and watch for digging under the fence," they said.

Shit.

I never loved this bird, but right now I'm equal parts creeped out, grossed out, and sad for her. And I have no idea what to do with the body.

"Why are you still here?" I ask the chicken. "If someone wanted you for dinner, you'd be gone."

Time to bring in reinforcements. Wayne has been living in the suburban wilderness for years, so he'll know how to handle this.

I walk through the opening in the hedges separating our properties. Wayne's yard is tidy but smaller than ours. At the back edge, up against a line of trees, Wayne steps out of a prefab tool shed holding a rake. Penny is lying in the grass halfway between us, panting at the exertion of just being Penny.

"Wayne," I shout across the lawn. "I need your help."

Wayne looks up and leans his rake against the shed.

"What's up?" he asks as I walk toward him.

When I get as far as Penny, she looks up at me, tail slowly thumping, her lips curled back into a doggy smile. That's when I see them, stuck to her gums and tucked into the thick mane on her neck. Red feathers.

I stop in front of the dog and start to cry. Wayne hurries to me.

"Ginny, Ginny, what happened? Is it Harri? Are you okay?"

I point at the dog. "She's dead!"

Wayne looks down at Penny. At first he is rightfully confused. And then he sees them. His face turns red with realization. There isn't a jury in the world that wouldn't convict the dog.

"Damn it, Penny! What did you do?"

Penny's ears flatten and she ducks her head. Then to add insult to injury, she licks her lips. My whimpers turn into sobs.

"What am I going to tell Harri?"

"Oh Christ, Ginny. I'm so sorry. I can't imagine what got into her. Christ, this is terrible. Are you sure? It's definitely dead?"

"Definitely."

"Oh crap, I'm so sorry. I don't know how she got to it. She's been with me all morning. I guess she was out here on her own for a bit—just while I was tinkering in the shed. But she never wanders. I'm telling you, she just hasn't been herself lately." He clasps his hand on my shoulder. "But this? I take full responsibility."

"No," I say. I take a deep breath and try to regain my composure. "I'm the one who left the gate unlatched last night. This is on me."

Penny pulls herself up with a groan and wanders on stiff legs toward the house, clearly not interested in admitting her part in all this.

"Can you just come over and help me get rid of it? I hate to sound like a baby, but I just don't want to touch it."

"Of course. Just hang on a sec."

Wayne puts the dog inside and comes back with a towel and a paper grocery bag. We walk back to my yard where Mrs. Clucklesworth is still lying, now surrounded by the dried leaves that have been stopped from crossing the lawn by her body.

"Looks like a broken neck," says Wayne. "Penny was probably trying to play with her."

He leans down with a grunt, wraps the towel around the body, and slips it into the brown bag.

"What the hell does one even do with a dead chicken?" I ask. "I'm guessing Harri's going to want a proper funeral. The drama is going to be unbearable. I'm sure it will all end with me on trial for murder."

Wayne rolls down the top of the bag so it looks like it contains an extra-large lunch.

"What if Harri doesn't have to know about this?"

"Huh? She's going to come out here and see the chicken is gone."

"Well, what if it isn't?"

I look at the brown bag of hen and half expect Wayne to pull a David Copperfield moment. *Ta-da! Watch closely as I bring a chicken back to life!*

"Look, these things all look alike. Can you tell one from another? There's no difference. I say we just go buy another one, put it in the coop, and keep our traps shut about it. That way we save Harri all the heartache. No tears, no funeral."

I twist my mouth. "Why put her through unnecessary trauma?"

"Exactly."

"I mean, if you think about it, it's actually better parenting to keep her from avoidable heartache."

My spirits start to brighten. We could pull this off.

"We'd have to go right now. The farm where we got Mrs. Clucklesworth is about an hour away. We'd be cutting it close. Harri gets out at three."

"I'll drive," says my partner in crime.

Bill's Fowl and Feed Farm might as well be in Kansas for how far out in the sticks of New Jersey it is. It's harder than you'd think to buy a grown chicken. Everyone has chicks, but unless we are willing to have a hen shipped FedEx, Bill's is the closest. Before we schlep all the way down there, I at least have the forethought to call and make sure they have a few grown birds. Which they do.

Wayne and I arrive, giddy with the thought that our evil plan will work and no one, meaning Harri, will be the wiser. We park in an unpaved lot facing a decimated cornfield and walk into the store. The building is more of a warehouse, with a corrugated roof and cinder-block walls. Inside, it smells like hay and wet dog and sour molasses. Eight-foot high stacks of fifty-pound bags of feed, for every animal you can think of that doesn't live in your house, lead to the back of the building where an industrial garage door opens to the hutches and coops and pens.

"I called about the chicken," I say to a weedy man in dirty jeans and an oversized faded Jets sweatshirt.

He takes us back to an enclosure with a flock of hens. Most of them are black and white or butterscotch or blue gray. My heart starts to race until I see the one lone rust-colored chicken pecking at the dirt.

"I'll take that one."

"The Plymouth Rock's a better layer," he says, gesturing to the much prettier black-and-white ones.

"I need her."

The man gives me a wry smile. "Replacement bird?"

Wayne and I look at each other.

"How did you know?"

"Happens all the time. What got it? Coyote? Raccoon?"

"Something like that," I say.

"Well, a raccoon can dig right under the fencing like this," he says, snapping his fingers. "You might want to considering sinking it. And going with screen, not chicken wire, if that's what you got. They can reach right through it."

"Yes, that's good advice," I say, wondering what is going to protect this chicken from me and my stupidity.

The man steps into the enclosure and the flock surrounds him. He must be the one who feeds them. He leans down and snatches up the new Mrs. C by the legs and tucks her under his arm. We follow him back into the warehouse. He puts the hen in a cardboard pet carrier decorated with drawings of dogs and cats and hands it to me.

"Good luck with this one," he says.

The bird squawks and complains as we walk up the aisle, past galvanized trash cans of horse feed and bales of green alfalfa, toward the cash register. Wayne's cell rings. He fumbles a little getting the phone out of his pocket.

When he looks at the caller ID, his face drains of color.

"I have to take this," he says. He ducks his head and turns his back on me as he answers the call. "Yes," he says solemnly. "Okay, yes. Uh-huh. Okay. Yes. No, I understand."

He leans against a stack of fifty-pound sacks of lamb kibble and places his free hand on his forehead.

"How long? Okay. I understand."

The chicken is getting angrier about being in the box. She throws her weight against the cardboard walls.

"How much is that going to cost?" Wayne asks. "I see," he says seconds later. "I understand. Thank you. I will. Yes, I will. Okay. Goodbye." Wayne turns off his phone and places it back in his pocket. The color returns to his face and darkens. He looks at me, his eyes wet. "That was the vet. It's cancer."

Chapter 21

I'M HAVING MY FIRST DINNER PARTY.

Actually, it's hardly a party.

My guest list consists of Wayne, who is devastated about his dog, and Harri, who would prefer a lovely dinner for two with her phone. The only hope I have of turning the evening around is my special invitee and secret weapon: Zaria.

I called her on the way home from the feed farm, needing reinforcements. I had already invited Wayne over, thinking he shouldn't be alone tonight. I figured Z would be the perfect person to distract him, if only for an evening. I've wanted to introduce them for a while, considering they are my two favorite people in the world right now and I was sure they'd get along famously. And for all her stonewalling about making the trip out to this wilderness, I think Zaria could tell from the sound of my voice I really needed her tonight.

I'm making Harri's favorite, mac 'n' cheese with cheddar chunks, wagon-wheel pasta, and a bread-crumb topping. Call it a preemptive peace offering. The kitchen smells like melting butter and cheese. Harri has taken Zaria outside to meet her pet chicken. Penny is asleep under the table, snoring lightly. Wayne and I stand in the kitchen window, holding cold beers in the warm room, and watch them walk down to the coop. The sun is setting, casting a weak golden light through the trees. Zaria is holding Harri's hand.

"You saved my ass today," I say to Wayne. "Thank you."

He takes a long sip of his beer and places it on the counter.

"You're welcome," he says quietly.

We have both stopped assigning any blame to Penny. She's got bigger problems right now. Besides, I left the gate open. I gave the dog the opportunity to come face-to-face with the chicken. It's on me. And Wayne no longer has the energy to share the responsibility. His mind is elsewhere.

"So, did you get any more details from the vet?" I ask, turning away from the scene in the backyard. "What did they say about treatment?"

"They are referring me to a vet oncologist. We have to make an appointment and then hear the treatment options."

"I can come with you to the appointment."

He takes another long swallow of beer but doesn't take me up on my offer. "It's lymphoma, you know."

I do know. That's one of the few things he told me in the car ride home.

"Mary had lymphoma."

He had not mentioned that. All the oxygen leaves my body, drawn out by the shocking realization that Wayne's beloved dog has the same type of cancer that killed his wife. As I stand there numbly, Wayne finishes his beer, rinses the bottle, and puts it in the recycling bucket by the door.

"Thing is," he says, walking over to Penny and scratching her ear, "no matter what they come up with, I don't think I can afford it. It'll be in the thousands—that much I know. Jesus, Ginny, I love her to death, but I don't know if I can do it."

I kneel down next to him and the dog. "We'll think of something," I say.

He looks at me with tears in his eyes, but before he can say anything, the sliding glass door flies back across its track so forcefully it bounces to a stop and comes halfway back on itself. Harri stomps into the kitchen, her fists clenched, her chin down, her brow furrowed.

"What happened to my CHICKEN!" she yells.

Wayne and I stand. The dog flattens its ears. Zaria catches up to Harri and steps in behind her, looking alarmed and confused. For a second I think the hen fled the coop again. Then I see the line of Harri's jaw.

"Where is Mrs. Clucklesworth?" she demands.

"Harri, honey," I say slowly so my thumping heartbeat doesn't steal my breath. "In the coop, of course."

I look at Wayne, who is standing there licking his lips and looking guilty as hell.

"That is *not* Mrs. Clucklesworth! That chicken is nothing like Mrs. Clucklesworth. It's bigger than she is. Its comb isn't right. And its eyes are gold. Mrs. Clucklesworth's eyes are RED!"

I consider myself an observant person. I was positive the two hens were dead ringers for each other. A chicken is a chicken, isn't that what Wayne had said? I'm afraid to look at him. How did we get it so wrong?

I might just lie. I might say I have no idea. Maybe someone came into the backyard and switched chickens. Maybe someone is playing a practical joke on her. My mind can't come up with plausible theories fast enough.

"I can explain," says Wayne.

For a moment the room is silent. The air hangs thick with the heat of the oven and the smell of my daughter's favorite dinner and the anticipation of Wayne's explanation. Harri folds her arms across her chest. Zaria puts her hands on her hips. I stupidly cock my head as if I don't know what's coming. Maybe there is still time for lying.

"It was a terrible accident, Harri." Wayne says. "I'm so, so sorry, honey."

Harri's face flashes from anger to panic. Her eyes widen. She holds her hands in front of her as if she's bracing for a fall. "What?"

"She got out of her pen." he continues, "and she met up with Penny."

Harri's eyes fill with tears and she glares at the dog under the table.

"I'm pretty sure they were just playing. But Penny must have got too rough."

Zaria, who is closest to her, puts her hands on Harri's shoulders.

"Baby girl," she says.

Harri shrugs out of Z's grasp.

"Is she…dead?"

I step forward. I can't let Wayne take the fall.

"Yes, she is. I'm so sorry, honey."

The sound that comes from my daughter shatters my heart. It's the cry mothers work their whole lives to prevent.

"No! No! No!" she sobs, burying her hands in her face while the helpless adults look on. "I hate Penny," she wails.

"Oh, sweetie, please don't blame the dog. She was probably just following her instincts. She's part retriever—didn't you tell us that Wayne? Retrievers are bred to bring back birds. I'm sure she just thought she was doing her job. She didn't know any better. And besides, if you are going to blame anyone, blame me. I'm the one who left the coop unlatched. This is my fault."

Harri slowly lowers her hands and raises her chin toward me. Her glasses are smudged and askew. The hair escaping her ponytail hangs in her face. A tear runs over her top lip.

"Then I hate you too," she growls before she storms out of the kitchen and up the stairs.

"But I made your favorite!" I yell like a moron. "Mac 'n' cheese."

The pictures on the kitchen wall jump as her bedroom door slams.

"Shit," I say.

Wayne and Zaria look at each other. I'm sure they'd both rather go home.

"We might as well eat," I say, knowing full well the meal is ruined.

I pull the casserole from the oven, place it on the table, and spoon it out onto Stacey's French country stoneware. My guests watch me as I hit the spoon too hard against the plates but say nothing. I go to the refrigerator and pull three beers, the strongest IPAs I have, and pour them into Stacey's fancy beer goblets. I could have used the pilsner glasses or the thick steins or the English pints. That woman had a frigging glass for everything. I'd like to smash each and every one right now.

We eat in silence. Our forks scrape at the plates. Penny, who had retreated deeper under the table, sees the coast is clear and positions herself at Wayne's elbow waiting for her share of the dinner.

Finally, Z speaks up. "I think you should go talk to her."

"She doesn't want to talk to me. I killed her pet."

"Ginny, you did not kill anything. You made a mistake, maybe. Who's to say it was you who left the latch open?"

"It was me who left the latch open. I was the last one in the coop."

"Maybe it was faulty," adds Wayne. "Maybe Jeff installed it wrong."

"Oh, I'd love to blame Jeff for this right now, believe me."

"Just stop," says Z. "No one's to blame. It was an accident. It's just unfortunate it had to happen during this time."

"What's that supposed to mean? This time? What time?"

"I'm just saying, with Harri being so depressed, these sorts of things weigh so much heavier on a young girl."

"Depressed? What are you talking about? Harri has never been happier. She's got all these new friends. She's got her little coven on the street. They are always together, and she's even starting to look like them."

Z twists her mouth and gives me a what-other-stupid-thing-do-you-want-to-say look.

"What?" I ask. "She's so caught up with her new friends she barely gives me the time of day. And to be honest, I'm a little surprised she so 'devastated' about the damn chicken. She's barely looked at the thing in weeks. Who do you think's been taking care of it?"

I see myself saying it. The old, normal, reasonable Ginny is sitting on the granite counter where Butcher Pig used to be, watching this crazy Ginny competing with eleven-year-olds for her daughter's attention. *Best mom ever*, my ass.

Wayne has his eyes on his plate, busying himself with large forkfuls of mac 'n' cheese. He wants no part of this.

"You've got to look beyond all that," says Zaria. "Just look into her eyes. It didn't take me a minute before I saw it. That girl is not happy. And it's taking a toll."

"I thought it was just typical preteen behavior. That's what the women on the street said."

"The women on this street don't know your daughter."

I feel a heavy pressure on my chest and shoulders like the lead apron that protects you from X-ray radiation. "Did she say something to you?" I ask.

"She didn't have to. I've known that girl since she was a baby."

"So have I," I whisper.

"You're too close to her. It's like not noticing your child is getting taller. I have the benefit of distance. And of not being her mom."

"I thought she was fitting in. I thought she was shedding some of the 'Harri-ness' that always stands between her and other kids. I'll be honest, I was a little relieved. I thought it was going to make life easier for her."

"That Harri-ness is the best part," Zaria says gently.

"I've got to go talk to her." I push my chair from the table. The scraping startles the dog.

I go to the cabinet, grab a Flintstones jelly glass, and spoon in a mound of mac 'n' cheese. It's something we used to do before we moved here—eat out of a glass, just because it was silly. I leave Zaria and Wayne at my kitchen table to maneuver past the awkwardness my daughter and I have created. If anyone can do it, they can. I take the stairs slowly, working on my case as I go. This is on me. I should have known my own daughter, my own heart.

I knock lightly and open her door slowly without waiting for a response. I know I won't get one. She is on her lower bunk, lying stomach down, legs bent and feet in the air, typing on her phone.

"What?" she says without looking up.

I sit on her mattress, but she won't scoot over to make room for me so I end up with one butt cheek hanging off the edge. She continues to type. I look around the room. It still echoes the boy who grew up in here. But although the walls are papered with baseballs and footballs, there are signs of Harri everywhere—stacks of books on the bedside table and the floor, posters from *The Hobbit* and The Chronicles of Narnia over her desk. Her collection of bottled sand art from summer day camp sits on top of a bookcase overflowing with more books.

"Har, I want to talk to you," I finally say.

She rolls onto her back and looks at me. "Well, I don't want to talk to you."

"Look, I'm sorry. I'm so, so, sorry about Mrs. Clucklesworth."

Harri goes back to her phone.

"Hey, I brought you your favorite—cup o' dinner!" I hold the glass of noodles up like a prize.

"I'm not hungry."

"You know, you've been saying that a lot lately."

Harri looks up from her phone, her eyes challenging me.

"Well, I'm on a diet."

"Oh, for Christ's sake, Harri. A diet? That's ridiculous."

"That's a classic response from you. God, Mom, you are so predictable."

"Excuse me?"

"Madison says you don't get it because you don't care about your appearance the way the other moms do."

That stings. I'm sure it will leave a mark. My knee-jerk response is to shout, *What the fuck does Madison know?* But I don't.

"Harri," I say slowly to control my breathing, "don't let your friends bully you into thinking—"

"I'm not getting bullied!"

She kicks her leg against the mattress.

"Hon, this is silly. You are beautiful just as you are."

"You have to say that. You're my mother."

"Hey, you know me," I say, tugging at the end of her ponytail. "I don't *have* to say anything I don't want to."

Harri harrumphs and rolls away from me. She picks at a seam of wallpaper.

"Well, I need to lose weight for the fashion show."

I look down at the cup o' dinner still in my hand. The cheese has become congealed and shiny. The wagon-wheel pasta is limp and twisted. What is the matter with me? Where has my head been? I now see them all lined up like dominos, the missed meals, the half-eaten pizza, the food pushed around her plate. My heart sinks. This has gone too far. I might not have seen it before, but I sure as shit can stop it.

"You know, Har, I'm sorry I pushed you into doing the fashion show when you didn't want to. It turns out you were right. It is a dumb idea. I think we should quit. Both of us. Who needs it, right?"

That gets her attention. She rolls away from the wall and sits up quickly.

"What? No! What are you talking about?"

"I just think all this isn't us. You know, this dressing up all fancy and parading around. You said it right from the start. I should have listened to you."

"No, Mom! I want to do it. All my friends are doing it!"

"Harri, I know you are trying really hard to make new friends and keep up with these girls. But you don't have to change yourself for them or anyone else. People love you because you are you. It's too much, don't you think, all this emphasis on the materialistic and superficial? We can still like everyone and stay friends, but Harri, we have to stay true to ourselves. Be our authentic selves. Like we always have been. We can't lose what is important to us just to fit in."

"I'm not doing that! I don't even know what you're talking about!"

My daughter is a smart, intuitive kid—wise beyond her years in so many ways. She knows exactly what I'm talking about.

"I'm sorry, I just think the pressure is too much for you. You don't seem happy, your moods are crazy, and you haven't been eating. That scares me."

Harri's breaths become short and quick. Her face reddens and tears fill her eyes.

"I'm doing the fashion show and you can't stop me!"

"No, Har. You're not. I'm your mother. I love you. And I have to make decisions for you to protect you from harm. And I think this whole thing has gotten out of control. You're not going to end up with an eating disorder over a stupid fashion show. I didn't see it before. And I'm so sorry. But this is for the best."

Harri wails and contorts her body, flopping onto her stomach and throwing her face into her pillow. Her words are muffled but crystal clear.

"YOU RUIN EVERYTHING!" she shouts.

Chapter 22

As I CLIMB THE STAIRS AFTER MIDNIGHT, HEADED TO BED WEARY from the chicken debacle, the dog news disappointment, and the daughter disaster, I hear Jeff's voice coming from Harri's room. They are FaceTiming. She's woken him up for sure, but Jeff would never say that. I'll bet she's telling him how I ruin everything. Is he defending me or siding with her? My inclination is to swing open her door and yell that it's past her bedtime. Maybe take her phone away. But I don't. I can't. Instead, I get in bed, unhook my bra and slide it off without taking off my shirt, squirm out of my jeans and kick them onto the floor, and go to sleep in the clothes I'd been wearing all day.

I'm woken up by my cell phone glowing in the pitch-black room, telling me there is a text. At this time of night? I reach out, slapping the bedside table for the phone and squinting from the light of the screen and the size of the type. I see it's from Jeff.

Hey so Harri really wants to do the fashion show. All her
friends are doing it. Maybe you'd reconsider? Oxo

I feel ganged up on. And I resent the long-distance parenting. Maybe he should be here to see what's really going on before he weighs in. I toss the phone to the foot of my bed without responding and then spend the next few hours staring at the ceiling.

The next morning, I give Harri an ultimatum.

"Okay, your stepfather thinks I should give you another chance. So, you can stay in the fashion show on one condition."

"What?" she asks so sullenly that I want to reconsider my offer.

"No more dieting. I'm serious, Harri."

I want to believe she is reasonable enough to stop this nonsense and snap out of whatever spell these girls have over her. After all, we have a long history, an ingrained value system, and a few months on Elderberry Lane can't change that.

"Okay, fine," she says less enthusiastically than I'd hoped. Still, I'd made my point. Disaster averted.

Now we are at the fitting and "loose rehearsal," as Margot calls it. The fashion show is in two weeks and she doesn't want any surprises. The venue, a wedding/bar mitzvah/PTA fundraising hot spot called Le Chateau, wouldn't let us practice there, a kink that has infuriated our leader, so we are in the school cafeteria. Most of the lunch tables have been folded up and rolled against the wall, except for two where after-school program kids are making bracelets with plastic beads.

Twenty-eight girls are running circles around each other while we committee members try hopelessly to corral them. We didn't invite the boys to rehearse. Margot thought it would be futile to try to get them to do this twice, they wouldn't have the kind of fit issues as the young ladies, and really, they will just be too disruptive when we have so much work to get done. The girls jumping around and chasing each other are just trying to prove to Mrs. Moss-Marks that her gender stereotyping needs a twenty-first-century update.

We are not allowed to alter any of the clothes because they have to go back to Neiman Marcus after the event, so Margot's contact at the store has sent over multiple sizes of most outfits. They are arranged on four rolling racks and are like sirens calling to the girls who can't keep their sweaty hands off them. I think it's a lot for the store to expect their merchandise back in one piece, but I still try to fend off the wide-eyed catwalkers.

Margot has set up a dressing screen (she just happened to have one at home, doesn't everyone?) so that no one takes their dresses into the girls' bathroom where there are too many possibilities for damage. Evelyn is stationed in front of the screen, trying to give the kids privacy but also stepping back there to zip up and untwist and generally keep the process moving. Otherwise, we could be here all night.

When it is Harri's turn to try on her gown, she takes Madison behind the dressing screen with her. In a different lifetime it would have been me back there. I remind myself this is a good thing.

I am trying to stop a wispy girl in leggings and high black boots from doing cartwheels too close to the wall and thinking you couldn't pay me enough to be a teacher, when Harri steps out from behind the screen. I gasp at the sight of her in a sleeveless emerald-green taffeta gown. She looks nervous and takes small, tentative steps toward Evelyn, who holds her hands to her chest as if she's praying. From the chin up, I see Harri, my Harri, with her messy ponytail and her slipping glasses. But beyond that, I have no idea who I'm looking at. She is gorgeous and elegant and grown-up. I feel off-kilter, in awe of my beautiful daughter and devastated at the same time. It's almost as if a fold in the time continuum reached forward and brought back the Harri from the next decade. And I'm not ready for that.

I'm about to step forward to claim the space next to my daughter when Cartwheel Girl gets too close to the aforementioned wall and crashes into it. I have to turn my back on Harri and pick the child up off the floor. An egg-shaped bruise is already forming on her forehead. I bite my tongue before I say, *I told you so*. Over the whimpering, I hear the oohs and aahs as Margot and the other committee women surround my daughter. I quickly MacGyver an ice pack by dumping the leftover ice in Amber's Starbucks drink into a ziplock bag formerly containing uneaten Cheez-Its from the injured girl's own lunch and give it to her to hold up to her head.

By the time I reach Harri, Margot has stepped back, her finger tapping her lip in contemplation.

"Harri, I think you've lost weight." She says it with the pride of a lioness whose cub has just made her first kill. "We're going to have to go down a size for you."

"Thank you," says my daughter, beaming.

Her face lights up and reveals a smile I haven't seen in weeks. My hands curl into fists. My fingernails bite into my palm. My daughter skips back behind the screen to await her new dress.

"Margot? Can I talk to you for a sec?"

"Yes?"

"Over here, please." I cock my head toward the door of the cafeteria and then walk out into the hallway.

Margot meets me out there—followed by Amber, Evelyn, Kim, and Noah. I guess they think we're having an impromptu committee meeting. Well, that's fine. I do have something to say to all of them, a scheme I came up with last night after Jeff's text. But first I need a word with Margot, and if I have to have an audience, so be it.

My "friends" create a half circle around me with Margot at the apex. She folds her arms and waits.

"About Harri," I say.

"Yes?"

The group leans in, their arms folded like their leader's. I hover above myself, seeing where I stand in this pack and realizing I'm going to try to win a battle, but I may lose a war. I change my mind about confronting her. I want to tell her to knock it off with this body-image-destroying crap. But if I do, then the next thing I want, the brilliant scheme I have to propose, will fall on deaf ears. Besides, look at Margot, a creature of shadows and angles, a woman who accepts nothing less than her idea of perfection from herself. She's not going to understand how damaging it is to encourage my eleven-year-old to lose weight. Nothing I am going to say is going to flip her perspective.

"I have a proposal," I say instead.

Last night, annoyed at Jeff, annoyed at Harri, annoyed that I couldn't fall back to sleep, I thought about the fashion show. What a stupid idea, I realized, to make little kids parade around on a stage as if they were on *Toddlers & Tiaras*. I had been so happy to be included, to be part of an existing social circle that could have so easily closed its ranks to me, that I didn't question the concept. And I never stopped to consider what the "fundraising" was going toward. An end-of-year picnic? This is a community that throws wedding-sized birthday parties for their five-year-olds with tents and clowns and real pony rides. Does it really need to raise money for a party any one of them can afford to host ten times over? I had a much better idea for the funds.

"Well, I recently heard very sad news," I say, treading carefully, trying to build an ironclad case. "Wayne's dog, Penny was just diagnosed with cancer. It's lymphoma. You know, the same exact cancer that Mary, his wife, had."

"Wait," says Margot, holding up her palm. "Who's Wayne?"

There is a little murmuring among the minions. They look as confused as Margot.

"Wayne? My next-door neighbor?"

"The creepy old guy who lives in the ranch," Amber says, rolling her eyes.

I glance at her, unappreciative of the tone. "Yes. Anyway, Penny is everything to Wayne. She's all he's got since Mary passed away. He's just devastated. And the problem is, he can't afford the treatment. I googled the cost of chemo for dogs, and it could be thousands and thousands of dollars."

The sounds coming from the cafeteria are reverberating through the heavy doors. We've left the girls alone in there with no adults other than the after-school aide. Amber and Kim's eyes shift toward the noise. I'm losing the group. I start talking faster.

"So I was thinking… Do we really need to raise money for a picnic? Our kids have everything. A party a week. A holiday a month. Every day around here seems to be another excuse to send in cupcakes or hand out a goody bag. It's sugar, sugar, sugar. Am I right? Do they even *need* a picnic? Would they even notice if it didn't happen? But, what if the money we raise went to something really worthwhile? Something altruistic. Something compassionate. Helping a neighbor. Supporting our community. Think of the lesson we could teach our children. What great citizens of the earth that would make them."

"What on earth are you getting at?" asks Margot.

"I'm saying I think it would be a fantastic idea to use the money we raise to create a fund for Wayne and Penny."

Margot clenches her jaw. No one speaks.

"For her vet bills."

Evelyn blinks. Still, silence.

"To help our neighbor."

Noah and Amber look at each other.

"That's kind of sweet," says Noah.

Margot shuts him down with a sidelong glare. "Look," she says focusing back on me. "I know you are new. But I can't tell you what a ridiculous idea that is. On so many levels."

"That's right," adds Amber.

I feel the heat rising in my face. Now my arms are crossed. "Why? Why is it ridiculous?"

"The funds are allocated. The fashion show has been advertised as a fundraiser for the *picnic*. The parents buy tickets because they know the money will go to the benefit of their children."

"Well, that's stupid."

Margot's head jerks back as if I'd slapped her—which by the way is not the worst idea right now.

"Ginny!" scolds Kim.

"No, I'm sorry. But these kids don't need the money. Wayne does. His dog is going to die. And then he'll have no one. Where are your priorities?"

"Where are his?" asks Amber. "If he needs money so badly, he should sell that ramshackle house and move somewhere he can afford. Then maybe *he* can take care of his own dog."

I gasp.

"Okay, Amber," says Margot. "We don't need to go there."

"I'm sorry," she says. "I just don't like it when people ask for a handout before they try to help themselves. Too many people do that these days."

"He's not asking for a handout," I bite back. "He doesn't even know I'm doing this. I just thought you'd have a heart. Boy, was I wrong."

Margot puts a few inches between herself and Amber.

"Ginny, we are not a heartless bunch. We feel for your friend, we do," she says. "But there is a protocol. We work within the Board of Education guidelines. There have been proposals submitted, planning meetings attended, and votes taken. This is not a random neighborhood lemonade stand."

"If the great Margot Moss-Marks asked them to do this, I'm sure they'd ask, 'How quickly?'" I bite down on my cheek so hard I can taste blood.

Margot's hand flies up to her chest, protecting herself.

"Maybe you should try to live in this community for more than five minutes before you presume to know how things work around here," she says.

I just lost this one. I know it. My diplomacy skills are crap. But I can't help myself. I've had it with all of them.

"So I'm afraid the answer is no. Now, please, can we all get back to work? The parents will be here to pick up in twenty minutes, and we haven't finished the fittings."

Margot and her lemmings turn in unison and head back toward the cafeteria door.

"It *was* a sweet idea," whispers Noah as he walks past me and pats my arm.

I stand up straighter, locking my shoulders back and raising my chin.

"Well, then, I quit."

My announcement echoes off the walls of the empty hallway. That stops them.

"Oh, Ginny," says Noah. "Don't do that."

"I'm sorry. I just think my time would be better spent, um, elsewhere."

"But the show is in two weeks," Evelyn whines. "And you've done so much already. Your centerpieces are so unique and funky. They are going to be the hit of the night. You have to finish them!"

"Kim can do it. I'll bring her all the finished towers and the remaining shoes. Heck, she can even have my glue gun."

Kim looks panicked, as if I've said she should figure out the mathematical equation to determine the landing coordinates of the next Mars mission. Amber's mouth twists into a small smile. Does she think this is funny?

"This is a shame. But it's up to Ginny," says Margot to the others. "We can't make her continue on with us."

She turns to go back into the fitting but stops and faces me again.

"Of course, you realize if you quit the committee, we will have to switch out Harri's outfit for the show. Only committee members' children walk in formal wear."

"What? Why would you do that? She has nothing to do with this."

"It's the rule. And we can't break the rule, or the next thing you know, everyone will be asking us to do it."

Stupid fucking formal wear. It's what started all the trouble with Harri in the first place. Maybe she will be happy about this. Maybe it will take the pressure off. She can still participate in the fashion show with her friends, but now she can wear something more in line with her own aesthetic. She can walk that runway showing her true self. And that will be the end of the ridiculous body-shaming and unnecessary dieting. This could be a winning situation for both of us.

"That's fine," I say. "I don't think Harri was all that interested in wearing a gown anyway. She basically agreed to do it under duress. I actually think she will be happier with this new plan."

Chapter 23

In the car, Harri is in a rare good mood. She is chattering on about the dress and the emerald-green color and how Jacqueline's mom is letting her do a semipermanent red hair dye that washes out in six shampoos and maybe she should do that too because it will look so good with the gown.

The dagger in my heart twists. "I quit the committee."

"Mom! No! You said!"

"Circumstances have changed."

"What circumstances?"

"Because of Penny."

"What does Penny have to do with this?"

I hadn't told her about Penny. I wasn't sure she was ready to hear it on the heels of the Mrs. Clucklesworth debacle. In fact, I was hoping not to tell her until I could pair it with the amazing news that the community was going to step up and help with the dog's treatment. Time for Plan B.

Harri takes the news of Penny's illness as expected. She cries quietly, keeping her face turned toward the window, occasionally wiping at her nose with the sleeve of her coat. At least the loving, compassionate part of my daughter hasn't disappeared into a cloud of preteen angst. Finally, she takes a deep breath and faces me again.

"I don't understand what this has to do with you quitting the fashion show."

"Well," I say, "when it comes down to it, it's a matter of shared values. I think raising money to help a friend in need is more important than throwing a lavish picnic for a bunch of entitled kids. Clearly, the committee doesn't agree with me." I'm sure Harri will be on my side.

"Oh, why can't you just be like the other moms?"

"What is that supposed to mean?"

Aside from the fact that we've already established I don't care about my appearance. What else now?

"It means, why can't you just go along with things? Why do you always have to 'take a stand'? It's so embarrassing."

"Embarrassing?" I laugh to keep my voice from rising. "How can you say that? You are always first in line for a cause. Who are you, and what have you done with my daughter?"

"It's not funny. I'm serious."

I'm trying hard not to lose my cool. Harri, my Harri, the Harri I showed up in this town with, knows better.

"Well, I'm sorry I'm embarrassing you. But I feel strongly about this. Wayne is our friend. And Penny is all he's got. We have to find some way to help him. That's where I'm going to be putting my energy. And I'd love it if you were part of it. Whatever *it* is."

Harri doesn't answer. She's back to looking out the window.

"Besides, my quitting doesn't mean you have to. You still get to be in the show."

I pause a beat. I see the next thirty seconds of my life so clearly. It's like I'm speeding toward a brick wall with my brakes cut. "Just not in formal wear."

"What?"

"Formal wear is just for the committee's kids. And they are being sticklers about it. But look, now you don't have to wear that dumb dress. Isn't that what you wanted from the start?"

"Mom! No!"

"And I have an even better idea. Remember that artist we loved at the

Manhattan Armory Crafts Fair? She made clothes from recycled materials? You loved the romper made out of eighties band T-shirts. I think Aunt Z knows her. I'll bet she'd love for you to model one of her pieces. Talk about a showshopper! Wearable art—what a statement that will make!"

"Oh my God, Mom. You've got to be kidding!"

"I'm not kidding. I think it would be great. It would represent your true aesthetic. It would support the artistic community that raised you. And to be honest, it would be adorable."

"I want to wear what my friends are wearing."

"Well, that's not possible. They won't bend the rules."

I could go back to Margot and apologize. I could make the rest of the Cinderella's glass-slipper centerpieces. Heck, I could even volunteer to chaperone the big end-of-year picnic. But I won't—because this is about so much more than a disagreement over money and the coldheartedness of my neighbors. I do not want my daughter walking a catwalk in a tight evening gown—no matter how gorgeous an emerald green it is. I do not want Harri seduced by these girls anymore. Despite my ultimatum this morning, I don't trust that Harri is going to hold up her end of the bargain. She thinks I didn't notice that she left for school without eating breakfast. I don't like that she feels she has to starve herself to fit in. I don't like the spell they have cast over my beautiful, independent, quirky, brilliant child.

I can't explain it to her. She won't hear what's in my heart. All she'll hear is that I'm depriving her, punishing her, that I'm mean and I ruin everything. She isn't in a place where she will understand I'm doing this for her own good. I'm trying to protect her from becoming like these superficial people who encourage their children to be the next Kardashian. Maybe after this fashion show is over, I can convince Harri to try something new. She can join a club more in line with her actual interests—maybe a science club or handbells—where she can find kindred spirits, friends who can lift her and not suck the life out of her, which I see so clearly now is what's happening.

We ride in silence. Harri is slouched in her seat, her arms tightly folded, her chin tucked into her neck. The days are getting shorter, and the sun is starting to set as we reach the turnoff for Elderberry Lane. As I am about to turn, I get an idea. It's a small idea, but getting my daughter back is going to take one small idea at a time.

"You passed our street," she growls.

"I've got to run a quick errand."

Harri grumbles. She wants out of this car and away from me. We are back to radio silence as we roll into the town center, past the eyelash-bar strip mall and one of our town's two Starbucks. When I pull into the parking lot a few doors down, I can see through the shop's front window that it doesn't have much inventory. It is late in the day. A girl in a bright-pink T-shirt is wiping down tables.

"Why are we here?" Harri asks.

"What, you never had cupcakes for dinner?" I ask as I jump out of the car and go into Buttercupcakes to buy everything they have left.

Chapter 24

HARRI CAN'T GO TO SCHOOL TODAY AND I HAVE ONLY MYSELF TO blame. The idea of eating a plate full of cupcakes for dinner was a good one—in theory. I wanted to go back to a time when my daughter and I did silly things. And I wanted her to eat. Even if it was a cupcake. Or two.

When we returned from the bakery, I put the sum total of Buttercupcakes inventory on a gold-trimmed serving platter that matched the setting for twelve stacked on glass shelves in the dining room hutch. Stacey's wedding china, I assumed.

I brought the dish and two glasses of milk into the family room and searched through our old DVD collection for our favorite movie, *When Harry Met Sally*. I used to tell my daughter she was named after the Billy Crystal character, which would make her laugh. I was also known to claim her namesake was Harriet the Spy and occasionally, Harriet Beecher Stowe, depending on my mood and the tale I wanted to spin. Regardless, it always got a laugh. The truth is, she is not named after anyone. She isn't even named Harriet. She's just plain Harri, one of a kind.

I took it as a good sign that Harri didn't go straight to her room and slam the door when we got home. Instead, she sat cross-legged on the couch looking exhausted as I inserted the disk and fumbled with the collection of remotes on the coffee table.

"What flavor is this?" Harri asked, holding up a yellow cupcake with pale-pink frosting. It was the first thing she'd said to me since we'd been home. Sure, she was half talking, half whining, half grumbling, but I was adding it to my win column.

"Piña colada, I think. And that one is rum raisin. This one might be key lime," I said, dabbing my finger in the green frosting and taking a taste. "I had to take what I could get. It was slim pickings this late in the day."

Harri shrugged, chose the piña colada, and broke it in half, making her famous cupcake sandwich. I was feeling better already. By the time Harry and Sally had driven from the University of Chicago to their new (but separate) lives in New York, Harri had eaten four cupcakes.

The meal wasn't exactly going to pass the government's food-pyramid guidelines, but I had gotten her to eat. It wasn't the joyous, giggling, getting-away-with-it experience that usually accompanies having dessert for dinner, but more of a glum, robotic shoveling of food into piehole. Still, I was patting myself on the back for my stealth and sly parenting skills. Until the vomiting started. It came up like baking soda and vinegar lava from a science fair volcano, while Harri's eyes widened in shock and filled with tears. The piña colada landed on her chest. The rum raisin hit the sofa. The key lime splashed on the rug. And the judges came back onstage and took away my parenting award just as I was delivering my acceptance speech.

So when Harri woke up this morning complaining of a tummy ache, I sent her back to bed. Letting her skip school is the least I could do. After the way she'd been eating lately, or should I say, not eating, I should have known her stomach would have shrunk to the size of a pea. And there I was, treating her like a foie gras goose just to try to prove a point. I got what was coming to me—a sick kid and a stain on Stacey's cream-colored sectional that I don't think is coming out.

When I come downstairs for the third time—after checking Harri for a fever, swapping out a melted glass of ice for a fresh one, and just generally checking to make sure she was still breathing—Wayne is in the kitchen pouring himself a mug of coffee. Penny is in her spot under the table, already fast asleep and snoring.

"I hear you quit the fashion show," he says, searching the refrigerator for milk. It's already on the counter. I pour some into his cup.

"How'd you hear that?" I ask, knowing there was only one person I spoke to after I put Harri to bed and cleaned up the mess. Well, hum me a few bars of *Fiddler on the Roof* and call me matchmaker. I smile.

Wayne takes a sip of his coffee and places it on the counter. "Zaria told me you walked out on them. And why. Look, Ginny. I can't tell you how much it means that you went to bat for Penny and me. It was a crazy idea, I'll tell you that. And I would've been shocked if they'd taken you up on it. But really, I don't want you to jeopardize your friendship with those ladies because of me. I don't think you want to get on their bad side."

"Don't you worry about me. Remember, I'm from Queens. We don't take any shit in Woodside."

"I'm serious. It's a small town."

"Honestly, it's fine. We parted amicably—enough. They got their decorations, so they don't need me anymore. And besides, I think the whole thing was making Harri nuts."

"So Harri quit too?"

"No, she still wants to do it. But they are making her change outfits—no evening gown. Which, to be honest, is pretty petty. Still, I think it's going to work out for the best. She doesn't need that kind of pressure—you know, trying so hard to live up to everyone's standards in this town. And the little girls are as bad as their moms. It's like no one can just play and get dirty and be a kid; everyone has to be a little beauty queen. Now I just have to convince her of that."

"Okay, if you say so. So, what are you going to do with all your free time?"

I look out the kitchen window at my nearly abandoned art studio above the garage.

"Well, for one, I've got a stack of commissions backed up. I'm not complaining. I can't tell you how long I waited for my business to catch on. It's wild how many people want pet portraits these days. It's almost a craze."

"I'd love one of Penny. I mean, before…you know. But I need to save my dough. Every cent I have is going to go toward treatment. I'd even try my hand at it myself, but it would look like a five-year-old did it."

"Ha, like I'd charge you for a pa—"

A lightning bolt hits me.

"Holy cow, Wayne. You are a genius!"

"What did I say?"

"You just gave me the most amazing idea for a way to raise the money for Penny's treatments!"

"Again, what did I say?"

"I'm going to organize a Paint Your Pet event. I've seen them done before—mostly to raise money for animal shelters. You sell tickets, people send a photo of their pet ahead of time, and you sketch it out for them. It's practically paint by numbers. And I could get Z and some of the other artists I know to donate their time to help with the drawings. Throw in some wine… Bada bing, bada boom, vet bills paid!"

My ideas of how to pull this together are making my heart race.

"Ginny that sounds like a ton of work. I can't ask you to do that for me. You just told me how behind on your work you are."

The cogs in my head are turning.

"It's not really that much work. I can look into having it at a 'paint your own' place. That way all the materials are already there. It will be a piece of cake. And I could take what I learned from working on the fashion show—like we could have raffles and gift baskets. And I'll bet Noah would help with the financial end. He's a great guy. And with the people in this town, we could charge a hefty price, and they wouldn't even blink an eye."

"Ginny, I couldn't ask you—"

"Ask me, Wayne, please ask me. I'd love to do this for you and Penny. It would mean so much to me. It would be an actual *good* use of my creative time. It would give me a chance to reconnect with my artistic self and my old friends from my craft fair days, and honestly, it would be great for Harri. I'll bet she'd love to be part of this. It will be such a good opportunity for her to get engaged with something that really matters. I don't mean to be overly dramatic, but it will help her remember who she really is, what she really cares about."

I stop and take a deep breath. I realize I am shaking. This idea has become so much bigger than helping a dear friend. It might just be a chance to bring Harri back to me.

Chapter 25

I FEEL LIGHTER THAN I HAVE IN MONTHS. YES, I HAVE A disgruntled daughter who is barely speaking to me, a good friend with a dog dying of cancer, and a husband who is three thousand miles away unnecessarily trying to prove his worth that no one, save for his ex-wife, is questioning. But something is different about today. Today, I feel like the Ginny I used to know.

Wayne has left to take Penny on an amble around the block. They could be gone all morning. I pad up the stairs one more time and slowly open Harri's door. My catlike reflexes don't allow me to avoid a loud, whining creak. I freeze like a burglar and hold my breath. But my daughter doesn't move. She is on her side, facing the door, one cheek jammed into the pillow, the other slightly flushed. She's out for the count. It's the perfect time to reintroduce myself to my studio and apologize to my dried-out paints. I'll text Harri to let her know I'm up there in case she wakes up and needs me.

Fallen leaves on the back deck and lawn crunch under my feet as I head to my studio. If Harri is feeling better later, we can rake them up. She's never had a chance to jump in a leaf pile. It's things like that—leaf piles and snowball fights and waiting for the bulbs planted in the fall to bloom in April—that made me so excited to move Harri here when Jeff proposed it.

My beat-up Subaru sits in the driveway, and I stop to admire it before I head into the garage. The stickers, some of them old and weatherworn, tell the story of our life before Elderberry Lane: a paisley peace sign, a Hillary2016 bumper sticker, ovals with large initials—VT, NH, MB for my parents' place in Myrtle Beach—like decals on a steamer trunk, all reminders of places visited, craft fairs traveled to, cheap vacations where I showed my daughter as much of the world as I could afford at the time. I start to pick off the remains of a flower power sticker that has only two petals left.

As I lean over my back bumper, I see the white caravan—Margot's Lexus SUV, Amber's BMW SUV, Colette's Porsche SUV and Noah's Land Rover—rolling down the street. Each turns into its own driveway with the harmonization of synchronized swimmers. I pull my phone out of my back pocket and look at the time. So they are back from their power walk slash committee meeting in the park.

I feel the bite of being excluded, disinvited to the party, FOMO—fear of missing out, as Amber calls it. But I stop myself. This was my choice. Besides, I've left the committee, not the street. Just because we don't see eye to eye on the fashion show doesn't mean we can't be good neighbors. We are all still moms who are trying to do the best for our families. We just have different views on what "best" is.

My studio is cold but smells heavenly as my body kicks up the stagnant air and awakens the aromas of paint and oil and paper. I breathe in deeply. *Yes*, I think, *I can finally strike a balance in this place. I can exist in this new world as the OG Ginny—original gangster, city girl makes good in the burbs. And who knows, maybe some of it will rub off on a few of her new friends.*

I turn the knob on the baseboard heater, and it snaps and cracks to life. The reading chair looks at me accusingly from the corner. If it could fold its padded arms, it would. Not only has it been abandoned by the girl who used to balance her library books on its side arms, but it has been relegated to act as a holdall for the high-heeled shoes not yet turned into magical, modern-day Cinderella centerpieces. *Shit.* I've got to get rid of that stuff.

I try to ignore them. Now is my time to paint. I take a large canvas from the clean ones leaning against the wall, balance it on the easel's ledge, and turn screws until I readjust the height. A photo of a black Labrador is pinned on my wall. Black dogs are my least favorite to paint; the textures and highlights of their fur have to be brought out with a series of lighter tones that can get tricky—at least for me. But the owner has been waiting patiently and the larger canvas will bring a higher price, so Black Dog jumps to the head of the line.

I tape the photo to my easel and pick up a pencil to start my sketch on the canvas. I want to see how quickly I can do this. If my Paint Your Pet idea works out, I'm going to have to draw a lot of these, and even with recruiting Zaria and some other artist friends, it's going to be a challenge. I need to run this event soon. Penny's treatments can't wait.

I start with the lab's big, square head and bulky shoulders, but something is nagging at me, like the pointy heel of a shoe poking me in the back. It is the damn pointy-heeled shoes piled up on the reading chair, and the silver sprayed ones lined up on newspaper on the floor, and the half-finished centerpieces, and the glue gun lying next to them, and the seven already completed shoe towers that were meant to mark my debut into the stay-at-home-mom, volunteering, fundraiser world.

"That's it," I say out loud. "Everything's got to go."

I pull out my phone and call Kim. She doesn't answer, probably not home yet from taking my place at the walk-meeting.

"Kim," I say into her voicemail. "I'm on my way over. I'm going to drop off all the centerpieces and other materials for you." I'll figure out what to do with it all if she's not home when I get there. I just need them gone.

Kim lives in a section of town whose homes make Elderberry Lane look like affordable housing. Each driveway is circular and paved with pale cobblestones instead of asphalt. Some have three-tiered fountains sprouting up in the manicured circle between the driveway and the street. To the one, every house sports an elaborate and professional-looking autumnal arrangement: urns filled with mums and cabbages, pumpkins and gourds atop full bales of hay, dried cornstalks standing guard at imposing double front doors hung with wreaths of wheat and berries.

A young woman answers the door soon after I ring.

"Is your mother here?" I ask, doing the quick math of my estimation of this girl's age plus how old I think Kim looks minus the Botox. "I know they had a fashion show walk, er, I mean meeting, but I thought she'd be home by now."

"I'm the personal assistant," she says. "And Mrs. Biaggio didn't attend. She's got another matter. Can I help you with something?"

Assistant? I know for a fact Kim doesn't have a job, doesn't run a business, and certainly isn't a celebrity. What does a stay-at-home mom need with an assistant?

"I just left a message for Kim," I say. "I'm dropping something—"

Just then Kim and a young, muscular man in a tank top and track pants walk into the foyer. Kim, wearing a sports bra and multicolored leggings, is dabbing at her décolletage with a towel.

"Ginny," she says, her voice echoing in the cavernous, two-story entryway.

"She's here to drop something off, Mrs. Biaggio," says the assistant to my former assistant.

"Yes, Andrea, I heard her."

"Goodbye, Mrs. B. Great workout today," says the young man.

"Thank you, Michael."

I step back as Michael ducks out the door. Now I'm back on the front step with the cornstalks. I don't have all day. Harri was still flat out when I left, but she'll be waking up soon. I step into the house and past Andrea.

"So, I don't know if you heard it, but I left a message. I have all the material for the centerpieces—and all the finished ones in my car. I'm passing the torch as it were," I say with a forced laugh.

Kim sighs impatiently and does not seem amused. "Andrea, please take everything out of Ginny's car and put it in the pool house. It's closed up for the winter so you'll be able to spread out in there with no interruption. Ginny, before you go, you'll explain to Andrea what she needs to do."

Andrea looks at me like she's trying to send an SOS signal. I get it now. Kim is just another Margot, except when she's with Margot. There is a pecking order. Andrea and I are at the bottom of the pile.

"Sure, no problem."

I start to follow the assistant outside but Kim stops me.

"So you are really quitting?" she asks. "After all the work is almost done? Seems silly, if you ask me. You're going to miss the fun part." She spreads her finger apart like Bob Fosse's jazz hands. "The Big Show," she says breathily.

"The fun part for me was the creative process," I say. "I was glad to be a part of that. But right now I have a lot on my plate."

"Yes, we heard. And, I'm sorry," she says. "We've all been through it. Stick to your guns. And get a good lawyer."

"What are you talking about?"

"Oh, don't be embarrassed, Ginny. Amber told us all about it. Honestly, it's shocking these days if things *don't* end up in court. Keith wasn't my first, you know. And at the rate we're going"—she looks up at her four-tiered crystal chandelier—"he won't be my last."

I don't know who Keith is. I don't know what answers lie in a chandelier. And I certainly have no idea what Amber told them that is evoking such sympathy in the normally icy Kim. Without further explanation, Kim turns and walks out of the foyer and into her kitchen. I follow mutely. We can't be done with this, whatever this is.

I have become used to restaurant-sized kitchens in this town but this one is colossal, all white and glass and stainless steel, like the futuristic galley on a luxury cruise ship to outer space. Kim opens a walk-in glass refrigerator the size of a closet and pulls out a pitcher of water infused with lemon and cucumber and mint. She pours two glasses and hands one to me.

I put it on the white marble counter. I'm not interested in luxury water right now.

"What did Amber tell you?" I ask as casually as my growing anxiety allows.

She pulls the elastic out of her hair. Shakes her head and takes a long sip before she answers me.

"She told us about you and Jeff. Trouble in paradise and all that. About how things are falling apart since he took that job overseas."

The zing starts in my feet and rushes so quickly up my body that I can't control the tears welling up in my burning eyes. *What the fuck is wrong with Amber?* I rack my brain to remember if I said anything to her, anything that would give her the impression…

"What exactly did Amber say?"

Kim puts a manicured finger on her lip. "She said that you feel like he's deserted you—which I don't blame you for, by the way—and that your marriage is too new to withstand that kind of distance, and she gives it a few weeks—or maybe a few months—after he gets back and the whole thing is going to collapse."

Now I feel the hairs on my scalp rising. I take a deep breath and lean against a countertop. "I don't know where Amber got that idea," I say, trying to laugh it off but betraying myself with the squeak in my voice. "Jeff and I are fine. Totally fine. Yes, he's away on business. Sure, that's not ideal. I mean, because I miss him. And Harri misses him. But we're fine. Totally. And we speak every day. Well, almost. And he's coming home soon."

I'm starting to sound like Hamlet's mother. Protesting way too much. And I know why. Buttons have been pushed. Salt has been poured.

Kim smiles sympathetically, but I can tell she doesn't believe me. "Well, that's a relief."

"Yes." I go for the forced laugh again. "So it's fake news!"

"Amber must have gotten the wrong end of the stick. Classic Amber. You know how she is."

No, I think. *Clearly I don't know how she is.* But I'm going to have to make it a point to find out.

Chapter 26

WHEN I ARRIVE HOME FROM KIM'S, THERE IS A STRANGE CAR IN MY driveway. My heart starts racing as I think of my daughter, hopefully safe and sound in bed. I park in the street and walk up to the driver of the car, a young man in his early twenties. The racing turns to pounding as I approach him. His window is open and a hand holding a vape pen is dangling out of it. As I get closer to the car, I smell the strawberry smoke and pine car freshener.

"Can I help you?" I ask as I scan my property for a possible accomplice. *Dammit, why did I leave Harri home alone, why did I have to go to Kim's today, why isn't Jeff here?*

He points to a decal on his windshield that says Uber. "She asked me to wait."

I look at my front door, expecting to see whoever "she" is standing at it. No one is there. "She" is inside.

Not wanting to take the time to fumble with my keys, I race around the back of the house where I know the sliding door is unlocked. I step into the kitchen and there is Harri, sitting at the breakfast table in her pajamas, looking intact and unharmed. A black parka with a fur-trimmed hood is draped over the chair next to her. I turn my head and see the coat's owner leaning against the island with one of my thick, ceramic, cream-colored mugs in her hand.

I step between Harri and this woman. "Harri? What's going on? Are you alright?"

She looks up at me. "I was going to call you—"

"Now, don't be mad at Harri," the woman says taking a step toward me.

"She's a smart girl. She knows all about *stranger danger*. But when I told her we were practically related, she was kind enough to let me come in out of the cold."

She smiles at my daughter with thirty-two perfect white teeth. There is nothing familial about this person. But she seems familiar, another wiry blond cut from the Margot/Amber mold—minus the jewelry and the lash extensions and the gel nails. And while her face shows the signs that I've become acquainted with—lips too plump, forehead too smooth—an inch of brown growth tells of a missed appointment at the hair salon.

"Mom," says Harri. "It's Stacey."

The woman turns her smile to me and throws out her arms.

"Ta-da!"

It's like seeing someone you thought was dead. Stacey, as legend goes, left with her clothes and what jewelry her underachieving husband could afford to bestow on her, and never looked back. Oh, there was the anecdotal evidence of her showing up to see Brendan once in a while, including her shadowy appearance at his college graduation, but for Jeff, aside from through her lawyers in the early days, he hadn't heard from her since.

And now here she stands, exhumed. That is, of course, if she is who she says she is. I've actually never seen a photograph of Jeff's ex-wife. There are no family photos on the shelves and walls—only sweet school and graduation pictures of Brendan—and no old albums hidden away in any closet I've come across.

"Not even from a family vacation?" I asked Jeff about it on that first tour of the house he gave me. I picked up a photo taken in a forest of a younger Jeff with his son in a baby backpack. I had assumed it was taken by Stacey, although surprised she had agreed to be out in the wilderness after what he had told me about her.

"Why would I save those?"

It had made me sad, but also relieved. There was no question about Jeff pining for his ex.

This woman standing in front of me certainly looks like a dulled-down version of someone who could have lived on this street. But the Queens girl in me has to be sure. After all, whoever this is, she's standing in my kitchen, drinking my coffee, within arm's reach of my daughter.

"Well, Stacey. You won't mind showing me some ID then."

The woman lets out a short, aggressive laugh. "Oh, Ginny, I see Jeff landed himself a funny one."

I hold out my hand and she realizes I'm serious. After rummaging through her bag, she hands me a California driver's license with an I-told-you-so look on her face, as if I'm a bouncer at a club who didn't believe she was of legal age. Unlike the person standing in front of me, the woman in the photo has a deep tan, large diamond hoop earrings, and perfectly arched and painted eyebrows, but it is Stacey.

I hand the card back to her. "What can I do for you?"

"Well," she says as she surveys the kitchen, "I'm sorry to pop in on you unannounced, but I need to speak to Jeff."

It's ten in the morning on a Thursday. She has to know Jeff wouldn't be here. "Jeff's at work."

She doesn't need to know his office is in Dublin.

Stacey glances into the family room and then walks around the island to the archway leading to the dining room and looks in. Harri and I exchange glances. Harri knits her eyebrows as if to ask, *What is she doing here?* I raise mine to answer, *I have no frigging clue.*

"You haven't changed much," she says. She stops at a set of hand-crafted ceramic canisters found at an arts fair in Bangor, Maine, and set on the counter to replace the glass containers filled with decorative, oily vegetables. "Not my style. But, okay."

I certainly don't owe her an explanation. I wait for her to state her business. She does another circle of the kitchen, stopping at the sink. "Where's the pig?"

"Gone. Smashed. An accident."

I don't have any desire to tell her it's up in the attic along with a lot of her other crap. I wanted to get rid of it all, make a donation to a very deserving and grateful thrift store, but I didn't say a word when Jeff and Harri hauled it upstairs. I was so touched by the gesture of getting it out of sight and out of mind.

"Oh, that's a shame," she says, running her hand along the granite. "It was an antique. I brought it back from the most marvelous shop in Paris. It was worth a lot of money," she adds almost wistfully.

Then maybe you shouldn't have left it behind, with all your other possessions and your family.

"I can tell Jeff you were here. You can leave your number," I say, knowing Jeff will never call her.

"Well, Ginny, maybe you can help me. If I think about it, we don't really need Jeff to sort this out."

"Sort what out?"

I look over at my daughter who has her chin in her hands, rapt. Whatever's about to go down is way more enthralling than anything she can find scrolling through her phone.

"Harri, why don't you go upstairs and get dressed?"

"Nope," she says.

Great, today is the day my daughter decides she's back to her old self, sticking to me like glue to find out what the hell the grown-ups are up to. I let it go. One adversary at a time.

"Sort what out?" I ask again.

Stacey picks up the copper-bottomed teakettle resting on the stove top.

"This is from Le Sur," she purrs as if she's sharing her family history with me. "You see Ginny, the thing is, I've been away, as I'm sure you know."

I'm starting to wonder if the California sunshine has baked this woman's brain. She's been away? No kidding.

"And six months is a long time, especially when you have nothing to do but think—and work out." She adds that last bit with a beauty contestant turn, as if I am supposed to give her points in the swimsuit category.

"So I've decided I'm not waiting for him. I'm going to restart my life. A complete do-over. Back here. In Jersey."

"Six months? Back here? Stacey, I have no idea what you are talking about."

"Oh, really?" she asks, hand to chest. "I just assumed Jeff told you, you two being married now. It was all over the news in LA, and even then it died down quickly, what with all the shit going on in this country. But unless you knew to google it, I'm positive it didn't get to Jersey. Of course, I had to tell Jeff, you know, because of Brendan, but I asked him to keep it from the gossipmongers on the street. That was the last thing I needed. Can you imagine this kind of information in Amber's hands? You know her."

"I'm sorry, I honestly have no idea what you are talking about."

"Oh really," she says. "That's interesting. And telling. Never mind, it's none of my business. I just would have thought. Well, anyway..." she says, cupping the outside of her hand around the side of her mouth and winding up for a stage whisper. "I was in *prison*."

Harri's mouth pops open like the top of a jack-in-the-box. Mine probably has as well.

Stacey reads my face. "Don't worry, honey, I'm not here to shiv you." She is the only one who laughs.

"It wasn't like hard time or anything. Don't get me wrong, it was awful. But it was minimum-security white-collar time. My only crime was being stupid. I signed some papers. I didn't ask what they were. Went down with the damn ship. Now, Ronny—the bastard—he's the one in real trouble. Mortgage fraud, mail fraud, lying to the feds. The most expensive lawyer in

Los Angeles couldn't get him any less than twenty-three months. And, like I said, I'm not waiting for him. I mean, how would that work out? Where's the trust?"

My head is spinning. I don't know who has more gall right now, this woman who showed up out of nowhere with her *Orange Is the New Black* backstory or her ex-husband who kept this story to himself.

"So, the thing is, I left him. He'll come out, eventually, and no one will be there to pick him up. And I left California. Like I said, fresh start." Stacey walks off into the dining room.

Harri and I follow her. She crosses her arms and surveys the room.

"But here's the problem," she says, opening the hutch and taking out the gold-trimmed gravy boat. "They seized everything, the bastards, everything down to my pearl studs. The code to the front gate was changed. Can you believe it? I couldn't even get down the driveway of my own house. Such an invasion of privacy."

"Who is they?" Harri asks, enthralled.

"The government, honey. The feds," she says. She turns the gravy boat over and inspects the bottom. "This was my wedding china. Royal Worcester. Two hundred and fifty a place setting. I loved this pattern."

She reaches back into the cabinet and pulls out the same platter I served cupcakes on last night. "Anyway, I'm back and I've got a lead on a great job. There's a dermatologist in Tenafly who's looking for a receptionist *and* going through a divorce."

Stacey winks at Harri as if they are both in on her little scheme to snag herself a rich doctor. "But I'm kind of stuck. I had a credit card they didn't find, but it's almost maxed out. What I really need is cash. You know, to set myself up." She pushes at her hair and glances down at her nails. "And God, do I need a spa day. After everything I've been through."

And there it is. I step forward and look at the platter she has tucked under her arm.

"Stacey, we don't have any—"

"Oh, Ginny, I'm not asking for *money*." She laughs. She walks over to the credenza and picks up a porcelain statue of a mother and child in Victorian dress that was missed in the big clearout. I am half expecting her to start to juggle the gravy boat, the platter, and the figurine.

"Believe me, I'm aware Jeff has no spare cash lying around," she says, throwing a dig that doesn't land well.

If I weren't so pissed at him, my heart would break for my husband. How the hell did he put up with her as long as he did?

"Here is what I'm thinking though," she says. "I'm going to take some of the things that are clearly mine—the wedding china, for example—and sell it." She holds the statue out toward me. "This Lladró alone is worth five, maybe six hundred. And I'll bet that it hasn't been touched—or dusted— since I've been gone."

"I don't think Jeff is going to… Never mind, I'll speak for myself. I am not a fan of this idea."

I had spent so much time convincing Jeff I was fine about moving into his ex-wife's house. I swore blind that I didn't care about material posses- sions, that all that mattered was we were a family and we were here together. But right now, as I follow Stacey back into the kitchen and watch her cover *my* Lladró with a dish towel and put it in her purse, I feel like I'm being robbed.

"It's only fair," she says way too casually. "Half of all this should have been mine. But I didn't ask for a thing. I left it all for him, which was more than generous if you ask me. In fact, I'm entitled to half the house. I could have made him buy me out. That was my right."

Knowing what I know now, I'm sure had she done that, it would have destroyed Jeff financially and wiped him out emotionally.

"In fact, I think I might to talk to a lawyer. I'll bet the statute of limita- tions on property co-ownership hasn't expired."

My pulse is racing. Harri ducks behind me, sensing the storm brewing here.

"You can't do that," I snarl.

This woman is trespassing. She's endangering the welfare of my child. She is even potentially robbing me. I watch, feeling helpless, as she shrugs into her coat and tucks the fine china under her arm. And then I snap out of it.

"Hang on, Stacey," I say feeling the cork—the one that's been bottling up my emotions since this woman walked into my house—twist and loosen. "You're not leaving with any of my things."

I hold out my hand, expecting givebacks.

"Your things?" Jeff's ex-wife laughs in a pitch that brings to mind a certain witch from a certain land called Oz. "You clearly haven't been listening to what I'm saying."

"Oh, I have." I take a step closer to her and she stiffens. Slowly and deliberately, I relieve her of the wedding china and place it gently on the kitchen counter. This woman isn't taking anything else from Jeff. Not if I can help it.

"Well, aren't you one tough cookie?" she asks mockingly. "What does Jeff think of this ugly side of you?"

I set my jaw. I can feel Harri grabbing onto the back of my sweater. She's rarely seen me like this either. But I hold my resolve. "And the statue," I say, opening my palm to her.

Stacey waits a beat. She scans the kitchen, maybe hoping the likes of Amber will burst through the doors and help her fight me for the Lladró. After a moment, when she realizes the cavalry is not arriving, her shoulders drop.

"Okay, fine. Suit yourself." She pulls the ceramic figure out of her bag and tosses it on the counter. Only the dish towel it's wrapped in saves it from breaking. "I'm going to have to come back anyway," she says sweet as pie.

"I'll pick it up then, with the rest of the dinner set. Oh, and I think I'll bring a truck and a few strong men. That dining table and chairs are Palais Royale. I paid twenty grand. If I get half that, I'm all set."

Chapter 27

WHEN *THAT WOMAN* LEFT, HARRI STARTED CRYING. IN THE TOO-SMALL pajamas she had put on after showering off thrown-up cupcakes, with her wrists and ankles sprouting from the doughnut-patterned fabric and her chin bent to her chest, she looked like a shadow of the girl who moved out to the suburbs with enthusiasm because her mother had promised her a great new adventure, an amazing new life.

"Is she going to take our house? Are we going to have to move again?"

"No, of course not!" I said, sweeping her up into my arms. It seemed like years since she'd let me hug her, and I could tell from the feel of her she had lost weight.

"I'm so sorry I let her in, Mom," she said between small gasps. "She said she was related to Jeff. She said I should call her Aunt Stacey."

"It's okay."

I don't actually know if it's going to be okay. I don't know if Stacey's threat is legit or if she's desperate enough to follow through with it.

"No, it's not. She's going to take our house and it's going to be all my fault!"

The second Jeff answers his cell, I can tell he is in a pub. I look at the clock on the microwave. Five ten in Dublin. I can't stop myself from thinking of the phrase most often said with a laugh, *It's five o'clock somewhere.*

This time, I'm not laughing.

"Ginny, my love," he says, putting on a fake Irish lilt.

In the background, I hear men singing with deep, loud voices. *How long has he been there? What happened to being too busy to come home to your family?* My rising irritation meets my stomach acid like the Mentos and Coke challenge.

"Guess who was just here?"

"Who?" he asks, merrily playing along.

"Stacey."

"Who? Hang on, I didn't quite hear that."

"Stacey, your ex-wife," I say, raising my voice, and not just so he can hear me better. "Was here. At this house."

I hear a rousing round of cheers in Jeff's pub and then the background noise cuts out. He must have stepped outside.

"Shit, Gin," he finally says. "I'm sorry."

"Guess where she's been for the last six months."

"Where?"

"Guess."

I hear a tittering of laughter from a group of women passing him on the street, but nothing from Jeff.

"Jail, Jeff. She's been in jail."

I look over at Harri, sitting in front of an uneaten bowl of Cinnamon Toast Crunch, her eyes still glassy and red from crying, and step outside onto the deck. The sun is casting short shadows of the trees onto the lawn. A cold wind cuts through my sweater.

"And apparently, you knew all about it."

"Ginny, let me explain—"

"Jeff, why wouldn't you tell me something like that? For God's sake, I think that's an important piece of the backstory. 'We met in college, she ran off with some rich guy, she's in *jail* now.' I have a daughter, Jeff. I had a right to know there is an *ex-con* in the picture."

"It's not exactly like she killed anyone, Gin. She's not dangerous. She got duped."

"So, now you're defending her?"

"No, of course not."

Now it is my turn to stay silent. I want to hang up on him. It might be better if I do—before this turns into something neither of us can take back.

"This is exactly why I didn't tell you," he finally says. "I was afraid you'd react like this. I was afraid you'd think her shit was a reflection on me, that you wouldn't want to marry a guy with so much ugly baggage."

"You think that little of me?"

"No, Gin, no."

What else didn't I know? What other parts of our marriage are like delicate, newly formed ice, one misstep and you plunge into the unknown? Three thousand miles is too far to begin to figure it out. I can hear Kim's voice. *"She said...your marriage is too new to withstand that kind of distance... After he gets back, the whole thing is going to collapse."*

I nestle the phone into my collarbone so I can pull my sweater tighter around me. Something drips onto my chest, and when I put my hand up to my face, I realize my nose is running from the cold. I look through the sliding glass doors and see Harri is gone.

As I step back into my warm kitchen, safe from ears that have heard too much, Jeff asks, "So what did she want?"

"Well, she's out," I say flatly.

I tell him the whole story, including trying to tuck the Lladró into her purse. I almost stop short of including the threat to get a lawyer and claim her half of the house if we didn't let her cash in on what she thought was rightfully hers. It is my natural inclination to protect him, to not let this go to the deepest place where my husband's insecurities lie. But, fuck it. The rules of engagement have shifted.

"She can't do that," he stammers. "We're divorced! Everything was settled. She didn't want anything. She didn't *need* anything, she gloated, if I recall. The papers were signed, are signed. She married that What's-his-name. She has no claim to anything now!" His voice spirals upward.

"Alright, calm down. I'm sure it's not legal, what she's saying. She is just trying to bully us—well, me—into letting her take what she wants."

"Do me a favor, talk to Brian down the block. He's Noah's partner. And a lawyer."

"I know who Brian is."

"Yeah, okay," he says, the acrimony in my voice escaping him. Jesus, what does he think I've been doing on this street while he's gone, locking myself in and not interacting with *my own* neighbors? Noah is my friend. I know who his damn husband is.

"So can you just call him? Ask him what he thinks. Can you just confirm that she's full of shit?"

"Jeff, he's a general counsel at a bank. I'm not sure he's going to know—"

"Can you just ask him, Gin?"

"Okay, sure, fine. But what are we going to do about the bigger issue, Jeff? I don't want this woman showing up here whenever she feels like it. I don't want her thinking she can just walk in and take stuff."

"I thought you didn't care about material things?"

That was a low blow borne out of his anxiety about his ex-con ex-wife showing back up in his life. I get it. But it hurt like hell, and I refuse to become the collateral damage between them.

"Fuck you, Jeff."

"Alright, I'm sorry. Gin, I'm sorry. That was uncalled for. It's just…you call me and spring this on me. What am I supposed to do from here? I can't really manage this situation with an ocean between us."

"Well then, Jeff. I think it's time for you to come home."

"I'm afraid I've made a terrible mistake," I say to Zaria as soon as I hear her voice. I wish she were sitting here with me, offering a warm shoulder.

"Let it dry completely and paint over it. Jeez, that's Painting 101. You always were so impatient," she says, laughing.

"If it were only that easy." I sigh.

"Oh, this is one of those phone calls? Sorry, let me switch gears. So, what's up?"

I begin to clear the breakfast dishes from the table. I dump Harri's uneaten cereal into the sink, and the soggy squares clog the drain. I realize that she's avoided another meal, and my heart feels like a stone in my breast.

"What am I doing here, Z?"

I'm waiting for a snarky remark about the dreaded suburbs and an I-told-you-so, but thankfully, I don't get it.

"Hang on, I've got to put up a kettle," she says. I hear the faucet running and the burner clicking before it lights. "Okay, you've got my full attention."

First, I tell her about the visit from Stacey.

"Unbelievable." She laughs. "You can't make this stuff up."

Then I share my phone call with Jeff.

"When I asked Jeff to come home, he hesitated. Actually had to think about it. And then he said it would be 'soon.' I've heard that before."

In fact, this whole thing is starting to feel very familiar. Another man distancing himself from my daughter and me. Last time it was only painful for me. Colin's declaration, "I'm not cut out to be a dad," left me to fend for myself, but at least Harri was too young to remember her father in her life. This time, Harri doesn't escape unscathed.

"You don't really think it's the same thing," Zaria says when I tell her my newly realized theory. "You can't compare Jeff to Colin. He abandoned you, Ginny. Abandoned. Jeff is coming home. Maybe not as soon as you'd like, but you know he misses you like crazy."

"Does he, Z?"

"Of course! Look, I know having that batshit-crazy ex show up rattled you, but she's got nothing to do with you and Jeff. Nothing's changed. Most people have to deal with exes all the time. It comes with the territory. Jeff lucked out with the great disappearing Colin. And now you know you got yourself a real winner."

"It's more than that."

"Is it?"

"I'm just wondering if this was a big mistake. All of it. Why did I agree to move out here? Into a house that is so foreign we might as well be in another country. Why did I push Harri so hard to fit in? Look what it's done to her. Was I so desperate to find a way out, so tired of trying to do it on my own, of struggling and failing, that I married the wrong man? I feel like I don't know Jeff. Not like I thought I did at least. Maybe I just jumped into all this too soon. Jumped into a pool of sharks. And now we're getting eaten alive."

"Take a deep breath, baby."

"Oh, and did I tell you what Amber's telling everyone? That we won't last. Who goes around spreading shit like that?"

"Now, don't start drinking the neighborhood gossip Kool-Aid. All you have to ask yourself is, do you love him?"

"It's not that easy, Z."

"Sure it is. Do you love him?"

Zaria's kettle goes off like an alarm. It gives me time to wipe the tears rolling down my cheeks and answer her question.

"Yes," I say. "Of course. Yes, I love him."

"Then that's all you need to know. Everything else is just noise. Turn down the volume and you'll work it all out. The two of you will. He'll be home before you know it, and you can figure out how to get the life you two really want. But first, march yourself across the street and set that trouble-making Amber straight."

Chapter 28

"MOM, MOM, MOM!" HARRI SHOUTS AS SHE THUNDERS DOWN THE stairs making it sound as if there are ten of her up there. She bursts into the kitchen fully dressed, which is unusual for midmorning on a Saturday. Even more surprising is her hair, brushed and pulled back into a tight pony, a skill she seems to have mastered when I blinked.

"Wow," I say. "What's all the excitement?"

I almost don't care. It is such a relief to see her like this that it's infectious.

"Madison and all them are going to the mall, and they want me to come! One of the moms is driving us all, and another is picking us up later. You don't have to do anything. Can I go?"

And the bubble pops.

"What about what happened yesterday?" I ask her.

Harri returned to school yesterday. Her social studies class was in the middle of ancient civilizations, and if she skipped another day she'd miss all of Mesopotamia. No amount of cupcake-induced distress was going to stop her from giving her report on life at the banks of the Euphrates River. So I was surprised when the school nurse called to say she had my daughter in her office complaining of stomach pain and I needed to come pick her up.

She was quiet on the ride home and only shrugged her shoulders when I asked for specifics about the location and intensity of the pain.

"Well," I said as we turned on to Elderberry Lane, "I guess we'll just have to go to the doctor this afternoon. Maybe she can get to the bottom of all this."

"I don't need to go to the doctor," she said flatly.

"No?"

"No."

"Do you think your belly issues have anything to do with what happened yesterday? I don't want you to worry about Stacey."

"It's not that," she said as we pulled into the driveway. "I just had a bad day."

She grabbed her backpack and slammed the car door. I followed her into the house, talking to her back.

"Do you want to tell me about it?" I asked.

"Not really," she said as she started up the stairs.

"Hey, no," I called to her. "Enough of hiding up in your room. Come here, sit down, and spill."

I didn't expect her to listen to me. So many times over the last weeks she would blatantly ignore my requests, acting like at the very moment I'd spoken she'd gone temporarily deaf. But this time she turned around and came back into the room. She pulled the chair out from the table and dropped herself into it with a groan. I grabbed two banana yogurts from the fridge and put them down in front of us.

"It was just a bad day, okay?" she said, peeling off the foil lid and licking it.

I had to contain my excitement. *Sustenance! Victory is mine!* "What kind of bad day?"

"With friends, I guess."

"Okay."

"Madison and Jacqueline and them were kind of mad that I wasn't in formal wear anymore. They said I ditched them and now Blake S. doesn't have anyone to walk with."

Guilt started its slow climb up my body like a vine of poison ivy.

"Can't you still walk with him? You are still *in* the show."

"He's wearing a *tux*, Mom. You can't match up a tux with plain, ordinary clothes."

Oh boy.

"And then they said it was probably just as well because I don't have the look for a fancy gown. They said my lips are too thin, and my eyes are too close together and I would look bad with professional makeup on anyway."

Suddenly, I was the one with stomach pain. I pushed the yogurt away from me.

"And then they said I had to eat lunch somewhere else, because their table was for formal-wear models only."

This morning, it seems, my daughter has a short memory.

"I want to go to the mall with my friends," she says.

My better angel sits on my shoulder and tells me not to let her go. But little girls are fickle and stories get twisted. Maybe Madison and Jacqueline's despicable behavior has been exaggerated. If it were me, I'd tell them to F off, but my daughter is more forgiving than I am.

"Sure, okay," I say. "But text me when you get there. And when you are on your way home."

Harri springs on her toes. "Yes, thank you!"

She runs out of the room, beaming.

After Harri leaves, I go up to my studio and stand in the center of the room, hands on my hips, sizing up my options for my free time. My to-do list is a mile long—inventory and general housekeeping, finishing up the black Lab piece, and getting my benefit for Penny off the ground.

I've decided to partner with a studio called Canvas & Cocktails that does wine and paint events—girls' nights out, birthday parties, and fundraisers. These places are as popular as the pottery studios that let you paint on unglazed ceramics and *boom* you're a potter! Anyone can be an artist! How that idea makes my old friends back home laugh. Still, I need a turnkey situation like this, even if it is going to cost more and make less. Penny's first treatment is in a week. Canvas & Cocktails had an opening for a few days after the fashion show. I'm not worried about people feeling tapped out after a night of raffles and tricky trays and a chicken dinner. Not in this town.

Of course that means some fast work. Luckily, Zaria is on the case. She's commandeered the members of her artists' co-op to sketch the canvases in advance. I will email them the files and pick them up the day before the event. Easy-peasy, thanks to my fairy godmother Z.

I sit cross-legged in the oversized reading chair, mercifully free from the pile of high-heeled shoes now in Kim's pool house being hot glued together by her personal assistant. I open my laptop and search for the email Margot sent me when I was working on publicity for the fashion show. It contained all the parents' contact info. *Why not?* I think, dragging the list into the address bar of a blank email. I type in the subject line: Fun Event, Paint Your Pet & Save a Dog's Life. I add the date, time, and place, and decide to go over to Wayne's later to take a photo of Penny to add to the announcement.

Then I set to work on a free graphics site Harri once showed me. It will let me make a professional-looking design to post online or print out to make posters I can put up around town. That is, if I can figure out how it works. I bite my lip and squint my eyes as I struggle to get the type the right size and rotate the image I found of a paint palette. This part is frustrating. I need a kid who was born into the technology and social media culture to help. I'm going to give myself two more tries, and if I don't get it, I'll wait for Harri to come home from the mall and fix it for me. I should have had her do this part right from the start. Not that she would have been willing. She's still mad at Penny about Mrs. Clucklesworth. And the jury is out on whether she has any interest in helping me. It all depends on which Harri shows up on any given day.

I'm so determined to figure this out and avoid having my daughter laugh at what an old fogey I am that I don't hear the footsteps on the stairs until a head pops above the floor level.

"Ginny, you up here?" he asks before he sees me on my chair in the corner.

"Rand," I say, feeling nervous before I know if I have to. "What are you doing here?"

Now he is standing in my studio, blocking the stairway, smiling his slightly condescending smile. He is wearing faded jeans and a soft button-down shirt. His hair, which has always been slicked back with some sharp-smelling pomade when we've been in social situations, is newly washed, still wet and flopping over one eye. The very fact that he looks younger, casual, approachable, um, *handsome* makes my anxiety swirl. I stand up so we are at least closer to eye level.

"I just came by to say hi," he says as if my question was amusing. "I told Jeff I'd check in on you, remember?"

"And I told you I didn't need checking in on, remember?"

Rand strolls over to the window that faces the street and looks out.

"I knocked at the house, no answer. I figured you were up here," he says, ignoring my question. I've got another one for him.

"Where is Margot?"

"Out. Hair appointment? Nail appointment? I can't remember." Then he adds, "She won't be back for a while. So how are you doing, Ginny? Asking in an official capacity, you know, for my report."

He winks. My stomach tightens. *Relax, he's probably just trying to be a nice guy. He's got some stupid ingrained macho chip that makes him think a woman alone can't take care of herself. He doesn't think he's being sleazy—he thinks he's being chivalrous.*

"I'm great, Rand. You can check that off your list," I say, laughing. "But I'm kind of in the middle of something right now, and I don't have much time before Harri gets home. So thank you, really, for coming over. Tell Margot I say hi."

I step closer to him and open my arm toward the staircase. It's the universal symbol that I'm showing him the door, but instead of getting the clue, he takes a step closer to me. He smells like soap and toothpaste.

"You know, Ginny. You are different than the other women on this street."

He reaches his arm up slowly and rests a large, heavy hand on my shoulder. I take two quick steps back as if we are playing an uncomfortable game of Mother, May I? He takes another step forward. *"Mother, may I?"* No, you may not.

"Rand, really. I've—"

"You are like a breath of fresh air around here." He moves his hand to my throat and touches my rose quartz necklace. "So artsy and creative. It's kind of sexy in a dirty hippie kind of way."

Now it's three steps back as my hand flies to my neck, covering the spot where he touched me.

"Rand, you need to leave! You are making me very uncomfortable."

He laughs. "Jeez, Ginny, I'm just kidding. I'm joking around with you."

The heat roars to my face. Why am I the one who feels stupid?

"Although," he says, moving ever closer, "Jeff has been away for a while. You must be, well…lonely."

My studio is not that big. His last move has pushed me right up against the arm of the reading chair. There is no room to back up any farther. My heart is pounding, and I can feel thumping in my ears. I look over his shoulder toward the top of the stairs. My cell phone, always in my back pocket, is on a shelf across the room. I was using it to take notes while I was inventorying my supplies. *Shit.*

"Come on, Ginny. Admit it. You've been throwing off vibes since you got here. Remember dinner at our house?"

"You've got it wrong."

He leans forward and tucks a strand of hair behind my ear. "I don't think I do."

I jerk back and fall into the chair. I taste bitter bile in the back of my throat. Rand leans against the chair, his hands clasping each of my arms. His knees are pressing against mine. He bends toward me, his hair falling over his eyes. I am trapped.

"No one has to know," he coos almost like he's singing a lullaby. "No one is around. It's just you and me. You know you want to. You've been asking me for it since we met."

His breaths are becoming more rapid. Now I smell something sour under the mask of the toothpaste. "I see how you've been looking at me. You can't possibly have been getting it as good as I'm going to give you."

He drops to his knees, tilts his head, smiles cruelly, and places the back of his hand on the inside of my knee. Slowly he moves it higher, up my thigh until his hand stops between my legs where he runs a finger up the length of the zipper of my jeans. But he has made a terrible mistake. So confident in his ability to subdue me, sure I will see things his way, he has not thought to bind my arms. A white-hot anger explodes behind my eyes and replaces my fear. Who the fuck does this guy think he is?

I pull one arm back as far as it will go considering how deep I am in the chair, make a fist, and swing it as hard as I can, hitting him below his left eye. The sound is awful, his reaction instant. The shock on his face tells me he wasn't expecting a fight. In quick succession he puts his hand to his cheek, jumps to his feet, and stumbles backwards. I scramble out of the chair and rise, full of rage.

"Get out!" I scream.

He doesn't move. He pulls his hand away from his face and looks at the blood on it. There is a small slice across his cheek. I look down at the tiger's eye ring on the hand I hit him with.

"You bitch," he growls.

Nope, this is over. I throw my full weight at him, pushing with both arms at his chest, toward the stairs. Rand stumbles and trips backwards. I look down at his feet trying to regain purchase and I see what he's stepped on—one silver, spray-painted high-heel shoe. Hiding until now under the chair, it must have been kicked across the room in the scuffle. Rand is not regaining his balance. He grabs at the easel and pulls it over. The wooden frame makes a terrible slapping sound against the floor. The painting of the black Lab falls between his feet and tangles him up even more. Now he is at the top step. He staggers one last time too many and falls down the stairs.

I hear a series of ugly thuds and then nothing. I am frozen, standing in the middle of my studio, my hands covering my mouth. Then there is a groan. Afraid of what I'll see, I step over the toppled easel and look down the staircase. Rand has stopped halfway and is on his ass, one foot tucked under him. Blood is coming from his cheek and his nose. He slowly starts to right himself, holding onto the railing and pulling himself to his feet. He limps down the rest of the steps to the door. Before he leaves, he looks up and sees me watching him.

"Are you out of your fucking mind? You could have killed me!"

"Well, you could have raped me. Consider us even, asshole."

Chapter 29

RAND SLAMS THE DOOR BEHIND HIM. I GO TO THE WINDOW overlooking the driveway to make sure he's actually leaving and find some small relief in seeing him hobble away from my house, his forearm held up to his bleeding nose. I should run down and lock the door, but I realize my knees are shaking too badly to take a step, let alone negotiate a staircase.

As my heart thumps out of my chest, I replay the last few minutes in my mind. I don't know where things would have gone if Rand hadn't stepped on the shoe, starting the bizarre choreography that landed him bruised and bleeding on the stairs. He doesn't strike me as a guy who gets told no, or takes it for an answer.

I walk over to the toppled shoe lying on the floor, its side crushed and caved in from Rand's weight, and I turn it over in my hands. Then I go to the window and place it on the sill next to a fat succulent in a terra-cotta pot painted by Harri on a rainy Saturday afternoon in our old apartment. I was desperate to get these damn shoes out of my studio. But this one, this straggler, this holdout, I'm keeping—and in a place of honor.

I right the easel and pick up the painting of the black Lab. The canvas is torn across the dog's half-finished face. The whole thing is ruined. I'll have to start over again, but I lean the canvas against the ledge of the easel anyway. Was this my fault? Did I, as Rand had accused, send him signals that this was okay? What if I smiled too long or laughed too hard or, due to my own insecurity and inability to make a quick judgment of the situation, didn't move away fast enough when he "accidentally" or "inadvertently" or "innocently" touched me? What if I allowed myself to be seduced, okay that's the wrong word, to be drawn in by his confidence and charm? None of that justifies this attack. The presumption, the sheer arrogance, the take-what-you-want attitude, turns my shaking into seething.

There's blood on the wall at the top of the stairs from Rand trying unsuccessfully to catch himself before he fell. There's no running water in the studio so I grab a paper towel and spit on it. The blood hasn't had time to dry and it comes away easily. This is the closest my DNA will ever be to Rand Moss-Marks's again.

And what about Margot, so busy running her own fiefdom? How does someone so in control of every movement around her not see what's happening under her nose? Or does she? My heart, hardened by my anger toward her husband, breaks a little for Margot when I think maybe she does know exactly to whom she is married. No one, not even someone who has to climb over others to reach the highest pedestal, deserves that. What am I going to say to her, if anything? How am I going to look her in the eye?

There's another smear of blood under the railing where Rand's fall ended. Thank God I caught it before Harri wanders in here later and sees it. This is exactly where her eye would go—to an odd little thing that wasn't there yesterday. Of course, I could always tell her I'd crushed a spider. But then I'd have to hear about what a murderer I am. And I'm just living down the Mrs. Clucklesworth debacle.

Who else in this town, even on this street, has had Rand show up to "check in on them?" And who has given him an answer other than a bloodied nose and a sprained ankle? I remember those first days and weeks when Amber was showing me a different side of herself—Little Miss Welcome Wagon. She had warned me about Margot's husband. "Handsy" was how she put it. I didn't believe it, but I appreciated the gesture and thought we were on our way to being friends. She had my back already, and we'd only just met. But Amber's motivation has come into question. Maybe she was warning me off him because *she* was screwing him. At this point, nothing about that woman would surprise me.

Thinking about Amber sets my hair on fire all over again. Harri will be back from the mall soon, but I have enough time and certainly enough indignation to march over there and confront her right now. I throw the bloody paper towel in the trash can and wipe my hands on my jeans. On the way out of the garage, I look both ways, on the off chance that Rand is hiding in the bushes. With the coast clear, I stride down the driveway and across the street to Amber's house.

In my agitation, I rap on her door with my bare knuckles instead of ringing the bell or tapping the pineapple-shaped door knocker. That is a mistake. The cold air and my dry hands don't care for the abuse, and three knuckles crack and start to bleed. While I'm waiting for a response, I look down at the autumnal display on Amber's front steps. It's similar to everyone else's in this town, some variation on pumpkins and gourds and scarecrows and hay, only just a little bit less professional looking than the arrangements many women have hired expensive florists to install. An animal, most likely a squirrel, has chewed a big hole in the top of one pumpkin. Stringy pulp spills down the side like witch's hair. The potted mums are choking from lack of water.

It dawns on me that I have never been inside Amber's house. We have been many places together, and she's sat in my kitchen countless times, but I've never been invited over, nor have I ever thought to just wander by. Considering what "good friends" we are, that strikes me as odd now that I think about it.

It's taking Amber forever to come to the door. I know she's home. I see her car in the driveway. If she doesn't answer soon, I'm going to lose my nerve. Time to reconsider can be the demise of assertiveness. I am about to start banging away at the pineapple knocker when she finally opens the door, but only wide enough to reveal half of her body. She is wearing a pink velour tracksuit and her hair, out of her classic viselike ponytail, reveals a pencil-thin line of dark regrowth. So, there is a chill Amber. I've just never seen her in the wild.

"Ginny," she says, looking over my shoulder. Does she think I've come with reinforcements? "What are you doing here?"

"Amber, I want to talk to you. Can I come in?"

She bites her lip as she considers it. A cold wind picks up and blows a small green gourd off the front step. "Sure," she finally says.

She steps away from the door and pulls it open far enough for me to enter. Her foyer is like so many I've seen in this town—a two-story ceiling, curved staircase, gold paint, thick ornate molding on the doorways and ceilings. But that is where the similarities end. In Amber's front room there is no expensive Oriental rug, no marble-topped, carved-leg side table, no crystal vase filled with fresh, artfully arranged roses and daylilies. The chandelier has burned-out bulbs. The bare walls show outlines of artwork that is no longer there. Picture hooks dot the walls like blemishes on a face. She catches me looking up at the chandelier.

"They're impossible to change yourself. You have to hire a company to come in and do it for you. It's on my list." Her voice sounds defeated.

Nope, I'm not going to get sucked into a sob story about how Amber hasn't had time to bring in professionals to change her light bulbs. I'm on a mission.

"Look," I say. "We need to talk about these rumors—"

"Come in, sit down. Do you want a drink?"

She turns and walks away from me. On the ass of her track pants are big block letters that say NASTY. *Yup*, I think as I follow her into the next room.

"Amber," I say to her back as we walk down a hallway that also shows the ghosts of framed pictures no longer there. "I talked to Kim. She said you are spreading rumors about Jeff and me. About problems in our marriage. Why on earth would you do that?"

Amber stops and pivots. "Kim's a liar," she says flatly.

"Why would Kim lie?"

She turns and I watch the back of her head as she continues.

"Why does anyone lie, Ginny? Because she's jealous of me. Because I'm beating her. I'm thinner than she is. I get invited out more than she does. You name it."

We walk into a high-ceilinged room filled with windows and sunlight and not much else. Again, the walls are nearly empty except for one abstract painting leaning on the mantel of a large stone fireplace. It hardly seems like Amber's taste. But, then again, there are a lot of surprises in this house. The floor is cold ceramic tile and in front of the fireplace lies a hexagonal-patterned rug, the kind that is so popular they sell it at Costco and Walmart—two places I would have bet Amber had never been to. Kissing the edge of the rug is a couch, and to the right of the hearth a flat-screen TV rests on a small end table. Aside from a large glass-fronted curio cabinet on the far wall, the room is virtually empty. It's kind of shocking, really. Something is not right.

"What's going on in here?" I ask, abandoning my mission momentarily.

"What do you mean?"

"Everything is, well, where is everything? Honestly, it looks like you've been robbed."

Amber's shrill laugh makes me think I have good reason to worry about what's going on in this house. "Ginny, you are so funny!" she sings too gaily. "I'm redecorating! Giving the whole place a fresh, new look."

"But where's all your stuff?"

She looks around the room as if she's seeing it for the first time, but in a second she's back to her performance. "Stuff? Gone! Couldn't stand to look at it. Out with the old and in with the new!"

I walk toward the glass curio case. "What's this?"

"Oh, that's my collection. Eclectic isn't it?"

I get closer to the cabinet and peer in. It is indeed interesting, stuffed with random items—a pearl and gold brooch, a Princess Leia PEZ dispenser, a doll's shoe, a ceramic turtle, a cracked and worn leather wallet, the top of the teapot I saw Amber slip into her bag at Goodwill, and on the top shelf, right smack in the middle, towering over an embroidered handkerchief and a black plastic ashtray, is the Hummingbird, my lost wedding gift from Zaria.

Chapter 30

"WHAT THE HELL?" I SAY, PULLING OPEN THE CABINET DOOR SO aggressively that its contents of weird objects rattle and shake on the glass shelves.

Zaria had called the shipping company twice. "I got the tracking number online, and it said the package was delivered," she had said going from anger to frustration to sadness in one sentence. "But I just didn't believe it. There could've been a glitch in the system, I thought, so I got a human on the phone and they said the same thing. Still, *they* could have gotten it wrong. So, I called back and talked to a manager. They checked the driver's log and they swore black and blue it was delivered. The only thing they can do is report it stolen."

She was sick about it.

And now here it is.

The shipping company had been right.

It was stolen.

I take the Hummingbird off the shelf and shake it at Amber. "This is mine!"

For a flash, her face looks like one of those rubber toys you squeeze until their eyes pop out. I have caught her off-balance, but not for long. She is an expert at the spin, the gaslighting. She would have made a great politician, but I am no longer buying her party line.

"Ginny, what are you talking about," she says after she rearranges her face. "That most certainly is not yours."

She reaches out to take the vase from me, but I twist my body away from her.

"This was a gift from a friend," I say. "From the artist who made it. She sent it to me, and you stole it off my front step!"

"Ridiculous! Ginny, what is the matter with you? You are confusing it with something else. Something similar. I bought *that* vase at an art gallery in Soho. To say I stole this? What a terrible thing to accuse someone of!"

"Oh, cut the shit, Amber. This vase is one of a kind. There are no others similar. And I can prove it."

I turn the Hummingbird upside down. On the bottom is Zaria's mark, the letter Z pressed into the glass. The mark of Zorro. I used to tease her about the flourish of her signature initial.

"That proves nothing," she says.

"And what about the teapot lid over there? I saw you take it from Goodwill. You stole it like you stole my vase."

I look over at her odd, incongruous collection. "Did you steal all of this, Amber?"

Her face changes again, this time from benevolent queen to evil sorceress. Her jaw sets, her eyes narrow, her fists clench. "Be careful who you accuse of stealing, Ginny."

"What is that supposed to mean?"

She lifts her chin like a defiant child. "Nothing."

We are feet away from each other, me with my newfound wedding gift tucked against my side, her with her arms crossed under her breasts. A soundless clock ticks off the seconds.

"No, say it. Go ahead," I dare her.

Amber twists her mouth and moves her hands to her bony hips. "You fucked up everything," she finally hisses.

"Me?"

"Yes, Ginny, *you*! I had a plan. It was going perfectly. And then you showed up with your earth mother, artsy-fartsy crap and your 'Oh, I'm just so supersweet and want to get along and fit in' and your 'Oh, I'm just a poor girl from Queens, and I don't know how to function in the mean suburbs' and ruined it all! *You* stole from *me!*"

"What did I steal from you?"

Her cheeks are flushed an angry red and a fleck of spittle lands on her hoodie above her heart. "Jeff! You stole *Jeff!*"

I shake my head and blink as if I've just emerged from a cave. I don't understand what she is trying to tell me, but her tone makes me take a step back.

"Ask him who was there for him when Stacey left. Ask him who brought him home-cooked meals and cleaned his house and did his laundry while he mourned that stupid bitch who never deserved him anyway.

"We were connecting," she says, pointing an accusing finger at me. "We were falling in love. I was going to get out of this shithole house…finally be rid of the humiliation of losing my husband! Everyone saying it's my fault. How did *I* not know? How did *I* not see it coming? What did *I* do wrong? And look at this place. You think this is how I should be living? He took everything! All the furniture, all the art, took it all to set himself up in his loft in the Village. He took it all, and I'm the one who's at fault? That's rich, isn't it?

"And I was this close to putting it all behind me," she snarls, holding her thumb and pointer finger together to show me just how close she was. "There was Jeff just sitting across the street in that house all alone. I was this close and then *you* showed up."

I may have my doubts about Jeff in this moment, but I know one thing for sure. He would never be interested in a woman like batshit-crazy Amber. She is Stacey on speed. I don't doubt her story about bringing him food and helping him around the house. Jeff had told me after Stacey left, all the women on the street took turns looking in on him to make sure he ate and had a clean shirt to wear to work. It was a sweet story and another one of the boxes I checked when I considered moving out here.

It is so obvious to me that Amber was on a different stage than everyone else back then, playing out her own narrative in some phantasmagorical romance. I need to go. I have my answer about why she was spreading lies about me. But first I have one more question.

"Then let me ask you this. If you hate me so much, why were you so nice to me when I moved here? Why the best-friends act?"

"You know the saying," she says, in a frightening measured tone. "'Keep your friends close and your enemies closer.'"

"You are certifiable. I'm leaving."

She is standing between the door and me. I move to go around her when she growls. "Not with my vase you don't."

She lunges at me, and while I instinctively twist and jerk away from her, she is too quick for me and gets a good grip on the Hummingbird. We each yank the glass piece away from the other in an angry tug-of-war, but since I have it tucked under my arm, with only the other hand securing it, her perch is better than mine, and the vase slips out of my grip. Amber tumbles back, loses her balance and her hold, and my beautiful, one-of-a-kind, award-winning work of handblown glass falls to the ceramic floor.

And smashes into a million pieces.

The shards skitter across the room as far as the fireplace. The base of the vase, a now jagged circle, lies upside down, revealing Zaria's imprint, at Amber's stocking feet. A slow growing spot of blood blooms across the top of her sock where a blue sliver is poking out—a piece of the bird's beak. She stands there with her hands covering her mouth, frozen in a minefield of sharp glass.

My throat closes and hot tears form in my eyes. "Stay away from my family," I snarl.

I start to walk out across the littered floor, my thick Frye boots snapping and crunching the debris, leaving Amber to fend for herself, when her daughter Jacqueline appears in the room. We had not heard her come home.

"Mom, what is happening?"

She is holding two bright-pink bags, spoils from a successful afternoon at the mall.

"Jacqueline, get your mother a broom. I'll leave you to clean this mess up," I say to Amber. "Now that Harri is home, I'm going to see if she had a fun shopping day."

"Oh," says Jacqueline, putting her finger to her lip like a mini-Amber. "Harri didn't come home with us."

A fire alarm goes off in my head. "What do you mean?"

"Well...I remember she was with us at the beginning...because we were at Claire's and we were looking at the pierced earrings, but Harri couldn't look at them because she doesn't have pierced ears...but she wasn't in the car coming home."

"Where was she? Where did she go? Why wasn't she with you?"

Jacqueline shrugs. I want to wring her neck.

As I grab my cell phone out of my back pocket, Amber says to her stupid, vapid daughter, "Honey, weren't you all in a group? Did you warn Harri about the rule about sticking together?"

As I press Harri's number, I hear Jacqueline throwing my daughter under the bus. "Of course, Mommy," she says. The phone rings once and goes straight to voicemail.

"Who drove you home?" I bark.

"Mrs. Poncherelli."

"Amber, give me her number."

Amber looks at her bleeding foot and the broken glass surrounding her and says, "My cell is in the kitchen."

I storm into her kitchen, grab her phone, and shove it at her. She scrolls through, finds the number, and makes the call.

"Susan, hi, it's Amber," she says as gaily as if she were asking for a lunch date.

"Give me that," I say. "Susan, this is Harri's mother. You were supposed to bring her home from the mall. Why didn't you?"

I'm sure Susan Poncherelli is a nice woman, but in this moment she is the villain in my story. "You were supposed to pick up the girls, and my child did not get picked up. I want to know how that happened. And I want to know where she is."

Susan Poncherelli gasps.

"I had no idea," she says, sounding truly guilty and alarmed. "I didn't see your daughter. I don't even know who she is. I was told to meet the group in front of the Cinnabon and bring them home. I picked up the whole group. I said to the girls, 'Is this everyone?' and they all said yes. I didn't know!"

"Jacqueline," I say. "Why didn't you tell her Harri went to the mall with you?"

Jacqueline looks at me and then at her mother and shrugs again.

Chapter 31

I leave Amber with her broken glass and her brat of a daughter and her beaten-down life and run back home, willing Harri to be there.

The house is empty. I try her phone one more time but it goes straight to voicemail again, and for a moment I let my anger overtake my worry. This is exactly the reason I have hounded her to keep her phone charged. In case of emergency. This, and only this, is the reason to give an eleven-year-old a phone. A phone that, when she gets home, she is going to lose.

Only one person can help, and right now it doesn't matter if we have a little bad blood over a stupid committee, that her husband is a predator, or that I'd been hoping to avoid her for as long as possible. I call Margot. She answers the phone with a slightly annoyed hello. She may have been hoping not to deal with me either.

"Harri's missing," I say. I tell her what just happened as quickly as I can.

"Give me five minutes and I'll call you right back," she says.

While I am waiting for Margot, I call Wayne.

"What if something terrible happens to her?" I ask.

Saying it all out loud again has pushed all the anger aside, and fear fills in the cracks in my composure. Every horror story about missing girls I've ever heard floods back to me.

"We're going to find her. She's a smart girl, she'll be fine," he says, and within seconds he is at my back door, his cell phone still pressed to his ear.

He steps inside and draws me into a hug. His coat is already cold from the short walk between our properties. "I'll go to the mall with you. We'll find her."

"Maybe you should stay here, in case she comes back."

"I'll leave Penny here," he says, and I finally notice the dog at his feet. "And I'll call Zaria. She can drive out here pretty quickly. The bridge should be clear coming this way. They can wait for her."

Within minutes I receive a text from Margot. She has sent it to a group—Collette, Noah, Amber, an unknown number, and me.

Be in front of my house in 5. G, unknown # is S Poncherelli.

Margot has organized a search party in less time than it takes to make dinner reservations. That's why I called her.

When Wayne and I pull up in front of Margot's house, the telltale white caravan—including Susan Poncherelli's white Suburban—is already there. I see Amber's car in the lineup. Noah and the women gather at the curb around our leader, hugging themselves against the wind and the sharp temperature drop. I roll down my window as Margot comes up to my car with sheets of paper in her hand.

"I don't need Amber's help," I tell her.

She glances over at her recruits. Everyone is looking at me with nervous but hopeful faces—except for Amber who has her back to me. I'm sure she would have rather not come. She is probably gloating over Harri being left behind. What a fortuitous turn of events for her evil plan. Still, she would never say no when Margot calls.

Margot hands me a piece of paper that turns out to be a map of the mall with an entrance highlighted in pink marker. "Nonsense," she says. "There are six main entrances to the mall, there are six of us. We need everyone."

She turns to the others, handing out more maps. "Listen, everyone, when you get there, go to your designated entrance—it's marked on your map—and fan right. Keep going until you get to the next entrance. Then go up to the second floor and do it all again. Make sure you go into each store; don't just walk by it and glance in. Noah, your territory includes the food court. Be vigilant. Use the group text for any updates. Oh, and Ginny. Text a photo of Harri to the group—for Susan."

She's right about Amber, of course she is. Margot just organized an entire search party in under ten minutes, complete with color-coordinated accompanying materials. It's going to be hard to doubt her ever again after this.

The group breaks up and people get into their cars. Susan Poncherelli comes to my window and clasps her hands together.

"Ginny, I'm so sorry. I really didn't know. I feel terrible."

There is a long list of people who should feel terrible about this ahead of Susan Poncherelli—the little bitches who are supposed to be my daughter's BFFs and their mothers who are raising such mean girls.

"It's not your fault," I say as kindly as I can while my anxiety threatens to punch a hole in the roof of my car.

I don't wait for the caravan to pull out. Wayne and I head to the mall as I fight the urge to speed. I can't get pulled over and lose time. The sun has set quickly, as it does these days. As we pull onto the highway, we see a sea of red taillights.

"Shit," I curse, slamming my palm into the horn.

"She's okay," says Wayne. "Probably wandered off, probably doesn't even realize she's lost the group."

"Or she's been abducted. You hear about that all the time. Someone sees her by herself, vulnerable, easy prey. Or some creep posing as a nice, suburban dad offers her a ride home. That's who it always ends up being— some normal-looking dad who coached Little League and everyone swears was always a regular, quiet guy until…"

I swerve in and out of lanes, tossing Wayne back and forth in his seat.

"Ginny, you are spinning yourself up. Try to take a breath. She's going to be okay."

"Something must have happened. Those girls must have said something to her to make her leave the group. She knows better."

"She does know better so—"

"Not one of those brats said anything when they were picked up. Not one. They just left without her. What the fuck, Wayne?"

Wayne doesn't answer. He's been living on the street much longer than I have. He knows the terrain better than I do.

The mall is monstrous. There are at least four or five department stores anchoring two floors of chain stores, restaurants, and a ten-plex movie theater. I gasp at the needle-in-the-haystack aspect of our mission. This would be over in ten seconds if her damn phone weren't dead. I push away that thought. It isn't going to help me find Harri any faster.

Wayne has to turn the map sideways to find our designated entrance. It is around the farthest end of the mall, near the movie theater.

"Shit, there's no parking!" I say when we get there, frustration coursing through me and threatening to come out in a full-blown tantrum.

"Pull up to the door," Wayne says.

When I do, he jumps out of the car and comes around to my side. "Get out, I'll park the car. Go. I'll catch up with you in a few minutes."

I don't argue. I don't say thank you. I just move. I rush past the entrance that smells like ostracized smokers and into the busy mall. It's packed, so many voices swarming together creating a steady roar, so many bodies emanating heat and perfume. I lean forward and charge ahead, swerving around people like they are traffic on the highway. The ticket booth for the theater has a long line forming along a velvet rope. I scan the line, the people at the ticket taker, and as much of the popcorn counter as I can see from here. What are the chances of Harri choosing today to go to a movie by herself for the first time? I decide to keep moving.

I am traveling at a racewalker's pace. My jacket is building up greenhouse-level humidity, but I don't have time to stop and take it off. I pass a luggage shop and a men's shoe store. Despite Margot's instructions, I give each a cursory glance and carry on. I am in a juice bar, marching up and down between the small, crowded tables, when my cell phone buzzes in my back pocket. It's the group text and the message is from Margot.

What is Harry wearing?
With Security. Need description.

The idea of talking to mall security about Harri makes me dizzy and weak. I leave the juice bar and lean against the window of a Victoria's Secret. I try to think back to what my daughter was wearing before she left the house, but my mind only shows me images of her at three in her favorite watermelon-print bathing suit and at seven in a Madame Curie Halloween costume, holding a beaker and a test tube, and at eleven, before we moved out of our apartment, in her Mr. Bubble T-shirt.

I squeeze my eyes shut and try to focus. Finally, I remember her running down the stairs this morning and dashing out to the driveway with more enthusiasm than I thought was warranted, considering how sad these same girls had made her feel just the day before. Hadn't they just been telling her that her lips were too thin?

I tap my answer back into the phone:

Skinny jeans. Pink chenille cropped sweater. Adidas Super-stars sneakers.

I look at what I have just written and realize what I'd done. I've described every fifth-grade girl in this town. Well, I finally got what I wanted: a daughter who fit in, who would disappear into a crowd.

I check four or five more stores. My cell phone buzzes in my pocket.

Not at the food court.

Not in the Disney Store.

Not the Yankee Candle.

Wayne finds me, although I don't know how. I feel like I've covered a hundred miles. His face is flushed and sweat is dripping from his temples. "I'm sorry, I had to park in Outer Mongolia."

"I haven't found her," I say, and he doesn't point out that I'm stating the obvious.

"Do you want to split up?"

I don't know what I want. Except to find my daughter. When I don't answer, he takes my hand and pulls me toward the next store. "We'll stay together. We can cover ground faster."

He's right. We get through almost all the shops on this floor in less time than if I were on my own. Of course, we've come up empty-handed in each one. My panic has risen to tsunami level. The only thing keeping me from crashing is knowing that I can't. I have to find Harri. Meanwhile my phone keeps buzzing.

Not at The Cheesecake Factory.

Not at The Sunglass Hut.

The only place left to search on this floor is the department store.

"This is impossible," I say to Wayne. The store is packed with counters and carousels of clothes and racks upon racks of shoes. There are a million places a person could be in there.

"Go all the way back to the back of the store and work your way forward," he says as if he's been getting lessons from Margot. "You take the right side of the escalator, I'll take the left."

I march through the men's department, past tables of folded shirts and racks of hanging jackets. A counter filled with half-empty cologne bottles gives me an instant headache. When Harri was five, I lost her in a department store just like this one. I turned my back for only a second, to hold a dress up against my body in front of a mirror, and when I looked back, she was gone. I can still feel the panic that seized me in that moment. The feeling of having your guts scooped out and your knees betray you. It's not far from what I am feeling now. I had yelled her name over and over again, and finally within seconds that seemed like an eternity, I heard giggling nearby. I followed the sound. It was only feet from where I stood. I waited for the thumping in my ears to slow so I could listen again. It was coming from a round clothing rack in front of me. I pushed an opening between the hanging clothes and there was Harri, laughing.

"You found me!" she had squealed.

It's hard for me to imagine my daughter would be playing a game of hide-and-seek today, but I pull back the tightly packed clothing on a few round racks just in case.

Once again my phone buzzes. I almost can't look. I can't bear another fruitless update. Still, I retrieve my cell and look down at a message from Wayne.

Meet me at escalator.

I run to the front of the store to a double escalator bank. Wayne is standing there—alone. My heart drops. He takes my hand gently, and I see his face has changed.

"Look," he says, nodding toward the cosmetics department.

Standing at a glass counter and leaning into a round mirror, her face caked with makeup like a very sad clown and outlining her lips over and over in a deep-red color is Harri.

Chapter 32

I WANT TO RUN UP TO HER, GRAB HER BY THE SHOULDERS, AND squeeze her so tightly she laughs, "Mom, you're crushing me!" I want to cry for her safe return and scream at her for creating this disaster. But something in the curve of her back stops me. Instead I approach slowly, cautious of spooking her. She is so engrossed in the mirror she doesn't see me coming. It gives me time to look at my daughter, really look at her. And I don't like what I see.

There is something missing from her. And it isn't just her outline, the softness of it erased in front of my unseeing eyes by meals skipped and food thrown in the garbage. Nor is it her posture, curved in defeat and resignation. There is a light gone, a spirit evaporated. The girl who laughed so easily and thought so uniquely is hidden from me. She stops drawing on her lips and puckers them. She dips her finger into a flat tray of brightly colored eye shadows and swipes a deep purple across her lid. At the other end of the counter, two women in black smocks stand behind a large display for a skin-care line, deep in conversation and ignoring her.

"Harri," I say softly when I reach her.

She turns to me slowly, as if she's been expecting me, as if she doesn't assume she's in any trouble.

"Mommy."

The thick makeup is caking on a face that is perfect without it. Her red lips, filled out beyond their outline, seem angry and menacing. She looks ridiculous. If this were any other day or time, she'd be the first to admit it. We'd laugh and I would probably join her to see who could make themselves look more foolish. Then we would dare each other to go out in public like that, and at the last minute I'd back out. My fearless daughter would be disappointed and call me a chicken, and I'd admit it and tuck my arms by my sides and flap.

But this is not any other day. And this is not my fearless daughter.

"A lot of people are looking for you right now," I say to her.

I look over my shoulder and see Wayne, still standing by the escalator. After he had pointed to Harri, I gave him my cell phone. "Text the group. Tell them we found her."

I had started to walk toward Harri but stopped after a step. I turned back to Wayne. "Please don't tell them where we are. Just say thank you, really, sincerest thank you, and I'll call them all tomorrow."

I was grateful for their help but they were the last people I wanted circling around my daughter right now.

"Harri, what happened? Why aren't you with the other girls?"

She lowers her eyes. When she looks at me again, specks of black mascara are on her cheeks. "I'm sorry," she says.

"Did you get lost?"

"No."

There are cotton balls and Q-tips and Kleenex lined up next to the makeup display. I pull out a tissue and wipe her cheek. It dulls but does not remove a harsh, pink blush. Harri's eyes fill with tears and spill over. She wipes at them with her palms, and large black and purple smudges appear under her eyes like a defeated boxer.

"I tried," she says.

"You tried to what?"

"I really tried, Mom. I did everything they said. But they still hate me. Why do they hate me, Mom? I did everything they said."

Now I do pull her close and she begins to sob. I hold her too tight, but this time she doesn't complain. I want to absorb her pain. Pain I am now sure I've caused.

"I know you did. But you don't have try anymore," I whisper into her hair. "We're done with that."

I look over at my friend, my one true friend in this town. His arms are crossed and his chin is down as if he is waiting for my signal. I give him a small smile and he nods.

"Time to go home," I say to my daughter. "Time to go home."

———

When we get back to the house, Zaria is standing at the stove, a glass of red wine in one hand, a wooden spoon in the other. The smell of butter and onions sizzling in a frying pan make me want to cry with gratitude. I can tell by the cutting board of cubed meat she is making beef stroganoff, her specialty and my favorite. I throw my keys on the counter and they skid across the granite and land on the floor. Penny, who has been lying at Z's feet while she cooks, ambles over to see if they are edible. I'm too damn tired to pick them up, and I need whatever strength I have left to open a beer—or two.

When Harri comes in, smudged and tearstained makeup still covering her face so that she looks like an abstract painting of herself, Zaria doesn't ask any questions. I get the sense Wayne texted a full update while he was waiting at the escalators.

"Why don't you go wash up," Z says, gently pinching Harri's chin. "Dinner will be ready soon."

"Okay, Aunt Z."

Harri hadn't said much on the ride home. Wayne drove and I sat in the passenger seat, angling my body so I could steal glances over my shoulder at my daughter in the back. She had wrapped her arms around herself and leaned her head on the window. I could see her eyes flicker back and forth as she watched cars go by.

"If you weren't lost, where were you?" I'd asked.

Harri took her eyes off the road and looked at me, but only shrugged. It didn't matter. Eventually, she would tell me all the sordid details, but I already knew enough to assume that somehow the girls had turned on her, had criticized or excluded her, and she'd had it. I'm sure Harri just walked away. Anyone with an ounce of self-respect would have. In the midst of this shit show, it gave me comfort to know my daughter was one of those people.

I can hear the shower running upstairs. Zaria adds the beef to the hot pan, and it sizzles and throws up steam. Wayne sits at the table and scratches behind Penny's ear. I finish my beer, leave the bottle on the counter, and open another one. Zaria tries to approach the speed at which I am drinking diplomatically.

"Well, she's back now. So we can all take a deep breath."

As opposed to drinking ourselves silly.

I take a few long gulps like an insolent child. "Not when you've had the day I've had," I finally say.

It's unfathomable to think about how it all started—with a visit from Rand. I tell my friends about it, sharing everything except the part when Rand accused me of leading him on. A small spark in me feels a burning shame that there is some truth in that. It is such a classic piece of aggressor justification, laying blame to the victim. I know I did nothing wrong, but after years of living in a culture that insists you must have "asked for it," I can't fully shake my part in what happened to me. But I also don't want to talk about it and give it the oxygen it wants.

Wayne has stopped petting his dog and is sitting back in his chair, his face reddening by the second.

"That bastard. I'm going to go over there and—"

"No, Wayne." My eyes fill with tears at the sweetness of his chivalry. "I took care of it."

"Damn straight you did," says Z. "I hope you kneed him in the balls something good."

I have to laugh. "Well, he'll be walking funny for a while. But that will be from falling down the stairs. Just as effective."

My joke does not lighten Wayne's mood. "What are you going to say to Jeff?"

I take another long drink. I look at the label on my bottle. It's a strong IPA—8.2 percent alcohol content—double the average. It's as if I've had four beers already. And I don't remember eating today.

"Fuck Jeff."

Wayne's head snaps back.

"I'm sorry," I say. "But our last conversation didn't go well. I need my husband here, now more than ever, and he needs to be three thousand miles away."

Zaria lowers the flame on the stove, puts the lid on the pan, and walks over to Wayne, putting a hand on his shoulder as if he's the one who needs comforting.

"It's not an ideal situation, but Jeff will be home soon. This will sort itself out," she says.

"That's right," says Wayne.

I shrug my shoulders like an eleven-year-old girl. Even after all this beer, I don't want to tell them what I'm really worried about: that it won't sort itself out because maybe this was a mistake. I don't want to say to Wayne, my husband's staunchest supporter, that maybe I said yes too soon. Maybe I was so ready to jump out of the life I had that I never stopped to think it through, to understand what I was agreeing to—and where I had agreed to live. Now I'm questioning my motivation. Do I really love my husband? Or did I want a different life, an easier life, a bigger life for my daughter and myself so badly I jumped in blindfolded?

Careful what you wish for.

"Oh, there is something else," I say. "I found the Hummingbird."

Z breaks into a smile and smacks her hand down on the counter. "There you go! Some good news. I can't believe it, after all this time."

"Amber had it."

Zaria stops smiling.

"She stole it off our front step. She's a total klepto. And there's more."

This time I tell them the whole story, not leaving anything out, feeling a chill when I repeat Amber's words, "'Keep your friends close and your enemies closer.'"

"And she grabbed it out of my arms and I lost my grip and it... I'm so sorry, Z..." I'm crying so hard I can't finish my sentence. But I don't have to. Zaria knows exactly what happened to the Hummingbird. She inhales sharply as if a shard of the shattered vase pierced her skin.

"I always thought there was something wrong with that girl. Really wrong," says Wayne. "But I didn't count on her being a damn psycho."

Zaria hugs me and I fold into her. "Oh, Ginny, and then there was that business at the mall? What a day you've had."

I pull back from Z, gasping air to slow my crying. "I don't think I can do it anymore. I really don't."

Chapter 33

"BANANA PANCAKES?" ASKS ZARIA, BACK AT THE STOVE TOP.

"Yes, please," answers my daughter as if today is just another Sunday morning.

Scrubbed clean, hair expertly braided by her aunt Z so that even after a night's sleep it has all stayed in place, Harri looks like Harri again.

"But hang on. I just want to see if Mrs. Clucklesworth Too started laying yet."

I glance over at Zaria. The new chicken has a name? Has it been accepted? Can world peace be far behind?

Chicken victory aside, I feel rotten. Hungover. Wrung out. I'm at the kitchen table, but barely upright, my head in one hand, a mug of coffee in the other. The quantity of beer I drank last night is the least of my problems. I tossed and turned in bed, the events of the day rolling around in my head like stones in a polisher—although no amount of tumbling and spinning has smoothed out the thoughts I'm grappling with right now.

Z brings a stack of pancakes to the table and places the plate in front of Harri.

"Can you just move in?" I ask my guardian angel.

"Eat," she says to Harri. Then she turns to me. "I said I could stay for a few days. Penny's got her first treatment tomorrow and I told Wayne I'd go with him. This way I can keep an eye on all of you at the same time."

Yes, the fundraiser for Penny. I'll have to factor that into my plans.

"Is Wayne your boyfriend now?" asks Harri as she helps herself to breakfast.

I don't know where to look first—at my daughter who is cutting into and actually eating maple-syrup-drowned pancakes, or my friend who could be divulging some very interesting information. I should have bet on my daughter because Zaria isn't giving anything up. She harrumphs and walks back to the stove where she busies herself with pouring more batter onto the griddle.

Harri gives me a questioning glance and I shrug my shoulders. I'm going to keep my fingers crossed that Z is just playing coy. Seeing her and Wayne end up together would be the one silver lining of this whole disastrous experiment.

"Keep your secrets," I say to Zaria who doesn't turn around.

Harri giggles with a full mouth. Score one for me.

Z brings another stack of banana pancakes to the table and takes a seat. Within minutes Wayne and Penny are at the back door. So that's why she's made enough for an army.

Wayne says his good mornings, but Zaria doesn't look up. She's not fooling anyone anymore. Harri and I watch Wayne move around the kitchen with renewed interest, but he doesn't notice. He takes a place at the table, helps himself to pancakes and a long pour of syrup, and digs in.

I sip my coffee and fight back the acids in my empty, sour stomach. We fall into an easy silence. The only sounds in the room are forks and plates scraping against each other, the extractor fan, and the heavy breathing of the dog waiting under the table for her share of the spoils. We are one happy family. I am painfully aware of why that is a bad thing.

I should call Jeff, but I'm not ready yet. I need some time, some space in my own head, a little distance beyond the initial three thousand miles. Not to mention, there are a few things here that have to be dealt with first.

Harri helps herself to another pancake. Wayne watches her, his own bite paused midair. "Look who's got her appetite back."

I cringe. If it were I who had said it, the comment would have been met with angry, defensive fireworks. But this is Wayne, whose affable charm cuts him a lot of slack. That, and the fact that he is not her mother.

"Nobody passes up my world-famous banana pancakes," Zaria says, laughing.

Harri smiles with a mouthful of mashed food, and Wayne chuckles. "Good to see you're feeling better."

My daughter flashes me a look I can't read. I sit up a little straighter and put down my coffee. If I'm going to get in trouble for Wayne's forwardness, I want to be prepared.

"Mom, I want to talk to you about something."

A cold hand squeezes my lower intestines as I jump to every conclusion I can. Something terrible happened to her at the mall yesterday after those brats exiled her, and she is only now able to talk about it. A man approached. A teenaged boy offered her drugs. Someone tried to follow her into the parking lot.

"It's okay, honey, whatever it is."

Zaria sees how my face has turned white and puts her hand over mine. *Back away from the ledge*, it says.

"Mom," says Harri. "Don't be mad. But I was thinking that I don't want to be in the fashion show anymore. Is that okay?"

Relief washes over me—and not just because my daughter wasn't kidnapped at the mall. It's one more piece of my new plan coming together. "I think it's a great idea."

"You do? But you told me—"

"I was wrong, Harri. You were right. The fashion show is a dumb idea."

Harri visibly relaxes and the guilt of getting her into all this bites at me. "I hated the clothes they wanted me to wear," she says.

When the committee members took formal wear away from my daughter to punish me, they decided to dress her in athleisure wear—which consisted of skintight kaleidoscope-colored leggings and a midriff-baring top that was basically a sports bra. In my mind, the only thing more wildly inappropriate for an eleven-year-old would have been sending her down the runway in her underwear. But I had caused enough social homicide for my daughter up to that point, so I kept my mouth shut and hoped for the best—maybe a cardigan tossed in at the last second.

And this was the best. Harri, the girl with the right values and a good head on her shoulders, wanted out.

"And now they want me walk with stupid Kyle Finney. He's gross. He tries to hold my hand and his are sweaty and hot—like steamed dumplings."

"Well, now I can never go for dim sum again." I laugh, throwing myself off guard for what comes next.

"Besides, all of the girls are mean to me," she pauses, and I see the energy drain out of her. "They are not nice people, Mom. Especially Jacqueline and Madison. And they said they were my best friends."

My dismal mood returns. I'm itching to seek revenge, if not on the little girls themselves, which I know will only make things worse and very likely land me in a heap of trouble, then on their mothers. I already know where that will end with Amber—more lying, more stealing, more smashing, and nothing changed for my efforts except a few choice words off my chest.

I'm starting to think the problem is systemic, like there is something in the water that shrinks the hearts of almost everyone in this town. Although, my feelings about Margot are more complicated now. Not only did she organize and execute a search party on a moment's notice—without calculating the cost of her disappointment in me as a failed fashion-committee foot soldier, or my inability to fill Stacey's shoes when they were "one girl down" on the street, or even her general dismissal of my inability to live up to the grooming and style requirements of an Elderberry Lane wife—but we now share an ugly bond. We are both Rand's victims, each in our own way. The difference is that I defended myself and hopefully put an end to his shit. I don't know if I can say the same for my neighbor.

"I think I'm going to go over and have a word with Margot," I say, pushing myself away from the table.

"No, Mom! Don't say anything!" Harri looks panicked. "Madison will know it was me!"

She has learned quickly about the world of bullies. If she gets the girls in trouble, it will only make things worse for her. My heart breaks and my resolve thickens.

"Well, I do have to let her know you're out of the fashion show. But I'm going to tell her you are coming down with something. Something nasty and contagious. How about the bubonic plague?"

Harri seems relieved.

"Don't worry," I assure her. "That's all I'll say. I have something else to talk to Margot about."

As I walk across the street to Margot's, a light, pre-Thanksgiving snow falls, warning of the coming winter. I'll bet they go all out on Elderberry Lane with the Christmas decorations. And when I say *they* go all out, I mean the same trucks that brought the hay bales and the exotic pumpkins will be back with lights and ladders and the most fashionable and tasteful of holiday decor.

I ring the bell and panic. I forgot that it is Sunday. What if Rand opens the door? *Shit.* This isn't going to work if Rand is home. His Porsche isn't in the circular driveway, but that's no guarantee. Before I can turn around, Margot opens the door.

"Ginny?"

I get why she is confused. I have not made it a habit of being at Margot's door without being summoned for a meeting or a task.

"Hey! Margot," I say with too much nervous excitement. "I'm sorry to bother you. You must have the house full with everyone home. Actually, come to think of it, I can come back."

"No bother. Madison is in her room. Rand is at the gym. How is Harri?"

"Uh, fine. Good. Better. Thank you."

She steps back and lets me in. Her house is warm and inviting on a cold Sunday morning. Candles are lit in her large center hall, softening the edges of all the marble and crystal. I smell a fire going somewhere, and when I follow her into her great room, one is crackling in a fireplace surrounded by a high, ornately carved white mantel topped with photos in silver frames. I have a hard time imagining Margot building and stoking that fire. There must be a housekeeper somewhere out of view. Just because it's a weekend doesn't mean Margot Moss-Marks doesn't need assistance.

I am suddenly unsure of my purpose here. There are so many possible outcomes after I've said my piece, and most of them are not good. Do I really want to disrupt this woman's life? I need to know my own heart. Am I here to help or harm? I decide to start slowly.

"I wanted to thank you, again, for your help yesterday."

"It was nothing, but you are welcome."

"I can't believe the way you sprang into action. I think FEMA could use you for disaster relief. The way you assembled those troops."

Margot waves off the compliment. "We are mothers," she says. "We're good in a crisis. And you would have done the same."

"Well, certainly not with such military precision."

Margot smiles. "Well, I'm just glad Harri is okay," she says.

My daughter is far from okay, but there is no point in going into that right now. I have another purpose for my visit. Plus, I promised Harri I wouldn't start. She still needs to go to school on Monday morning. I've made things hard enough for her. I don't need to throw water on the grease fire I've turned her life into.

"Like I said, she's fine, thanks. Although I'm afraid she's not going to be able to participate in the fashion show. With all the excitement yesterday, I think she's coming down with something. And I know my kid... These things hit her hard and what with the event only three days from now, I can't see her being better by then."

I'm talking too fast to be credible. I can tell from Margot's face she's on to me, but she doesn't argue or accuse me of throwing a monkey wrench into her hard-wrought plans.

"I completely understand," she says. "We don't want to make her worse, or get the other children sick. It's no problem. I'll make some rearrangements."

That was easy.

"Well, then," she says, placing her palms together. Her arms make sharp angles at her sides. "Thank you for informing me."

I am being dismissed, but I'm not ready to go. "There is one more thing."

She waits but I feel the pinch of her impatience. How do you tell a woman that her husband is a scumbag? How do you walk into another person's house and change her life forever? And what will my role be, after it's all out in the open? How much support do I owe her after having been the one to throw this rotten fish at her feet? Offering Margot a constant shoulder might be a problem in light of my plans. Still, she deserves to know. If it were me, I'd want to.

"Yes?"

"Well, so, um, Rand came to see me yesterday."

Her face doesn't change but her arms cross. Again, she waits.

"He said he was checking in on me, as Jeff has asked him to."

If she were wearing a watch, she would be checking it right now. I need to get to the point. "I'm sorry, Margot. This is so shitty. I hate this. I just think it's important for you to know. I mean, I'd want to know."

I feel nauseous. It's as if I've just received the news I'm about to share. Maybe this wasn't a good idea. Maybe I should just mind my own damn business. "So, yes, well, your husband—I mean, Rand—he, well, he went after me. I mean he assaulted me—well, tried to—sexually."

Before Margot can move a facial muscle, there is a bang above us. I jump as if I'm the messenger who's been shot.

"Linda," Margot calls toward the back of the house. "Please check on Madison."

The hidden housekeeper jogs past the great room and disappears up the staircase on quiet, sneakered feet. When she is out of sight, Margot looks back to me. She seems unmoved, unaware of the gravity of my confession. I wish I could see behind her eyes, past the studied composure, so I knew where I stood, what I was dealing with here.

"Nothing happened. I want you to know that."

I can see Rand's body hovering over mine as he pinned me in the chair. I can feel his hand between my legs, both pushing at me and grabbing at my zipper. I see his face looking up at me after he had tumbled halfway down the stairs, the blood running from his nose to his chin, the look of hatred in his eyes when he knew he'd been bested. None of that is for Margot. She doesn't need those details.

Margot looks into the fireplace. There are only tiny blue flames left licking at the charred wood. The housekeeper will be needed soon to add more logs. "Thank you for bringing this to me, Ginny," she says.

I blink with surprise. There is no ranting, no crying, only an unnerving steely calm. "I–I just thought you'd want to know," I stammer, feeling off-kilter.

At least throw something!

"I felt it was my responsibility to tell you," I say, defending my actions. "I couldn't live with myself if I thought—"

"I understand," she says.

And then *I* understand.

She knows exactly to whom she is married.

She's always known. And here I am, knocking at her door, pulling at the sutures of her loosely stitched wound.

The housekeeper comes padding down the stairs and stops in the door-way to the great room.

"Just some toys on the top of her closet she was trying to get down. I cleaned it all up," she says.

"Thank you, Linda," says Margot in the same tone she used with me.

Linda glances at the dwindling fire and walks over to the hearth.

"Leave it," says Margot. "I think we will let it die."

We both wait, like players on a stage as the lights go dark, for Linda to leave the room. When she does, I take a step closer to Margot. "I'm sorry."

"What on earth are you sorry for, Ginny? Did you seduce my husband?"

It's a rhetorical question. She knows the answer.

"Margot, are *you* okay?"

She sighs. I wonder how many people have stopped to ask her that question. I'll bet not many. Margot Moss-Marks is a hard hill to climb.

She lowers her shoulders as far as her finely sculpted deltoids will allow. Her eyes become hooded in defeat. "My husband is a confident and charismatic man. There are many women who have not turned him away."

I take her hand. She looks down at my paint-stained nails with a flash of alarm, but doesn't pull away. "And to those who have, I can only apologize so much for his behavior."

"You? Margot, no—"

She takes a short, deep breath, almost like a hiccup. "I'm thinking of having apology cards printed up on my husband's behalf." She forces out a small, defeated laugh. "Then I can simply pass them out at appropriate moments."

I smile and squeeze her hand.

"Good Lord," she says, straightening her blouse and smoothing her beautifully smooth hair. "I don't know why I'm telling you all this."

Maybe because there is no one else around here you can.

"Margot, why do you stay?"

She walks away from me to a glass and marble coffee table. She straightens an oversized art book, pulls a fading petal from an arrangement in a crystal vase, runs her fingers over the glass top and inspects it for dust.

"Where would I go?" She laughs softly.

"Anywhere? Nowhere? Stay here? Make him go?"

"It's not that easy."

"Of course it isn't. I didn't mean to suggest it was."

"Did you do it, Ginny?" she says, back to an antagonistic tone, back to the Margot I know.

"No, I didn't. I didn't get a chance. Harri's father disappeared little by little until he was completely gone."

"I'm sorry," says Margot.

I shrug. "Things worked out for the best," I lie.

"My situation is different. I have so much to lose. Everything. My security. My social life."

I ignore the implication that her loss would be greater than mine.

"What will people think of me? How will they look at me? With pity? As a pariah to be avoided? Do you have any idea what it's like not to be part of a couple in this town? I will not let Rand do that to me."

"I don't think that will happen. No one could blame you for—"

"And the last thing I will let happen to me," she says, lifting her chin, "the absolute last thing, is that I end up like Amber."

The light has shifted on Margot. I am so used to seeing her backlit, a halo around her. Now, the sun hits her directly, showing her for who she really is. Margot Moss-Marks, the queen bee of Elderberry Lane, is afraid. Now I see where all the bravado comes from, why she runs such a tight ship. She is trying to keep in check a life she has little control over.

It's not my place to convince Margot to leave her husband. Maybe she will come to that one day on her own. In the meantime, in this town full of women so willing to follow her, what she really needs is a friend.

Chapter 34

THE DROP-OFF LINE AT SCHOOL IS EVEN LONGER AND SLOWER than usual. A biting November rain has discouraged everyone from parking and walking their kid to the front steps of Acorn Elementary School. Whatever socializing, strategizing, and deal-making that usually occurs at the foot of those stairs will have to happen over skinny lattes or Greek salads with the dressing on the side or in the ladies' locker room after spin class.

The first bell has already rung by the time I'm close enough to let Harri out of the car without risking a sharp, impatient talking-to from the teacher on drop-off duty.

"Let me out here," she says. "I don't want to be late."

I should be comforted by the fact that with everything that has happened, my daughter actually wants to get to school on time. But I know better. Stopping at the office to get a tardy slip means walking into class after everyone else has settled, therefore drawing all eyes to the late person. And right now, the less attention Harri gets, the better. Tonight is the fashion show. Word will have gotten around that she's dropped out. The girls were not nice after her demotion to casual wear. Who knows what news of her bailing out on the whole shebang will bring?

"Don't forget tonight is movie night," I say as she steps out of the car and hoists her backpack onto her shoulder. "I'm making popcorn with extra butter and M&M's."

"A Pixar marathon is going to be way more fun than a stupid fashion show," I shout to her before she slams the car door and runs off.

The cars ahead of me move up slowly, like boats entering the Tunnel of Love. I have to stay in line even though my child is already in the building. Trying to cut out is another easy way to incur the wrath of the drop-off monitor. I suspect Margot and Amber and the committee are on their way to the venue. They don't have a ton of time to set up. I hope Kim's assistant did a good job on the shoe towers. Part of me wishes I could stop by to see my vision come to life—twinkle lights and silver tulle everywhere. But I'm persona non grata, for more reasons than one.

And besides, I have my own event to worry about. The Paint Your Own Pet night is only a few days away. The responses haven't been as gangbuster as I'd hoped. It breaks my heart to think we won't raise enough for Penny's full round of treatments. I spend the rest of my time in the drop-off line and on the ride back to Elderberry Lane racking my brain for a backup plan.

When I get back to the house, there is a U-Haul truck in my driveway. Standing next to it are two young men in light jackets with their hands shoved deep in their pockets. One of them is Jeff's son.

I park in the street and walk halfway up the drive. "Brendan?"

I remember that he's already picked up the few boxes Jeff had been storing for him. I guess Jeff forgot to tell me he'd be back for more.

"Hey, Ginny," he says, revealing his father's amiable smile. "This is my roommate, Tyler. She said she needed some help with the big things."

"She?"

Brendan lifts his chin in the direction of my front door. "She said she cleared it all with Dad and you're expecting us today."

Standing at my front door, leaning on the bell, is Stacey.

"Jesus Christ," I growl.

Brendan's face changes. He knows immediately that he's here under false pretenses. "So, you don't know anything about this? Do you?" I feel for this kid, I really do.

"No, I do not. Nor does your dad."

I had hoped she was bluffing, that she didn't have the nerve to come back and try to reclaim what she left behind. But here she is, with her hand held up to her forehead, peering into one of the narrow side windows framing our front door. Her Peeping Tom act won't yield any results. Harri is at school. I'm watching her watching my house. Zaria has already gone with Wayne to the vet for Penny's first chemo. And Jeff is, of course, in friggin' Dublin.

I stride across the lawn toward Jeff's ex-wife who's got some nerve. "Can I help you?"

She spins around toward me. "Oh, Ginny, perfect timing," she says. "I was just about to give up on you. I promised Brendan we'd be quick. He's got places to go, you know."

Brendan shoots me an apologetic look. "I've gotta get back. We're going out later."

Stacey waves Brendan and his roommate forward. "Come on, boys."

Tyler, who has no idea his friend has been duped by his own conniving mother and thrust back into the middle of his parents' (and now stepmother's) conflict, opens the back of the truck and pulls out quilted packing blankets. I hold up my hand.

"Wait right there," I say to him.

Tyler stops and looks at Brendan, who looks at Stacey.

"We'll be out of your hair in no time," she says to me. "Come on, boys."

"No, Mom," says Brendan. "You told me Dad was fine with this."

Stacey laughs in a way that even I, who has only been in her company one other time, can tell is insincere. "He is."

Her son shakes his head. Stacey leaves the doorway and meets me on the front walk. She crosses her arms and narrows her eyes at me. The wind blows a strand of hair across her face, and it sticks to her lipstick.

"We talked about this, Ginny."

"No, you talked about it."

She glances over at the boys who have gone back to stand by the truck.

"Look, it's cold out," she says with poorly acted civility. "Why don't we go inside and talk about it again?"

"You are not coming inside *my* house."

I think about what Jeff had said to me before he got the promotion, after a long, frustrating day at a job he didn't think valued him. It started with his disappointment about being stuck at the same level for way too long and no matter how hard he tried to move up, nothing changed for him. But then it turned to his ex. "Brendan was right, what he said at dinner the other night. She wasn't always so 'aspirational,'" Jeff had said with finger quotes to show me he really meant to use a phrase that was much more biting. "But when we got to this neighborhood and she saw what the women in this town had, things changed. At first, our kitchen wasn't nice enough. Then it was the car. And then it was the house. The one we were already mortgaged to our eyeballs for. It wasn't as big as her friends'. The envy turned her ugly. And didn't I understand, she'd ask me, how bad that was making her look?"

"You're not taking any of *our* things." I say to Stacey.

Her eyes widen, then her mouth twists.

"Have you forgotten what I said about getting a lawyer, Ginny?"

"I have not. And I have spoken to a lawyer of my own."

Okay, I didn't actually speak to a lawyer. I spoke to a lawyer's husband who had reported back to me after Noah had told him my side of the story. Noah said that Brian said chances were high Stacey didn't have a leg to stand on and the contents of the house most surely had been negotiated in the divorce decree, but Brian wouldn't say for sure without looking at the papers. I had said, sounding like a broken record, and giving me even more ammunition for my case that he should come home, that Jeff was in Dublin and I had no frigging idea where his damn divorce papers were.

"If you find them, Brian would be happy to help you," Noah told me. "But, honestly, you don't need papers to tell that bitch to go to hell."

Noah was right.

"And my lawyer says," I continue with my fingers crossed behind my back, "you are not entitled to anything in this house. In fact, you are currently standing on private property. I could call the cops right now and have you arrested for trespassing. And wouldn't that be a violation of your parole?"

I smile at the visual of Stacey being walked off in handcuffs—again.

"Well, you really stepped into it, didn't you?" she says.

"Beg your pardon?"

She moves her hands across the air in front of her as if she's a newsboy reading the headlines. "Poor, struggling artist with awkward, loser kid needs steady cash and place to raise her brat. Finds sugar daddy. Moves up in the world."

Only one person could have filled Stacey in on my backstory in such a disparaging way. And it must have been done recently, considering where Stacey's been the last six months. Wow, there had to have been some crazy, double-Dutch backstabbing going on for Amber and Stacey to conspire against me. Amber, who has had her sights on my husband since Stacey left, who was probably thrilled to see the back end of Wife Number One, teaming up with said ex to take down Number Two.

"Aligning yourself with Amber, I see. Makes so much sense."

"It just so happens that I ran into Amber in town. She filled me in on the story. The whole story. Oops, looks like there is trouble in paradise."

"Your source is unreliable," I say, thinking of her delusional, kleptomaniac informant. "You don't know anything about me. Or my marriage. Not that it's any of your business."

"Don't tell me what is and isn't my business. You are the stepmother to my son. You are living in my house. You are sitting on my furniture. Sleeping in my bed. You are getting chummy with my friends. You have basically stepped into my shoes and taken over my life."

"If I recall, you left. In fact, you were so quick to get out that you left everything behind. Including your son."

"Well, I'm back now, aren't I?"

Jeff's ex-wife has picked the wrong day to come back and start a fight with me. Not after the week I just had. I take a deep breath, steeling myself for the torrent I feel rushing through me.

"You're not back. You're here because your last 'financial transaction' didn't work out. You thought you'd traded up. You left Jeff because he wasn't giving you enough, didn't make it big enough for you. You tore him down for years and then walked away. You left him scarred. And not because he lost any great love—now that I've met you that is abundantly clear—but because you convinced him he had no value. All because your insane money-grubbing needs weren't met. Jesus Christ, me stepping into your shoes? No, thank you."

Stacey and I face each other as the cold wind blows between us. I don't budge an inch. She isn't getting into this house. She isn't driving off with one single item. There will be no profiting from Jeff today.

"You are just like Amber said," she finally says. Her nose is red and running now. "Hippie trash."

I shake my head and smile.

"Go nab yourself a rich doctor, Stacey. Build your empire back up. But get off my lawn. And don't come back."

"Oh, I'll be back. And next time it will be with my lawyer. And a much bigger truck!"

I step past her and let myself into the house. I lean against the heavy door, my heart pounding, my ears stinging from the cold, waiting to hear the truck pull away. Then I sink to the floor and cry.

Chapter 35

"*A Bug's Life*, *Finding Nemo*, and *Up*. Which one should we start with?" I ask the audience.

We're all set up for a long night in front of the television. The popcorn is popped. The M&M's have been poured into one of Stacey's Royal Worchester serving bowls. And to ensure that it is a full-scale gorge-fest, Harri and I made chocolate chip slice-and-bake cookies. She and Penny are lying on the floor in front of the TV. She is hugging the dog, whose rib cage raises and lowers Harri's arm with each deep, slow breath.

Wayne and I steal a glance at each other. All has been forgiven for the Mrs. Clucklesworth incident. My daughter's heart cannot hold a grudge, particularly after what her friend went through today. Wayne says Penny's wiped out from the chemo, but it's hard to tell with her. In the time I've known this dog, she's spent most of her day on her side, mouth open, tongue rolled out onto the floor like a red carpet.

Wayne, Z, and I are sitting on the sectional. There's a faint pink stain on the cushion from the cupcake fiasco. I cover it with a throw pillow. Wayne takes the *Up* DVD box off the coffee table where the offerings have been spread out.

"Hey, this old guy and his dog look like me and Penny. I vote for this one."

Harri and I shout our favorite line from the film in unison. "Squirrel!"

"What? Where?" asks Wayne.

Penny lifts her head. Z laughs, having watched *Up* with Harri more times than she will admit.

"You'll see," my daughter says, giggling easily.

I grab a handful of popcorn and lean back into the pillow now covering the vomit stain. Harri leaves Penny's side just long enough to pop in the movie. Zaria tucks her feet under herself and takes a long sip of her red wine. The bottle sits next to the cookies, at the ready. Wayne has brought two open beers from the kitchen, but after the other night and its subsequent terrible morning, I wave mine off.

The fashion show has already started. Margot will have the itinerary drilled down to the minute. The women, probably dressed for a night at the theater and not an elementary school fundraiser, wearing pearls necklaces and multiple diamond rings stacked on bony fingers ("This one was my push present after my first daughter, this one was for the twins...") will be mingling and stuffing raffle tickets into paper bags placed in front of cellophane-wrapped baskets filled with all manner of appealing objects, which they will win and most likely find they have no use for.

The bigger ticket items—seats behind the dugout at Yankee Stadium, a weekend in a villa in Belize, and a round-trip flight on someone's private jet—will be raffled off in a silent auction and the winner will be announced over dessert. But before that, the women will be herded to their seats and served a vodka penne appetizer that no one will eat. Margot will make a welcoming speech while the children backstage will be nervously acting out as the other committee members wrangle them into their outfits and ask them a thousand times to please calm down and use indoor voices.

I am in exactly the right place. Well, for tonight, anyway.

On the Monday After The Mall, Harri had come home from school and announced that she'd been permanently banned from the girls' lunch table. Apparently, Susan Poncherelli grounded her daughter—a month of no shopping for not speaking up about Harri's disappearance from the group—and the girls blame Harri for this injustice.

All I could say to my daughter at the time was, "I'm sorry." Again.

"It's okay, Mom," she said. "TBH, I don't really want to sit with a bunch of mean girls."

"TBH?"

"To. Be. Honest," she said like I'd just crawled out from under a rock.

"Oh man." I had laughed. "You have definitely been in the burbs too long."

And I meant it.

Now the popcorn is almost gone—half of it to Penny who has been mooching off Harri when Wayne wasn't looking. The movie takes a sad turn, and I kick myself for not remembering that the main character is a widower who is missing his wife. We could have watched *Finding Nemo*, which is about a fish whose wife dies… Damn it, Pixar! I look over at Wayne. A tear is running down his cheek. Zaria has her hand on top of his.

"Do you want to watch something else?" I ask quietly.

He removes his hand from under Z's and wipes away the tear. "Absolutely not. There's going to be a happy ending. There's always a happy ending in these movies. I want to see it."

I should have been a better friend to Wayne. I've been so wrapped up in my world collapsing around me that I haven't fully realized what he's been going through. Penny is his constant companion and now she's sick. He could lose her. He could lose her the same way he lost his wife. The cruelty of this strikes me down cold.

"She was a trouper," he said after he and Z got back from the vet. He had carried Penny from his house into my kitchen, staggering under her size and weight. It seemed like overkill; the dog looked fine to me. In fact, the second he put her on the floor, she wandered off to her spot under the table, looking over her shoulder on her way as if to say, "Relax, I've got it from here."

"They are optimistic," Zaria told me. "Lymphoma has the highest remission rate."

"She'll go back in three weeks, they said, probably four to six more treatments and then they'll do more blood work."

He didn't take his eyes off his dog as he spoke. "That is if I can afford them. It doesn't work if she doesn't get them all."

This little fundraising event isn't going to pay for all of Penny's treatments, but it will get her the next one and we'll go from there.

"Now, now," Zaria had said, patting Wayne's arm. "We said positive thoughts only, remember?"

He had smiled at Z. "Yes, I remember."

I gave myself a metaphorical pat on the back. *Well, at least I got these two right.*

We are almost to our favorite part of the movie, the part where Harri and I yell, "Squirrel!" at the TV, when my phone buzzes and does a vibrating dance on the coffee table. Jeff's photo comes up on the screen. I didn't answer when he called earlier today. Or yesterday. Now it's 1:00 a.m. in Dublin. That means he's most likely back from the pub, a few pints of lager under his belt. A lot has happened since I asked my husband to come home and he hesitated too long before answering. I'll never forget those few seconds of silence between us. Even thousands of miles away, I felt the gut-punching pain of it.

"I've got to take this." I grab my phone and start to leave the room.

"Mom, it's our part!"

"Do you want us to pause?" asks Z.

I wave my hand to tell them to keep going on without me as I walk away. When I reach the front hall, I sit at the bottom of the stairs and finally answer the call.

"Hey."

"Oh my God, Ginny, thank God. Where have you been? Are you okay?"

I release a snort-laugh through my nose.

"What's funny? Gin, what's going on with you?"

"I've had a lot on my plate this week."

"Right, I know the fashion show is soon. Margot's got you working your ass off, huh?"

"I quit the fashion show, remember? I told you."

"Right, yes, sorry," he says.

I can't remember whether or not I told him about quitting. It would have been one of those things couples tell each other over dinner after a long day, along with all the other details of their life. But oh, that's right, we don't have dinner together.

"Well, what else is going on? How's Harri?"

I can hear the movie music swelling. The old man and the Boy Scout are saving the day. My daughter is lying on the floor with her only friend, a dog.

"She's been better, Jeff."

"What's going on?"

"Harri is being bullied. She stopped eating because the girls told her she was too fat. She was abandoned at the mall because she didn't have fucking pierced ears."

"Oh Jesus, Ginny. That's awful. Little girls can be so mean."

"It's not just little girls," I say. "Do you know that Amber is *in love* with you?"

"What? Amber?"

"Apparently, you two were on the verge of living happily ever after before I came along and screwed everything up."

"Well, this is the first I'm hearing of it." Jeff laughs.

If he were here, he would know it's not funny.

"Come on, Ginny. Me and Amber? She must have been pulling your leg."

"She seemed deadly serious. She had it all planned out."

"Amber?" he asks again. "She is the last person I'd… I'm the last person she'd… Honestly, I don't even get it."

"I guess you were just a warm body. An available guy *and* just across the street. The lazy girl's guide to finding a new man."

I'm being passive-aggressive. Okay, I'm being plain old aggressive. Jeff pretends he doesn't notice it. This is not how I want to handle things, picking another long-distance fight. I need to tell my husband what is in my heart.

"I love you, Jeff."

"I love you too, Gin. And I'm—"

"Wait, let me go first."

There is that silence again, the one or two seconds that change the timbre of our conversation. My husband can hear my tone, even if he doesn't know what's coming.

"Okay, sure," he says quietly.

"Jeff, I love you. But I can't do this anymore."

I stare at the wall in front of me. Stacey had it painted with a faux finish to mimic gold marble. I'd never paid it much attention. Now I see how gaudy and dated it is. I need a second to organize my thoughts. I wasn't planning to do this now. But here we go.

"I thought we could be in love and be a family and be happy anywhere as long as we were together," I say. "But it's not true."

"Ginny—"

"I didn't think it through, Jeff. But I have a child I have to consider before anything. Even you. You don't know what it's like here. Somehow you've been blissfully immune to it all. But just *playing along* can't protect me like it does you. Harri's been beaten down by this place, by these people. She doesn't deserve that. It's not what I want for her. I want her to grow up somewhere she is accepted and nourished. I know kids can be mean everywhere. I'm not naive. But this place is some next-level shit.

"And this distance between us, Jeff. I'm not blaming you. You had your reasons for going. I thought they were misguided. You didn't need to do it, you didn't need to prove you were anything other than the person we love, but that was your choice. And I tried to be as supportive as I could, because I love you. But the distance, added to everything that's happened, is making me question if we made a mistake getting married. Did we jump in too quickly? Maybe I am guilty of what they are accusing me of—finding someone to get me out of a life that wasn't going anywhere, jumping into another woman's shoes."

"Ginny? What are you talking about? Where is this coming from? Who is accusing you of—"

"Jeff, please just let me finish."

"I don't understand, Ginny. Why is this the first I'm hearing about this?"

"I'm sorry, you've been thousands of miles away. And not just by physical distance. I was handling everything myself. Until I couldn't anymore."

"That's not fair," he says. "You said—"

"A lot of things happened that aren't fair. Look, I've been thinking about this, Jeff. I know they are wrong about me. I married you because I loved you. And I still do. Of course I do. And you have been wonderful with Harri. That means the world to me. But my mistake was agreeing to come here. This is not the life I want, Jeff. These are not the people I want around me—or Harri, especially Harri. The energy drain is incapacitating. I love you. But I have to choose my daughter. I know you don't want to leave this house. Or you can't. I get it. It breaks my heart. But I've made up my mind."

"Ginny, please, don't let a bunch of jerks chase you away. You are stronger than that. Stay."

"You're right. I am strong. And I've fought back hard. But I don't want to have to. How many more times is Harri's spirit going to be crushed just for being different than the mini reality TV stars they are producing in this town? How much more backstabbing should I endure? How many more Rands am I going fight off?"

"Wait. Rand?"

I tell him about my visit from his old pal in excruciating detail.

"Motherfucker. Goddamn piece-of-shit motherfucker. Jesus, Gin, why didn't you tell me?"

"I took care of it."

"Yeah, well now I'm going to take care of it."

I don't argue, but I'm not sure what he can do from an ocean away... send Rand a nasty text?

"Ginny, please. Don't let that lowlife chase you off. I'm so, so sorry that happened. That guy has been a slimeball from day one. I never trusted him. But you can't give up on us because of him. Stay. Show these people they can't destroy you. Stand up for yourself. But stay. I love you."

I've been pacing, doing laps between the front hall and the dining room, twenty laps around Stacey's oh-so-valuable table. My head is pounding and my mouth is dry.

"I know you do, but I don't know if that can be enough," I say. "If we stay, I could knock heads every day and take a stand for my values and be the outlier—but I don't want to. That is not how I want to live my life, among people who judge me, who force me to constantly defend my beliefs. I want us to be somewhere where I am who I am. Where I am enough. Where I can be my authentic self. And that's what I want for Harri. I wish you could be part of it, Jeff. But if you can't, Harri and I are going anyway."

I see a reflection in the glass front of the china cabinet. I spin around quickly toward the archway separating the dining room from the kitchen. Harri is standing there, her mouth and eyes open wide.

"We're moving?" she asks.

"Jeff, I've got to go," I say quickly. "Let's just both sleep on this and talk in the morning."

"But, Ginny—" he is saying as I hang up.

Nothing more can be resolved over the phone. But now it's time to talk to my daughter.

When I slip my cell into my back pocket and walk into the kitchen, Z and Wayne are standing there as well.

"So, everyone heard?" I ask rhetorically.

No one looks me in the eye.

"Hey, guys. I need to talk to Harri alone, if that's okay."

"Of course," says Wayne. He slips his arm around Z's shoulder and they go back to the popcorn and the slice-and-bake cookies and the uplifting movie that no one wants to watch anymore.

Harri and I sit at the kitchen table. I put my hands over my daughter's. "I should have talked to you first. I didn't want to make this decision without you. But Jeff called, and well…I wasn't expecting to have that conversation just yet."

Harri pulls her hand out from under mine and placed it on top. That simple gesture changes the dynamic of the moment. Who is here to comfort whom?

"It's okay, Mom."

"I wanted things to be better for you," I say. "But it turns out I just made a huge mess."

"I don't think you're the one who made a mess," says my smart daughter.

I laugh half-heartedly. "Well, it was fun while it lasted, right?"

Harri smirks. "Was it?"

I get out of my chair and hip check her so we are sitting on the same seat. I press my shoulder into hers.

"You are an extraordinary human being, do you know that?"

"Are we going back to Queens?" she asks.

"I don't know."

The questions come in rapid succession.

"When are we leaving? Do I have to start a new school? We will still see Wayne and Penny, right? The paint-your-pet thing is in two days. We're not going before that? We can't ditch Penny!"

"Okay, slow down. I don't have any answers yet. But we are definitely not ditching Penny."

"Do you think when we move Jeff is going to be sad about leaving his old house?"

"There is a lot that needs to be worked out," I say, knowing full well I'm not answering her question.

Chapter 36

CANVAS & COCKTAILS IS LOCATED ON THE FIRST FLOOR OF AN OLD Victorian house on a street that gave up its other stately homes to flat-fronted, boxy storefronts sometime in the sixties, judging from their level of dereliction. This store is like a prettily painted "kindness rock" waiting by a drab roadside to be discovered, and I love it right away. The owner, Rita Hepplewhite, is standing at the door, holding it open while my merry band and I haul in our supplies. Wayne, Zaria, Harri, and I each have a box or a bag or two in our arms.

"Welcome, welcome." Rita laughs. "Are you moving in?"

"We've brought snacks and wine," I say. "Lots of it. And of course, the canvases. And some extra brushes and paint, just in case."

"I've got enough paint here for the Sistine Chapel!" Rita's voice is warm and husky. Her blue apron, with the store's name and a silk-screened image of a martini glass in a frame, covers a long, printed peasant dress. Beaded and silver bracelets embrace her wrists and jangle as she takes a bag from Harri. "There's a table in the back where you can set up your food and drinks. Follow me."

The studio's faded and uneven wooden floors creak as we walk. Paintings, highlighting all levels of artistic ability, paper the walls. Long tables set with short-legged easels and brushes and palettes line up one behind the other and face a low stage where another easel and a paint-speckled side table stand ready. I breathe in the smells of old house and new paint. My blood pressure drops. I want to live in this room.

My daughter, looking a lot more like her old self—excited, enthusiastic, and engaged— pulls a small table up to the front door. She has given herself the official title of greeter and money-taker. Everyone who signed up and sent in a photo of their pet has already paid. But we are hoping for walk-ins. Between the snacks and the wine and Rita's percentage for the use of her studio, we are going to need a few more tushes in the seats.

Harri takes a poster out of a box and tapes it to the front of the table. It's a selfie of her and Penny—she's squinting into the sun with her arms around the dog's neck—taken on our back deck the first week we moved in. Before we knew what an important a part of our lives Penny and her owner would become. In the background is Wayne's head as he soaks in the hot tub. In large, stenciled letters Harri had written:

"♯ DOLLARS FOR PENNY ♯"

As we pour bags of pretzels into plastic bowls, people start to trickle in. Harri looks up each name on her list, Wayne searches for the canvases that Zaria and I, along with help from a few friends at her artist co-op, sketched of their pets. I don't recognize most of the women. Some may have responded to the flyers Harri made and helped me put up around town. One has brought her son.

"We have two cats, so we're each going to paint one," I hear her say to Wayne.

"Thank you for coming, means the world to us," he responds.

Once Harri has checked off every name and the box of presketched canvases is empty, I see that the room is only half-full. I do the math in my head and chew on a cuticle.

"I'm sorry," I say to Wayne.

Wayne takes a step forward and kisses me on the top of my head.

"Stop. We are beyond grateful," he says. "And you with your own—"

He doesn't finish his thought. He doesn't have to. I rest my cheek on his warm chest and he give me a tight squeeze. I realize how long it's been since I've had such a hug. I could stay here for an eternity, but I pull back after a few seconds, afraid of what emotions will be pried loose by his hold. I'm the hostess today and I've got to be onstage. Everything else will have to stay tucked away for now.

With Rita's help, we get everyone set up. We hand out aprons and give the budding artists a plastic palette on which we've squeezed a dollop each of the primary colors plus black and white. On the wall at the front of the studio is a large color chart illustrating what colors mix to make others.

Rita explains, in a simple and practiced way, how to follow the chart. "And then once you have your colors sorted, the general rule of thumb is to fill in the background first," she says. "And then work dark to light. Use the photo you gave Ginny for guidance. Don't worry about making mistakes. You can always go over them and make everything right."

"The most important thing is to have fun," I announce from the sidelines. "And get yourself a glass of wine. Or two. That will definitely help."

There's a smattering of laughter, and the room fills with the sounds of people chatting among themselves as they lean into their projects. It seems as if everyone has a question. Hands raise and Rita, Z, and I run around the room to offer advice. I'm helping a woman who is painting a beta fish in a small bowl when I heard the bells hanging from the front door of the studio ring and my daughter squeal, "Yay! More people!"

I turn around as Margot Moss-Marks and a group of ten or twelve women (and a few men, Noah and his husband Brian among them) file in and line up at Harri's little desk. As the newcomers unzip their coats and open their wallets, I excuse myself from the fish painter and walk over to Margot.

"What's this?" I ask.

"Community support."

"I thought you weren't interested in helping—"

"I said, if I recall, that I couldn't reappropriate the funds from our event. There was no mention of not caring about your cause."

I break out into a smile so wide my face threatens to crack from the unfamiliarity of it. Never underestimate Margot's ability to pull a crowd together at a moment's notice.

"I could kiss you, Margot Moss-Marks!"

She holds her hands up to me.

"Not necessary," she says sternly, but I see a small grin.

I laugh and address the new group. "Come on in, everyone, find a seat. If you have a photo of your pet, we'll help you draw it out on a canvas real quick. And then you can get started. You still have plenty of time."

"And what if you don't have a pet?" says a voice hidden behind a clutch of women.

"What do we paint then?" asks Amber, as she steps out from the shadows.

I can't believe Amber would have the nerve to show up here. I know that when Margot was gathering "volunteers" she hadn't heard about what went down between us, but I would have thought Amber would have the sense to decline the invitation. I'll never understand this woman. And thank God, I don't have to.

Rita has overheard Amber's question and saves me from throwing her out on her ass by offering a solution to all the walk-ins. "Don't worry if you don't have a pet to paint, folks," she says. "I have the lovely van Gogh Sunflowers. We can all work on it together. I'll take you through it step by step. I promise you, the finished product will be museum ready!"

Rita shepherds the group to the empty tables. Wayne and Zaria, who have just realized Amber is here, mime wide-eyed, confused looks at me, but jump in to help everyone get settled. Margot does not join them. We stand by the door like two chaperones at a dance.

"This is a great idea," she says. "A painting party. I'll have to add it to my list."

"Thank you. And thank you for bringing all these people. You're a life-saver." I hesitate, then I say it anyway. "I could have done without Amber."

"Who couldn't?" she says.

I snort so ferociously I think something flies out of my nose. Margot smiles conspiratorially as she surveys the room. I let a few beats pass before I fill her in on the latest. I finish with, "You know she had her sights set on Jeff? Apparently, I ruined her plans when I showed up."

"That would have never happened. Jeff has much higher standards."

"Was that a compliment?" I laugh.

"Never," she says, but she's smiling again.

I wish I'd met this Margot earlier. And I wish it didn't take a bond formed over an asshole husband to give her permission let her guard down with me. "So, I hear you are leaving us."

"Wh-what?" I stammer. I hadn't thought about how to tell the neighbors, but it certainly wasn't going to be before Jeff and I had talked everything out.

"News travels fast around here," she says as she watches me search for my words.

"How can you know? I haven't told anyone yet."

"Harri told Madison."

I specifically remember asking Harri that we keep this to ourselves for now. I can't be mad at my daughter, though. I can imagine she might have needed to tell someone, to wield the news like a sword against the harassment she's been getting from the other girls. The balance of power changes when you have the ability to walk away.

"I hope it wasn't… Well, you know, I hope he didn't push you to go."

Margot bears the burden of her husband's misdeeds already. I don't need it to pile more on. Besides, Rand Moss-Marks is the least of my concerns.

"Oh, no. Certainly not," I assure her.

"I'm sure a move will be wonderful for Jeff," she says. "He always seemed to be on the periphery of things, even when Stacey was here. Never really looked like he had his heart in it. I got the impression she was the one who managed their social life. I think he just went along with it. I'll bet he'll be happy to get a fresh start."

I can't tell her Jeff might not be starting anything. I haven't spoken to my husband since the phone call the night before last. "Well, the details aren't worked out yet."

"You'll keep us posted," she says.

And then she looks over my shoulder toward the door, and her eyes widen.

"Ha, speak of the devil," she says.

Chapter 37

"JEFF! YOU'RE BACK!" YELLS HARRI AS SHE THROWS HERSELF AT him so hard he stumbles.

I don't understand. It's like seeing something you know shouldn't be there, a crocus in heavy snow or a twenty-dollar bill on a dirty sidewalk.

"I'll leave you to it," Margot says before she walks away.

Harri takes Jeff's hand and pulls him toward me. "Look who's here, Mom! He surprised us!"

"What are you doing here?" I ask, still confused and disoriented.

"I went to the house. I found this on the counter." He reaches into his coat pocket, pulls out the flyer Harri made, and unfolds it as if he needs to prove to me that it's authentic. "So I came here."

"No, I mean, what are you doing *here*, in New Jersey?"

Harri is standing between us, looking to me and then to him, waiting for his answer.

"I got on the first flight I could. We need to talk. And not on the phone."

I look at Jeff. I haven't seen him in almost two months. His long-flight-tousled hair and clothes make him look younger, even more carefree, than when he left. But the circles under his eyes tell a different story.

"Look, Jeff. This isn't the best time. I'm right in the middle of—"

Wayne interrupts us before I can finish. "Jeff! You're home! When did you get back?"

"Just now. I came straight from the airport. Well, I stopped home, but… Hey, hi, Zaria… What's going on here?" he asks as he looks from Z to Wayne and the lack of physical distance between them.

"Penny has cancer," Harri tells him. "And Mom is doing this fundraiser to get money for her treatments."

"I know, Har," he says, holding up the flyer she made. "Wayne, man. I'm so sorry."

Wayne nods his head. I know it's still hard for him to believe.

"Harri," says Z. "Why don't we let your mom and Jeff say hi. The pretzel bowl is almost empty. Let's us go over and top everything up."

Wayne puts his arm around Harri's shoulder, and the three of them walk to the back of the room.

"Great to see you," he says to Jeff before he goes.

Jeff takes me by the elbow and leads me away from the scrum of neighbors and artists.

"Jesus, that sucks about Penny. Cancer. That's bad," he says. "Mary died of—"

"I know."

"Look, we can talk later. But there is just one thing I need to say, and I need to say it now."

But he doesn't get to. Because the bells on Canvas & Cocktails' front door chime again and Rand, fucking Rand, walks in.

"What the hell is he doing here?" Jeff says instead.

Rand is standing at the front of the studio, looking around, but he doesn't see either of us.

"I have no idea," I say.

I walk over to Rand with heavy determined steps. As I get close, I see that the cut on his face hasn't healed, and a faint purple-and-yellow bruise has bloomed around it. "What are you doing here, Rand?"

He seems shocked and none too happy to see me. "What are *you* doing here?"

"This is my event. And it's by invitation only."

He gives me a dismissive look. "I'm looking for Margot. I tracked her here on my phone. But she's not answering my call. My racquetball bag is in her car and I need it."

Before I can offer to find his wife and get him out of here as quickly as possible, Jeff steps in between Rand and me. His face is red and his jaw is clenched. Rand seems as surprised to see him as he was to see me. "Well, looks who's back," he says to Jeff.

"You've got a set of balls on you," Jeff says.

Rand smirks but before he can open his mouth, Jeff puts both his hands to the man's chest and shoves him.

"What the hell?" Rand shouts.

The whole room turns toward them and falls silent. Margot sees her husband for the first time and narrows her eyes.

"You stay away from my wife," Jeff bellows.

I quickly search for Harri. She is at the snack table with Wayne, her hand over her mouth.

"Jeff, stop!" I hiss. "Not now!"

"I haven't gone near your wife. Why would I? Look at her."

Jeff lunges at Rand, his hands spread wide toward his throat. Rand steps back a half step, leaving Jeff to grab at the neck of his sweater. He pulls at the fabric until Rand straightens his arm, puts his hand over Jeff's face, and pushes him away. Voices from the watching crowd gasp.

Wayne holds on to Harri, preventing her from getting in the middle of this nonsense. Jeff lets go of the sweater, and the two of them stumble backwards. Rand backs into a wall and knocks two paintings to the floor. By then Margot is standing next to me, her face twisted in anger.

"That's enough!" she commands.

But Margot Moss-Marks is not the queen bee in this moment. Rand rights himself, runs his hand over his mangled sweater, and lunges at Jeff. They grab each other with vicious bear hugs as they fling themselves against tables and easels and stools that topple over.

"Get them out of here," Rita yells.

"I'm so sorry," I say, drowning in embarrassment.

"Rand, stop!" Margot barks as she opens the front door.

Rand does not stop, but somehow in all the grabbing and tussling they manage to tumble out onto the street.

Harri breaks free from Wayne and runs up to me as the rest of my guests press themselves against the windows.

On the street, a series of high-school wrestling moves ensues. Rand puts Jeff in a headlock, but my husband corkscrews and breaks free. He rushes toward Rand and barrels into him with one shoulder. Rand staggers back and then comes at Jeff, swinging wide, catching only air. The fight continues— twisting and grabbing and pushing to the ground—but somehow, not single punch lands. Finally, they stumble back away from each other. Jeff has his hands on his knees and is breathing hard. Rand runs his hand through his hair. They are like two old bulls that have fought to exhaustion. Finally, Jeff straightens and there are words spoken that none of us can hear. Rand tugs on his lapels to straighten his jacket and gives Jeff the middle finger. Then he turns and walks off.

"Who's for another glass of wine?" shouts Zaria over the murmuring crowd.

Rita and Z usher everyone back to their stools.

"Well, that was a bit of excitement," Rita says to her group of Margot's walk-ins.

I busy myself with righting the paintings that have been knocked off the wall. I can't bear to see the look on Amber's face right now. Margot and I steal glances at each other as she steps behind the snack table and pours wine into plastic cups. Our husbands just had a knockdown drag-out fight, but all we know is that neither of us will be declaring victory.

"Mom." Harri is standing next to me handing me one of the fallen paintings. "That was so scary. Is Jeff okay? Why were they fighting?"

I look out the window. Jeff is leaning against a mailbox, dabbing at his lip with his sleeve.

"I think he's fine, hon. I think Mr. Moss-Marks just got on his every last nerve. That man is a bully. And an ass."

"Mom!" She is faking her shock at my language, of course. She gives me a smile wiser than her years and hangs the painting on the wall.

"Shh," I say, holding my finger to my lips. "Don't tell anyone."

"I won't."

"Do me a favor, will you? Can you go help everyone get settled? See if they need anything. More paint? Or a snack? I've got to talk to Jeff."

I throw on my coat and step outside. Jeff looks up and walks gingerly toward me. When he gets close, I see his lip is split and a purple bruise is forming under his eye.

"That's going to be some shiner," I say.

"You should have seen the other guy." He laughs quietly.

"I did."

I pull a crumpled tissue out of my pocket and press it gently against his lip.

"That was quite a show you two put on for my guests."

"I'm sorry, Gin. I ruined your event. But he pushed me too far."

"No, it's okay. But I wish I'd known there was going to be entertainment. I would have charged more."

Jeff smiles and then winces. "I've been wanting to do that for a long time," he says. "That guy's a jerk, always has been."

I nod my head. In that, we agree.

"Let me ask you a question. If you've always thought Rand was such a jerk, why did you ask him to check in on me while you were away?"

"What? No! I never did. He's the last guy I'd ask. Is that what he told you?"

I shrug my shoulders. It doesn't matter anymore.

"Listen, Gin, I know you have to go back in there. But just give me a minute. Will you? I have something I need to tell you, and I'd really like to get it out now. If that's okay."

I dig my fists deep into my coat pockets. "Go ahead."

"After you hung up the other night, I didn't sleep at all. And then first thing in the morning I booked the next flight I could get on. I didn't sleep then either. My point is, I've had a lot of time to think about what you said and what I've done. And why. And the first thing I need to say is, I was wrong. I should never have left you here."

"I told you to go. I wanted you to do what was right for you."

"I know you did. And I'm kicking myself for not realizing at the time what an extraordinary, selfless act that was. And how stupid I was to take you up on it. You said it at the time and it didn't sink in to my thick skull, but I was going for all the wrong reasons. I was chasing expectations of me that didn't exist anymore. I'd been convinced I wasn't enough, couldn't provide for my family. I thought going to Dublin would be my chance to prove my worth."

"You were always enough for me, Jeff. More than enough."

"I couldn't hear you. All I could think was I had something to prove, and taking that job was my way to do it. I was an idiot."

"No, you weren't. I had a chance to spend some more quality time with your ex-wife the other day. It was very eye-opening."

"She was back?"

"I took care of it."

"That's just it. I shouldn't have left you to take care of my crap. And I should have been here for when Rand, when he... And God knows what else I missed."

"A lot," I say. "But I—"

"I know, you took care of it." He smiles dejectedly.

"It was never about me not wanting to handle my own life. Harri and

I always did pretty well on our own. That's not why we want you with us. I don't need a knight in shining armor."

"And now you want to go."

I look back at the front windows of Canvas & Cocktails. Harri is standing there with her forehead pressed to the glass. Zaria comes up behind her, says something in her ear, and leads her away.

"Like I said on the phone, I'm tough. I could duke it out. But this is not what I want for Harri. I'm not saying I've got to keep her in a bubble. The world is a tough place. We all learn from the challenges we have to face. From the failures we've picked ourselves up from. But she doesn't need to start out on such uneven footing. She practically destroyed herself trying to fit in. And the worst part is, I asked her to do it—to stop being herself and try get along with people who were never going to see how wonderful the true Harri is."

Jeff looks down at his feet. His right shoe is untied. He ignores it.

"I get it. I know what this neighborhood is like. I've lived here for a long time; I've seen them crawl on top of each other to get what they want. I've seen how more is never enough. I could keep my distance from it. I guess I thought you could too. That was stupid. I should have realized... I never should have suggested we live here. I was too worried about money. My priorities were screwed up."

"Please don't blame yourself," I say. "As I recall, you offered and I accepted. Maybe part of me wanted all this—the big house, the fancy friends. You know, from the outside where I was standing, it all looked like the perfect life. Who wouldn't want that? I just thought we could be ourselves here, bring a little Ginny and Harri sparkle and shine to the place. Show everyone what a couple of hippie chicks can add to their lives. Ha, I found out the hard way the grass isn't greener here."

Jeff smiles and rubs his beard. "Sparkle and shine. I like that. That's exactly what you gave me. That's why I fell in love with you. It was your beautiful spirit. For someone who worked so hard and had so little, you were filled with such joy. I'll never forget the moment I saw you at that craft fair. You and Harri were standing in your booth, talking and laughing. You seemed so free and alive. So beautiful. And your work, the most whimsical paintings I'd ever seen—the colors and the style made me smile. I wanted to go out and adopt a pet just so I could ask you to paint its portrait.

"I couldn't live with myself if I thought keeping you here would destroy that. So what I'm saying is—I don't want you to stay. I want you and Harri to live somewhere that feeds you and lets you be your authentic selves and where you can make your art and sparkle and shine.

"But here's the thing, Gin. I love you. You and Harri. And you two can move wherever you want. But I'm coming with you."

Chapter 38

I SIT IN MY CAR AND SCAN THE WALKING PATH. IT'S TOO COLD TO get out until I have to. Mornings have gotten so brisk, but Margot will not be deterred. And now that it's just the two of us, there's no hanging back in an attempt to catch my breath. Funny enough, in the few weeks since our husbands beat the crap out of each other, we've gotten closer.

A few days after the fight, Margot invited me to meet her at the park. She asked me to come at noon, not the regularly scheduled power-walk time, so I was only partially surprised when I showed up and it was just the two of us. Almost immediately, Margot took off at a clip, pumping her arms and striding like she was going to beat her own world record. I felt like she had something to say, if I could just keep up with her long enough to hear it. Just when I thought I was going to have to collapse on a nearby bench and let her do the last lap without me, she slowed down to a regular human pace.

"I owe you an apology," she said, panting slightly. So even Margot Moss-Marks needs a second to catch her breath, I thought.

"Margot, there's nothing to—"

"No, it was outrageous what Rand did." A long strand of blond hair had fallen out of her Chanel baseball cap. Sweat beaded above a perfectly pink lip.

"Well, Jeff started it."

She dabbed at her lip with a gloved hand. "For good reason."

She was right about that.

Margot lowered her eyes. "Still, it was humiliating," she said.

"Yeah, for them," I said, laughing.

That brought a begrudging smile to her face. She shook her head and said, "They did look foolish, didn't they?"

"Like idiots. Who taught those boys how to fight?"

"I don't think they adhered to the Marquess of Queensberry rules of boxing," she joked.

"More like Queens back-alley rules."

It was good to see an unguarded laugh from Margot, and from then on, our walks became an almost daily occurrence.

She finally pulls into the parking lot and I look at the time on my phone. It is so unlike her to be late. But these weeks have shown me a side of the queen bee of Elderberry Lane I never thought I'd see. There's been a softening, a release, despite the stress I know she's going through. My going to her about her husband's odious behavior, watching the ridiculous display of machismo in front of the Canvas & Cocktails, knowing the hard decision that I made to change my own life, has cracked something in her, she's said. She is pushing back at home in a way she never felt she could. And, according to the stories I've been hearing, Rand isn't taking it well. He's been unmoored by the change, unable to cope with a new reality, like a spoiled child who one day finds out he isn't the center of the universe as he'd been led to believe.

I jump out of my car and stretch my calves. I can see my breath in the cold air as I twist my waist and raise my arms over my head. I'm ready for the sprint. But as Margot gets out of her car, I see she has two large coffee cups in her hands. She bangs her door shut with her butt and holds up the drinks as a greeting.

"I thought we could sit today." She hands over the cup. "It's a nonfat latte."

"Are you trying to tell me something?" I ask.

"Oh my goodness, of course not! I just don't know how to order a coffee any other way, I guess."

"I'm just kidding. This is exactly what I would have gotten. Thank you, that was sweet of you."

We find a cold bench and sit. I curse myself for not bringing a scarf and for wearing ankle socks. At least the coffee is keeping my hands warm. Margot sits ramrod straight as if leaning against the bench is a comfort she doesn't deserve. She blows on her coffee and scans the soccer field. On the playground across the grass, a woman pushes a small child on a swing. Even with the wind blowing our voices will not carry over there. Margot seems satisfied with her surveillance and turns to me.

"I'm doing it. I'm telling Rand that he has to leave. I'm doing it tonight."

She lifts her chin as if I'm going to challenge her. Which I certainly am not. Instead I put my coffee on the ground and scoot closer to her. I place a hand on her narrow back and I feel her spine loosen.

"Good for you," I say.

"Trying to talk to him is going nowhere. It's just one fight after the other. He just digs in and accuses me of being insane. Or hysterical. He says he doesn't even know who I am anymore. Somehow he sees everything that is wrong with our marriage as an attack on him."

"It's sounds like it's all about Rand," I say.

"Yes," says Margot. "That's it in a nutshell. That's always been it."

A car pulls into the parking lot and a runner gets out. We sit in silence as we watch him relace his shoes and adjust his earbuds. When he jogs off, Margot says to me, "It's because of you, you know."

My heart races from zero to sixty in a flash as I feel the accusation flung at me. But the walks, the friendship, the coffee? How is this where she was going all this time? I begin to stammer. What is my defense?

"I mean, it's because of you that I can do this."

The blood returns to my heart and rushes to my face.

"It's not just that when you came to me about your, um, experience with Rand, you didn't judge me. I think the moment I realized everything had to change was after that stupid brawl. I watched you out the window with Jeff afterward. Of course, I couldn't hear what you were saying... Don't worry, no one could. But I realized, just from looking at you two, that Rand and I could never have that kind of intimacy. And that we probably never have."

"I'm sorry, Margot."

"No, don't be sorry. I'm trying to thank you."

"Well, I..." It's a strange thing to be thanked for being the catalyst for a marriage breaking up.

"Enough about me," Margot says, giving us permission to move on. This conversation isn't over; Rand isn't going to make life this easy for her. But I understand her not wanting to dwell. She'll have plenty of time for that.

"What did you decide to do about Amber?" she asks. "Are you going to press charges over the stolen vase? I honestly wouldn't blame you if you did."

"Zaria and I talked about it. We're going to make a deal with her. If she's willing to join a shoplifters support group, we'll let the whole thing go."

"That's very generous of you, considering what she did. All the scheming and the backstabbing you had to put up with."

"Well, everyone deserves a second chance. They just have to be willing to take it."

"Amen," says Margot, clicking her paper coffee cup with mine.

"So, I found a group not far from here that meets once a week. It's run by two therapists who do role-playing and journaling."

"Oh, Lord can you imagine the contents of Amber Franco's journal?"

"I'd rather not," I groan. We sit quietly again as the cogs in my brain start turning. "But you know whose thoughts I'd love to read?"

I take a dramatic beat and she raises an eyebrow.

"Yours, Margot. You are about to embark on a really important life journey. A journey that takes bravery and courage. Think about all the women out there going through the same thing who you could connect to. Maybe sharing your process would give someone else permission to be brave and courageous too."

Margot throws back her head and laughs like I've told her the funniest knock-knock joke ever. "Can you imagine? I can't think of anything worse. That's a story the women I know would dine out on for ages. Watch her tumble from her high horse! Look how far she's fallen!"

"That's not how I see it at all. Everyone falls. Nothing interesting about that. But it's how you get up that will inspire people. And I think you are the perfect person to share that story. Everyone wants to hear from someone like you who can admit her vulnerability. Look at all these women who try so hard to project a perfect life," I tell my friend who's made an art of it. "Just scroll their Facebook pages where they're making else everyone think if they'd only try harder they could have the same. And then they knock themselves out and still fail in big and small ways. If someone like you, someone everyone looks up to, gives them permission to fall and get up? That. That's what people want."

Margot leans back and squints at me as if she is trying to figure out just who is inhabiting my body. "You thought of all of this just now?"

"I did! And you know why it came to me this easily? Because it's a damn good idea."

"Well, your talents have been underutilized painting dogs and crafting shoe towers. You should run a think tank."

"Just tell me you'll think about it. You could start a blog. You could call it *Second Chances*."

"I'm not a fan of the name," she pushes back, but she's smiling.

"Fine." I laugh. "I didn't say I had *all* the answers."

What's left of our coffees have grown cold, and in a shocking role reversal, I ask Margot if we can walk so I can warm up. We talk about the chances of Amber agreeing to the support group and how much I raised for Penny's treatments and we brainstorm names of the blog on the slim chance, mind you, that Margot would decide to start it.

When we get back to our cars, Margot still has one more question. "Have you thought about where you'll move? And when?"

The answer surprises even me. "Well, actually. We're looking in Sherwood Heights."

The Sherwood Heights neighborhood is an enclave of smaller, older, charming Capes and ranch homes less than two miles from Elderberry Lane.

"Wait?" says Margot, hand to chest. "You're staying in town?"

I can't believe it myself.

"Harri wants to stay at Acorn Avenue. She doesn't want to start a new school, despite what happened. And last week she joined stage crew and, in her words, it's a game changer."

It looks like these techie kids who dress in black and are most comfortable running around wearing headsets in the shadows of the stage are exactly the home Harri has been looking for.

"Good for her," says Margot, who is taking no offense that my daughter has found a new friend group that doesn't include hers. "And you know, I run the drama mamas. You'd be perfect for stage design. We're doing *Once Upon a Mattress* this spring. Think of what an artist like you could do with that. We'd be so lucky to get you!"

I need no more information. I need no more convincing. I don't ask for time to think it over. There's only one answer to her offer.

"Oh, hell no," I say, laughing. "Hell no!"

Chapter 39

Jeff and Brendan come into the kitchen through the garage door, stomping off snow and blowing into their ungloved hands.

"I don't know why you had to put that thing up right now," I say, picking up their wet shoes and laying them on the small rubber mat that is there for a reason.

"You never know when the sun will come out and the driveway will be clear," Jeff says. "Besides, we've always had a basketball hoop, haven't we, Bren?"

"That we have."

"Hey," I say, "our guests are waiting for you in the other room. Can you grab some drinks and bring them in?"

Jeff leans into the refrigerator and takes out a few bottles of beer. When he closes the door, he knocks into me. This galley kitchen is long and narrow with counters and appliances running down both sides and room at the end for a small table, but not much real estate for maneuvering. He steps around me to reach into a cabinet and pull out a wineglass. Its stem is thick and short, unlike the extensive collection we left behind, along with most of the contents of our kitchen, for the renters.

I am at the stove, a mismatched pot on every burner. The water in the pasta pot boils over, and the flame under it turns blue and hisses.

"I'm not going to lie," I say. "I didn't hate having a six-burner stove top."

"All I can offer you is this." Jeff smiles, handing me a beer.

I take a long drink. The condensation from the cold bottle in the warm kitchen runs down my wrist.

"Perfect," I say with a sigh. "That's exactly what I needed."

Jeff laughs as he pours red wine into the glass. "Happy to be of service."

With beers in one hand and the wine in the other, he walks with Brendan into the living room where Wayne and Zaria have been waiting for them to finish their project.

"I'm sorry it took so long. I thought we'd be done before you got here," I can hear him say.

"I could have helped you guys," Wayne offers.

"Nah," he says. "We got it. Guests sit with their feet up."

Zaria makes her classic harrumphing sound as I come around the corner with a plate of cheese and crackers. Penny, who was spread out on the floor, making the small room even smaller, jumps to attention when she smells the food.

"Don't give her any," Wayne warns. "She's been putting on a few with all the treats this one has been giving her."

Zaria flaps her hand at him and scoffs. "She deserves it, don't you, sweet girl?"

"Wait until Harri gets home," I say. "She'll be sneaking her half this plate behind our backs, if I know her."

"I give up," Wayne says, laughing.

Brendan sits on the floor and puts his nose in the dog's neck. "I missed you," he says to a very old friend.

"This place is charming," says Z, taking the glass of wine from Jeff.

"If by charming you mean old and run-down," he says. "Then yes, yes it is."

Jeff is joking. He loves this little house. We were so lucky to find it on such short notice. The single-level home has a small fenced-in yard with a perfect spot for Mrs. Clucklesworth Too's newly reinforced and double-latched coop. Now that Jeff's bosses have agreed to let him finish the Dublin job from New Jersey, a low-ceilinged finished basement office has become a good place to telecommute a few days a week. An unused third bedroom with great afternoon light has been transformed into my new studio. And we're only blocks from my new part-time job assisting Rita at Cocktails & Canvas.

I sit in Harri's reading chair, the one item of furniture I insisted we squeeze into the fully furnished rental. We've tucked it into the corner by a wall of built-in bookshelves and a window that faces the street. When the previous tenants moved out, they took their books with them, giving Harri room to store her blossoming collection. She is in heaven.

"We're renting this place with an option to buy," I tell our guests. "Which works out great. We have time to wait for the market to change before we have to sell the old house."

It all happened so quickly. Margot recommended a real estate agent who found us this house *and* a corporate relocation for Elderberry Lane—a man named Chip Walker from Chicago who needed to move his family quickly before starting a job in New York City. They were thrilled to find a place that was fully furnished and move-in ready.

"I wouldn't be surprised if the Walkers end up buying it," I say. "Margot tells me they—these are her words—'fit right in.' She even has the wife signed up to be concession stand mom for the spring musical."

News of our renters isn't the only thing Margot has been keeping me up to date on. Rand is out. After a few weeks of keeping himself in the basement—"Hardly a punishment," Margot has said. "With a full bar, the home theater, and a sauna down there."—he couldn't take her "midlife crisis bullshit." She laughed when she told me, which was a huge relief. He's renting an apartment in Manhattan. Lawyers have been acquired. She's kept herself busy. School committees beg for her guidance. The Board of Ed needs to be wrestled with.

But the big story is that Margot's blog, *Begin Again, with Margot*, is an instant hit. It looks like I was right. Everyone wants to know how Margot Moss-Marks will navigate her second act. So many women have subscribed that she's close to taking on paying sponsors. And she's been begging me to write a guest blog about how I started over—twice. I told her I'd have to think about it. I'd rather face forward right now, not look back.

"I wouldn't hate it if they bought your house," Wayne says. "Penny likes the kids."

"Ha, that's the ultimate litmus test, the Penny seal of approval," Jeff says as he leans down and ruffles her head. Then he looks back at Wayne. "Hey, man, thanks for offering to keep an eye on the place. It's good to know if anything goes wrong—you know, a frozen pipe or anything—you are right next door."

"Yes, to call a plumber. You don't want me messing with the waterworks."

"Still," says Jeff.

"Are you kidding? It's my pleasure. After what you did for us?"

"Ah, you can thank my ex-wife for that."

After I told Jeff that Stacey wanted to reclaim her dining room set, he had had a better idea.

"Why don't *we* sell it?" he'd suggested. "If we can get half as much as Stacey thought she could, we could replace it with a cheaper set, something to leave for the renters. And the rest of the money can go to paying for Penny's remaining treatments."

Thanks to Jeff's ex-wife, Penny is now almost finished with her chemotherapy, and just yesterday the vet told Wayne that although they'd need to do more blood work in a few weeks, he was feeling confident about her chances for a full remission.

"To Stacey," I say, raising my beer bottle.

"To Stacey," the others cheer and we clink all around.

We can joke about Stacey now. But a few weeks after I kicked her off the premises, there was a poorly written but strongly worded letter in the mail from a lawyer.

"Isn't that the guy whose face is on all the benches at the bus stops?" Jeff asked me, showing me the name and letterhead I also recognized from the *Pennysaver*.

Jeff had given the letter to Noah, who gave it to Brian, who knew an actual divorce attorney who owed him a favor. A *well*-written and *more* strongly worded document was sent back, and we were assured that would be the end of Stacey trying to restock her life with our belongings.

We are laughing and drinking and blocking Penny from the cheese plate when the front door opens. There is no two-story, chandeliered center hall foyer in this house, just a square of tile at the door separating the outside from the living room carpet. Harri enters and squeals with delight when she sees her aunt Z and her (she's made a prediction I can't entirely disagree with) uncle Wayne. She peels off her coat, tosses it on an empty armchair, and drops to her knees to hug the dog and her stepbrother. In that order. Puppy love supersedes first crush. Behind her is a woman in a puffy down coat zipped to her chin and a girl with a round face and a head of curls.

"I'm sorry. I see you have company," says the woman. "I just wanted to make sure Harri got in okay."

"No, it's fine, come in," I say, waving her toward me. "Guys, this is our neighbor Mars and her daughter Kit."

"It's really Kit Kat," says the girl. "Like the candy. And mom is Mars Bar."

The mother and daughter break into an infectious peal of laughter.

"Oh, my. I'm sorry. My name is actually Marsha Malone. And this is Katherine. Kit for short. You all must think we're nuts, but Kit and I like to have a little fun whenever we can."

Zaria turns to me and gives me an approving nod. *Now this is more like it*, I can tell she's thinking.

"I hope you don't mind, Ginny," says Mars. "But we did a little shopping after stage crew wrapped up."

The girls stand side by side, proud and with conspiratorial looks on their faces. Harri is almost a head taller than her new friend. She is wearing her new favorite shirt, a purple tee that reads, *Nevertheless She Persisted*—found at the thrift store where we donated the cropped sweaters and skinny jeans Harri wanted nothing more to do with. The Adidas Superstars with the rose-gold stripes stayed. "You have to admit, they're pretty cool," she had said.

The girls giggle and pucker their lips together and wait until I realize that they are wearing matching pink, shiny lip gloss.

"Looking good, ladies," I say.

Harri laughs and does a mock fashion-model pose, flipping her hair, which she has been wearing loose these days, having abandoned both her signature braids and the requisite ponytail.

"Yes, and I'm loving your new 'do, Harri," says Zaria.

Harri smiles and Kit tugs at one of her own tight curls. She looks up at my daughter. "I wish I had your hair, Harri. It's *so* pretty."

Harri turns to her new friend and places her hands on the girl's soft, round cheeks. "Katherine Malone, you are beautiful just as you are," she says. "And don't let anyone ever tell you otherwise."

"Aren't you the sweetest," laughs Mars. "Ginny, you have done a wonderful job with this one. Now, I won't keep you from your company. We had a lot of fun today, didn't we, Kit? Oh, and don't forget, Ginny. I'm going to restorative yoga tomorrow if you want to come with."

After we say our goodbyes and nice-to-meet-you's, I throw my arms open to wrangle the crowd. "Okay, dinner is ready, folks. Let's move this party into the kitchen."

"I'm sorry, Ginny. I can't stay," says Brendan. "I'm meeting some friends in the city."

Jeff pouts like he's just been told his playdate is ending early. "You've gotta eat."

"I'll come back the next sunny day. We'll shovel the driveway and shoot some hoops. You and me against Dad, right, Harri?"

Harri's face lights up.

"Hey, unfair advantage," complains Jeff, but his face lights up too.

After Brendan leaves, we assemble around the table. Penny finds her spot underneath it, near Harri's chair. The table is scratched in places and smaller than the one on Elderberry Lane. Even with Brendan's plate cleared away, we sit so close our elbows touch. No one minds. Jeff puts another bottle of beer in front of Wayne and tops up Z's wine. I dish the food onto plates from the stove. When I finally take my seat, we toast again to our new home and our dear friends and to Penny's health.

"Oh, I forgot to tell you," says Harri. "The cast list came out for the play today. We're doing *Once Upon a Mattress*, Aunt Z. And guess what."

"What?" we all say in unison.

"Madison got Princes Winnifred. That's the star of the play. And Jacqueline got the queen."

My mood sinks. So much for my daughter's fresh start. I reach my hand across the table and lay it on top of hers. "You know, hon. Just because those girls are in the play, it doesn't mean you have to have anything to do with them. You can just stick with your new friends. Like Kit."

"No, Mom. I can't."

"You can't?"

"Mom, stage crew supports the cast. That's our job. So, if Madison and them need help, I'm going to help them."

Mars Malone got it wrong. I didn't do a wonderful job with this girl. This is all her. I squeeze her hand and then take it back to wipe a tear from my eye.

"You know who the star of that play is, Harri?" asks Jeff. "It's you. A toast to Harri Miller, our brightest star. And I propose that Harri gets Brendan's extra dessert tonight. I think she deserves it. What do you think, Harri? Double chocolate cake tonight?"

"Yes, please," laughs my daughter.

"Okay, okay! Dinner first," I say.

We are about to dig in when Zaria sits up straighter and places her hand on Wayne's arm.

"Oh, I totally forgot," she says, and Wayne seems to know instantly what she's talking about.

"Do you mind going out to the car?" she asks him.

"Of course not," he says as he pushes his chair back.

"What's going on, Z?" I get only a knowing smile as an answer.

Wayne returns with a large bag, which he hands to Z. She pulls out something swathed in bubble wrap and tape and hands it to me.

"Open it," she says.

Harri gets out of her seat and comes to help me rip off the tape. When I fold back the plastic, I find a stunning glass vase with a wide, fluid opening and a kaleidoscope of vibrant colors suspended like liquid within its walls. I turn it over and see Zaria's signature mark of Zorro stamp.

"Oh, Z! It's exquisite."

"They say you have up to a year to give a wedding gift," she says. "I'm heartbroken that the Hummingbird never got to you. I know you loved it. But hopefully this one will bring you the same joy. I'm just sorry it's so late."

"No," I say, handing the gift to Jeff for a closer look at our dear friend's artistic genius. "This is perfect. And the timing couldn't be better. After all, this is truly the start of our new life together."

Acknowledgments

I am so grateful to the many smart, talented, generous, and all-around lovely people who helped me get this book into your hands.

The list is long because I am one lucky author.

To my agents, Erin Niumata and Rachel Ekstrom, thank you for loving my "mom-com," for knowing exactly how to help my manuscript hit the high notes, and for your patience with this publishing newbie. And a big shout-out to Maggie Auffarth and everyone at Folio Literary Management for their behind-the-scenes magic.

I couldn't be more appreciative for the support and guidance of my wonderful editor, Deb Werksman. The team at Sourcebooks is top notch—thank you, Susie Benton, Rachel Gilmer, Jocelyn Travis, Stefani Sloma, and Jessica Smith. I can't think of anywhere I'd rather begin my publishing life. I hope we get to do this again and again.

My sister, Suzanne Gaby-Biegel, who has read every word of this book more times than anyone should have to and who is always available to discuss a plot hole, my sometimes screwy sentence structure, bad alliterations, and the Oxford comma.

My brother, Keith Gaby, for writing all those plays, movies, and manuscripts that gave me the audacity to think I could do something similar someday. And thanks, but no thanks for the wit and rapid-fire banter that's made me the sister (and writer) I am today.

Vanessa Gaby, my pet-portrait-artist sister, who tutored me in painting and made sure Ginny's color mixing came out just right.

My mother, Pat, and my stepfather, Jerry Kaplan, for their never-wavering belief in me.

I was so blessed to grow up in a family of artists and writers, where creativity and individual expression were a priority. My dad wrote and created art out of found pieces. My mom was a potter and, like Ginny, traveled to craft fairs to show her work. We were forever putting on plays in the backyard, making pottery out of river clay, and scribbling down our stories.

Ann Garvin started as my mentor and became the dearest of friends. Thank you for being there, even when I'd forget about the time difference and wake you up to answer my constant queries, calm my *shpilkes*, and always make me snort-laugh.

Lisa Duffy and Kristin Contino, two awesome writer pals who have been in my corner for years. (How has it been years already?)

My gracious early readers and friends—Suzanne, Ann, Lisa, Jane Paterson, Maria Oskwarek, Julie Mulligan, Christa Allan, and Karin Gilleran.

The many generous people who offered insight, advice, and often a shoulder to lean on—Lisa Bruder, Annette Dalton, Terry Meese, Maggee Messing, Erin Celello, Gwendolen Gross, Joanne Nesi, Carolyn Sapontzis, Martha Megill, Jennifer Pinney, and Cindy Hauptman.

The talented and enthusiastically supportive writers at the Women's Fiction Writers Association, many of whom have become mentors, critique partners, cheerleaders, and online and IRL friends.

A special shout-out to the booksellers, reviewers, bloggers, bookstagrammers, and librarians who helped you find my book.

And saved for last, because they are the best, my husband, David, and my children, Jackson and Jordan. Your love, generosity, creativity, humor, and faith in me are the only reason I've been able to fall down nine times and get up ten. Roe Clan Forever.

About the Author

After graduating from the S.I. Newhouse School of Public Communications at Syracuse University and spending many years as an advertising creative director and copywriter in New York City, Lisa Roe accepted the tougher job of stay-at-home mom and turned to writing fiction—mostly to entertain her kids, but then to tell her own stories. A classic firstborn, a reluctant empty nester, and a Dr. Dolittle wannabe, Lisa lives in New Jersey with her husband and three incorrigible dogs. *Welcome to the Neighborhood* is her debut novel.

WITH NEIGHBORS LIKE THIS

Uplifting, feel-good fiction from *USA Today*
bestselling author Tracy Goodwin

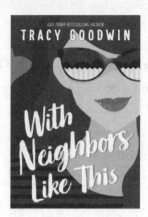

When divorced mom of two Amelia Marsh relocates to a northern suburb of Houston, all she wants is a bit of normalcy for her children. The last thing she needs is to be the center of community gossip. But that's what happens when Amelia clashes with the HOA representative over her children's garden gnome. HOA President Kyle Sanders could be a good friend—and something more—if Amelia wasn't gearing up for battle with the HOA in her determination to make her house a home and her neighborhood a community…

"Tracy Goodwin delivers every time!"

—Sophie Jordan, *New York Times* bestselling author

For more info about Sourcebooks's books and authors, visit:
sourcebooks.com

THE UNPLANNED LIFE
OF JOSIE HALE

Hilarious, heartwarming fiction from Stephanie Eding that reminds us it's always a good idea to expect the unexpected...

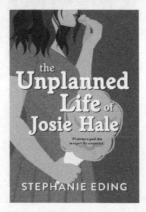

When Josie discovers that she's unexpectedly pregnant with her ex-husband's baby (darn that last attempt to save their marriage), she seeks comfort in deep-fried food at the county fair. There she runs into her two old friends, Ben and Kevin. While sharing their own disappointments with adult life, they devise a plan to move in together and turn their lives around. Soon Ben and Kevin make it their mission to prepare for Josie's baby. Maybe together they can discover the true meaning of family and second chances in life...

For more info about Sourcebooks's books and authors, visit:

sourcebooks.com

THE FAMILY SHE NEVER MET

An emotional multigenerational story that explores the resilience
of three Cuban-American women and the price they've paid
for their family, from bestselling author Caridad Piñeiro

Jessica Russo knows nothing about her mother's family or her Cuban culture. Every
time she's asked about it, her mother has shut down. But when the Cuban grand-
mother she's never met sends her right-hand man, Luis, to offer Jessica the chance
to come to Miami and meet her estranged family, she can't help but say yes...

"You can't go wrong with Caridad Piñeiro."

—RaeAnne Thayne, *New York Times* bestselling author

For more info about Sourcebooks's books and authors, visit:

sourcebooks.com

LUCKY LEAP DAY

A whirlwind trip to Ireland is supposed to end with a suitcase full of wool sweaters and souvenir pint glasses—not a husband you only just met!

After one too many whiskeys, fledgling screenwriter Cara Kennedy takes a page out of someone else's script when she gets caught up in the Irish tradition of women proposing on Leap Day. She wakes the next morning with a hot guy in her bed and a tin foil ring on her finger. Her flight is in four hours, and she has the most important meeting of her career in exactly two days—nothing she can do except take her new husband (and his adorable dog) back to LA with her and try to untangle the mess she's made...

**"A fun and flirty read that I couldn't put down—
the perfect feel-good rom-com."**

—Sarah Morgenthaler for *Happy Singles Day*

For more info about Sourcebooks's books and authors, visit:

sourcebooks.com

SUMMER BY THE RIVER

Don't miss this heartfelt romantic women's fiction by
bestselling contemporary romance author Debbie Burns

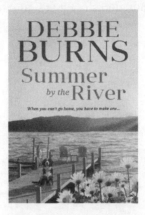

Making a fresh start in a new part of the country is challenging, but fate and good fortune lead young single mother Josie Waterhill and her six-year-old daughter to a cozy Midwestern town right on the river. There, Josie can raise Zoe away from the violence of the life she once knew and make a new home in the historic teahouse where they've been invited to stay. When a neighbor's interest in Josie inadvertently stirs up trouble, she thinks she might never outrun it. But her new community is more than willing to show Josie how to let go of her painful past and create a glorious future.

"A warm cuddly tale... This heartstring-tugger is certain to win fans who are yearning for a wholesome summertime read."

—*Publishers Weekly*, STARRED REVIEW, for *A New Leash on Love*

For more info about Sourcebooks's books and authors, visit:

sourcebooks.com

AND NOW YOU'RE BACK

International bestselling queen of romantic women's fiction Jill Mansell knows the importance of finding your way home in her new poignant, laugh-out-loud story that's sure to make you smile

Didi Laing met her first love, Shay Mason, on a magical winter visit to Venice. They were rapturously happy together and Shay came to work at Didi's parents' hotel in the Cotswolds. Then one shocking incident changed everything, and Shay disappeared.

Thirteen years later, Shay returns to fulfill his father's dying wish. Moving into the best suite in Didi's hotel sets off a chain of events that affects the whole town. Everyone has their own stories and secrets, more intertwined than anyone could have guessed...

"Uplifting, heart-warming, and supremely feel-good."

—Sophie Kinsella, #1 *New York Times* bestselling author, for *It Started with a Secret*

For more info about Sourcebooks's books and authors, visit:

sourcebooks.com

THE SISTERS CAFÉ

New York Times bestseller Carolyn Brown brings her unique voice to this poignant and hilarious novel.

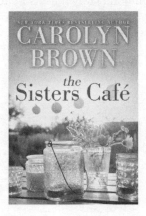

Cathy Andrew's biological clock has passed the ticking stage and is dangerously close to "blown plumb up." Cathy wants it all: the husband, the baby, and a little house right there in Cadillac, Texas. She's taken step one and gotten engaged to a reliable man, but she's beginning to question their relationship. Going through with the wedding or breaking off her engagement looks like a nightmare either way. She knows her friends will back her up, but she's the one who has to make a decision that's going to tear her apart.

"Fans of beloved Southern films, like *Steel Magnolias* and *Fried Green Tomatoes*, will flip for this charming small-town tale."

—*Woman's World*

For more info about Sourcebooks's books and authors, visit:

sourcebooks.com